Ada L Halstead

The Death Trust

A Novel

Ada L Halstead

The Death Trust
A Novel

ISBN/EAN: 9783337001728

Printed in Europe, USA, Canada, Australia, Japan

Cover: Foto ©Andreas Hilbeck / pixelio.de

More available books at **www.hansebooks.com**

A NOVEL

BY

ADA L HALSTEAD

OF CALIFORNIA

Author of THE SERPENT BRACELET

PUBLISHED BY THE AUTHOR

BOSTON AND SAN FRANCISCO

1889

ELECTROTYPED AND PRINTED BY
CASHMAN KEATING & CO 597 WASHINGTON ST
BOSTON MASS

.

TO

MY LOVING HUSBAND

𝔍 𝔒 𝔑

CONTENTS

THE DEATH TRUST

HARK to the hurried question of despair!
Where is my child? An echo answers *Where?*

BRIDE OF ABYDOS.

THE DEATH TRUST.

CHAPTER I.

EVELYN WELDON.

Love and hay are thick-sown,
And come up full of thistles.

SHE had dawned upon the fashionable world of
New Orleans with a splendor that made her
at once the envy of half a score of ambitious
belles, and the despair of as many designing
mothers, who had planned for their eligible
daughters the very success Evelyn had made,
with no apparent effort on her own part, ere the
season was at its height.

She was dark, almost, as a Creole; and beneath
the velvet smoothness of her cheeks, the warm
Southern blood surged, usually tingeing them with
that rich but dainty hue of red we ofttimes see in
mother-of-pearl, but at times firing them up to the
hottest glow of scarlet. Her features, of the small
type, were faultlessly moulded, save in a curve of
the red lips, which inclined upward with an abrupt-
ness that gave them a mocking, almost disdainful

expression. This, be it said, became most apparent to those who coveted her place, and were, consequently, ever ready and willing to dissect her.

Her eyes, however, were her grand weapons, wherewith to slay or charm at will. Splendidly black and mysteriously deep they were, and in them reposed a soft and passive languor, which occasion could awaken into brilliancy outrivalling her dazzling diamonds, or transfuse with hauteur coldly severe. Beautiful in face, tall and symmetrical in form, carrying herself with elegance which might well win her a position in any royal court, she became at once the centre of attraction in the ball, drawing-room, or opera-box. She was toasted at every feast and named at every club, as Queen of Hearts.

Yet among the many who adored Evelyn Weldon, who lived in a delirium of bliss over one smile, Monsieur Aubrey Deverell — a Frenchman, young, handsome as Apollo — alone received her obvious approval. Miss Weldon was present at all prominent social events, and Aubrey was her inevitable shadow. He danced with her; he enticed her away into dim conservatories, where they might share mystical *tête-à-têtes*. He sang and read to her by the hour, without apparent fatigue. They walked, they drove, they occupied Monsieur Deverell's box at the opera.

The season had not passed its meridian, when it was rumored that the ensuing spring would find the beautiful flower of Florida installed as mistress at Deveréll Hall, — one of the oldest estates of the South, whose windows overlooked the waters of the Mississippi, just beyond the domes of the Crescent City; but this rumor, blown from lip to ear with such assurance, proved an air-bubble.

The pomp and revelry of the season were over. The earth began once more to gleam in emerald attire. New Orleans heard no more the deafening roar of the Mississippi, as it plunged in white fury toward its eternity, the expanding gulf. As the watery thunder subsided, so did the noisy cymbals of society. As the tufted grass burst from the esplanades and carpeted the lawns, and the spring buds expanded their petals to the kisses of dew and sunbeam, Evelyn Weldon declared her intention of returning to her home, whence she had come for the winter's visit to her mother's sister.

It was the evening preceding the day set apart for her leave-taking, and Evelyn strolled with Aubrey Deveréll through the garden at Seymour Heights. The night was perfect. A delicious warmth mingled with the odor of new-blown flowers. Fair Isis sailed majestically in the heavens, making the firmament glad with silvery smiles, while countless stars twinkled in the quiver of the lake.

Myrtle Seymour, aged fifteen years, was in the drawing-room at the piano, interpreting one of her favorite Beethoven sonatas. The music floated through the open window, and mingled with the redolence of the blossoms. Deverell and his fair companion walked together in that dreamy night,—an Elysium which evokes the voice of love, where love exists; yet they walked in silence.

Presently the young Frenchman said, in his seductive tones: "Why can you not prolong your stay with us, mademoiselle? I can not realize — indeed, I do not want to realize — that you leave New Orleans on the morrow. It seems — forgive me! — unkind of you to run away, just when the drives are becoming so perfect and the opera is in full sway. In another fortnight the gardens at the Hall will be at their gayest. I should be much pleased to drive with you then, and show you my collection of roses, which is said to be the choicest in the State. Stay yet another month with us!"

He looked into her face with pleading eyes, which Evelyn dared not trust herself to meet, as she answered: "It is generous of you, monsieur, but I can not disappoint my parents again. Already have I named three dates for my departure. I must redeem my word, in this instance. Yet I should like to stay on forever! I adore life in a great city. After six months of it I hardly see how I can bring myself to endure our stupid and tasteless existence at Weldon Grange."

How the clear notes of the mocking-bird, hidden in a distant magnolia-tree, jarred upon her ear, as

she waited for his answer; but she waited in vain.
A weight seemed pressing upon her heart! How
pale her cheeks and lips, as she listened for the
words which she had repeatedly told herself must
come from his lips that night! Alas, they came
not!

At length the hour arrived for Farewell to be
said. Aubrey then asked for a Cloth of Gold rose,
which nestled, half-blown, against the purple-black
bands of her hair. Evelyn silently inclined her
proud head, as a sign for him to disengage it with
his own fingers. When she felt the soft touch
upon her cheek and hair, every fibre in her being
thrilled with the power of love; yet he spoke not
the words which would have made her one of the
happiest, perhaps the noblest of her sex!

He only pressed his lips reverently on the half-
withered rose, saying tremulously: "I will treasure
this forever, mademoiselle, as the dearest of all my
possessions." Then, bending over her cold hand,
he kissed it with the same profound respect, and
whispered, with low-toned fervor: "Adieu, *chère
amie!* Adieu! I shall long remember the past
winter as the happiest of my life!"

She was gone. He watched the door as it
closed between them, scarcely knowing his own
heart, and little dreaming what an icy grip had
suddenly seized Evelyn Weldon's; yet her white
lips really trembled with keen disappointment.

When the morning came, after a wakeful night,

Evelyn no longer felt disappointed merely, but chagrined, deeply chagrined, at what she had brought herself to look upon as only Monsieur Aubrey's imperturbable deliberation.

"He loves me!" she told herself. "His eyes have too often betrayed this truth, for his lips to belie it by their silence; and, though they suppress their story now, time will, *must*, bring it forth. I will return to Florida, and keep this love-affair secret, trusting the future for its happier sequel."

With a heart thus rendered less heavy by its new-born hope, Evelyn went back to Weldon Grange, only to learn, however, that old, old lesson, that hope deferred maketh the heart sick.

Months passed, and not one word did she receive from the knight of her dreams. Only the Spirit of the Past told her of his existence. From morn till night, from night till morn, she was haunted by a pair of brown eyes, — so loving, so true, as they gazed into her own. She was haunted by a voice, coming back from that beautiful past, which thrilled through her like an electric current.

With the incoming of summer every spark of hope had died out of her heart. One evening, as she stood at her chamber window, listlessly watching the amber cloud-wreaths mass their flame into a seething sea of fire, she shed the last bitter tear over her shattered idol, telling herself that Aubrey Deveréll either ignored their past acquaintance, or — what was still worse — looked upon it as but a

frivolous chapter in his book of social triumphs.
Doubtless he had flung away the withered flower
he had taken from her hair, promising to treasure
it as the dearest of all possessions ; or perhaps he
had consigned it to some relic-box, where dwelt
fifty other love-mementos, each with an individual
history as romantic as the tale of her Cloth of Gold
rose.

Now was the fire of vengeance kindled within
her bosom. " He is as false as Mephisto ! " she
cried within herself, " but I shall make him boast
of one conquest less than his record shows. I
will at once accept Wilford Hylton ; and the
coming winter will find me queening the *beau
monde* of New Orleans, just as I did last season.
Wilford's prospects as a barrister would be most
brilliant in the city, and he will readily accept any
change to obtain me, after these many years. He
will be an easily managed husband ! Oh unsuspecting Wilford ! I shall have my Evenings at Home ;
I shall dance ; I shall flirt ; in fact I shall no longer
be the ice-flower you have been pleased to call
me. You shall never surmise that my heart is not
wholly your own. I believe I love you less than
any of my wooers, but I can manage you better.
Oh innocent Wilford ! "

Evelyn danced away, bent upon making herself
as charming as possible. She knew the young
barrister would be at the Grange that evening ; for
Thursday had been his regular calling-night during

the past three years. He came ostensibly for social chat with the family, but really that he might be near the chosen of his heart, the ice-flower whose unfolding he had watched from its budding until its maturity, — a flower all the more beautiful because of its austerity.

Wilford went home from Weldon Grange that night with his brain in a delirium of joy, for his lovely ice-flower had smiled upon him more than once, and with such benignity! She had played selections from his favorite composers, and even sung the songs she knew he liked best, — sung them with such pathos as to send his senses whirling round and round, and make his heart beat like a muffled drum.

The following fortnight the young barrister lived in Paradise. There were moonlight drives, and walks through quiet paths. There were long and delightful evenings in the vine-clad verandas, and afternoons on the tennis-lawn. There were low conversations under the shady arbors, — all with Evelyn, who was, by the end of that time, his affianced bride.

CHAPTER II.

SHADOWS AND SUNBEAMS.

THE sky is changed, — and such a change! BYRON.
WOULD'ST let a serpent sting thee twice? - SHAKESPEARE.

THE loud clamor of the gong sounded for the third time, summoning the Weldon family to breakfast. Its sharp clang was significant of impatient servants, and of a breakfast spoiling, which should have been served half an hour before.

As the last vibration died away, Evelyn, clad in pale cashmere, appeared at the head of the stairs and slowly descended. She did not enter the breakfast-room as she reached the landing below; but, sweeping like a princess down the wide hall, she opened the low French window looking into the garden. Stepping lightly from the casement into this Eden retreat, she took a leisurely survey of its treasures, debating what flowers she should choose to adorn her corsage; for she was a veritable flower-worshipper, and never considered her toilet complete without radiant blossoms. She soon decided upon a cluster of rare roses. Hastening to the trellis, where this plant crept in wealthy confusion, she plucked a few of its delicate pink and dew-pearled beauties, and half buried them amidst the cascade of lace flowing over her bosom. Then,

(9)

humming a few low notes of perfect satisfaction with the effect, — which was, indeed, charming, the dainty pink contrasting with the cream of her gown, and also with her dark type of loveliness, — she was about to re-enter the window, when suddenly, from behind the corner of the conservatory, a young girl of about fifteen summers appeared, followed closely by a huge Saint Bernard dog, barking and bounding about in the very height of the ecstacy which a romp with his young mistress had inspired.

"Down, Bijou, down! No more play this morning," cried Hazel Verne, as she shook back the gold-brown tresses straying roguishly about her forehead, shading the dark-blue eyes which glowed with the fire of youthful animation.

Bijou was not to be easily subdued. In vain did Hazel caressingly stroke his glossy black hair, and talk to him in persuasive tones. He dashed forward again, with loud barks challenging her to follow. Wishing to elude him gently, Hazel glanced about her in search of some loophole of escape. Espying the open window, through which Miss Weldon had passed, Hazel gained the aperture with a sudden bound, just in time to plant her foot upon the edge of that young lady's train, as it swept over the threshold. *R-r-r-r-ip!* went the folds thereof!

"Oh you stupid!" snapped Evelyn, turning abruptly, her eyes and cheeks aflame with suppressed anger. "You disgraceful tomboy!" she

continued, slowly surveying the culprit from head
to foot with scorching gaze. "I've a mind to box
your ears well for this!"

Hood was right:

> Alas for the rarity
> Of Christian charity!
> Under the sun.

She was about to suit the action to the words,
when Hazel lifted tearful eyes to Evelyn's face,
and said tremulously: "Cousin Evelyn, forgive
me! I did n't, indeed I did n't mean to so offend
you. I was only trying to get away from Bijou."

"Oh, spare your apologies!". Evelyn returned
with contempt. "You have low manners, or else
you would be in the schoolroom preparing your
French lesson, instead of romping about the grounds
with that dog. Your conduct is beyond endurance.
It is insufferable!"

"But Cousin Evelyn," she said, with brimming
eyes still fixed appealingly upon her cousin's dark
and passionate face, "you know aunty objects to
my studying before breakfast, and, — and I delight
in being down by the lake, these beautiful summer
mornings, the water is so clear and still, and the
birds sing so sweetly. Bijou and I like to search
for their nests! Bijou is my only companion!"

Here the sensitive mouth quivered piteously;
but Miss Weldon, regardless of her cousin's agitation, was about to make some sneering rejoinder,
when the colored butler came hurriedly along the
hall.

"Fore de Lo'd," he muttered audibly, "I nebber see sich a bad reg'lated fam'ly as dis yah! I's done ring dat gong free times, 'n de breakfas done git cole! Missy Eb'lyn, missus done be in de breakfas-room a'waitin' foh you 'n Missy Hazel." With an impatient flourish from one shoulder to the other of the towel he carried, he retraced his steps, leaving the two girls to follow.

Evelyn did not again turn her glance toward the face which looked at her so pathetically. Shaking off the entreating hand laid upon her arm, she entered the morning-room, and greeted somewhat affectionately her mother, a sweet-faced, gray-eyed, little lady, who sat at the head of the table. Then she turned her attention to a letter which lay beside her plate, awaiting perusal.

As Hazel stooped to imprint the usual morning kiss upon her aunt's cheek, she could not conceal the tears which threatened an overflow. Being questioned as to the occasion of her grief, she no longer restrained it, but burst into convulsive sobbing, explaining her trouble somewhat incoherently. "Oh aunty," she concluded, "Evelyn hates me so! I am sure she hates me; else she would forgive me!"

Mrs. Weldon pushed back the locks of sunny hair, and gazed with compassionate eyes upon the clouded face of her darling, secretly wondering, as she had done many times before, at her Evelyn's implacable dislike of her foster-sister, — the child whom Mrs. Weldon had brought from her brother's deathbed four years previous, promising to love and cherish Hazel forever, as her very own.

Truly Hazel had been a continuous sunbeam at Weldon Grange, from the day when she first passed its doorway. What could have led to Evelyn's dislike of her mother's *protegée?* On the very day when Hazel came to the Grange, — a tiny, black-robed figure, fresh from her father's new-made grave, and innocent of all that pertained to the world's inhumanity, — that dislike asserted itself. It was then that the child had heard the first stabbing taunt about *dependence;* and it came from the lips of one who she had eagerly hoped would take her to her bosom, with something of a sister's affection.

Alas for Hazel's hopes! They melted like frost-work in the morning ray. She had not been alone with the daughter of the Grange fifteen minutes, before the child learned how vain was her heart's dearest wish; for Evelyn had said, in a tone so lofty that Hazel could never forget its bitterness: " Hazel, since you are to make your future home at the Grange, I presume you must needs address me as *cousin;* but I trust you will constantly bear in mind our different positions, and never forget to look upon me as your superior."

What a burden those unfeeling words added to the bereaved girl's sad heart! Despite this, however, the barrier which rose between the cousins from that moment had never seemed insuperable to Hazel. In her simplicity she believed that gentle perseverance on her part would, in time, win her the coveted place in her frigid cousin's favor; but that monarch of our lives, commonly termed Fate, thwarted Hazel's one ambition. Each day increased, rather than diminished, the wall of division. Try as Hazel might, to elicit, by her loving ways, a smile of approval from her cousin, she always received a frown or a sneer. The choicest flower, proffered by Hazel's hand, was declined with a politeness which was irony itself; while petty caresses were ignored with a resoluteness which chilled, though it failed to subdue the younger girl.

This morning the strife had arisen most unexpectedly, when, fresh from sunshine and dew, Hazel felt as free and happy as the delicate-winged butterflies she and Bijou had been chasing. Little dreamed she of the cloud threatening to drench the joy of her heart; but now the cloud burst, and tears rained in great floods down the fair young face, leaving not a trace of sunshine.

"Why did you wound her so, Evelyn?" at length questioned Mrs. Weldon, looking at her daughter over the bowl of new-cut flowers gracing the centre of the table; and in the mild eyes there was a look of reproach.

Evelyn was at that moment so deeply engrossed in the contents of her letter, that she failed to hear, or else to mark her mother's words. Why did her cheeks grow so pale, and then flush into crimson? Why did her hand so tremble, as she refolded the sheet of tinted paper, and looked up when Mrs. Weldon repeated her name?

"What were you saying, mamma mine?" she queried, in a voice wherein a sense of rapture was poorly suppressed. Evelyn's bosom rose and fell tumultuously; but Mrs. Weldon failed to note this emotion, so deep was her sympathy with the niece crouching beside her.

"I asked," repeated the mother, "how you could have been cruel to Hazel, over what you well knew to be the purest accident? You have wounded her sorely."

"But mamma, the child is insufferably awkward! She is forever getting herself into disgrace. My new dress, too! It was quite enough to provoke a saint. However," — this with a softening glance toward her foster-sister, who had quietly slipped into her place at table, — "Phebe's adroit fingers will repair the injury, and Hazel may consider the offence as condoned, provided she will be more on her guard in future."

Hazel said nothing, but her grateful heart fluttered, and her eyes said: "I will, oh I will, indeed, Cousin Evelyn!" and, with a face fairly aglow with happiness, — caught from the kind look which accompanied Evelyn's words, rather than from the words themselves, — she sipped her coffee in silence.

What could have caused this softening toward the object of Evelyn Weldon's wonted contempt, and even aversion? Ah, what indeed? That white-winged messenger, still trembling in her hand! Her heart was now at peace with all things under the blue canopy, for this messenger hailed from the Crescent City, and from Aubrey Deveréll! It breathed to Evelyn the sweet assurance that she was not forgotten, — even more, that he would soon be with her.

"Mamma," said the young lady, when they had finished breakfast, and Hazel had gone to the study-room, leaving the two alone, "let me read you my letter. It is from Monsieur Deveréll, of New Orleans. Aunt Lydia has doubtless named him in her letters to you." Mrs. Weldon assented.

DEVERÉLL HALL, June 7,

MA CHÈRE MADEMOISELLE EVELYN: As I have in prospect a trip to the Land of Flowers, I have determined, if agreeable to yourself, upon making a brief visit to Weldon Grange. I shall leave New Orleans on or about the 15th inst., and will telegraph you, immediately upon reaching Tallahassee, the exact hour I will be at your station. So, if the distance be material between Jasper and the Grange, I trust it will not be presuming too far on your hospitality to beg you to meet me at the former place, as I am somewhat wanting in courage, and should positively dread walking alone one mile on unfamiliar soil. Trusting therefore you will take pity on me, and yield me your most excellent protection, mademoiselle, — trusting, also, that you will look somewhat kindly upon my advent, — I await your reply.

Obediently your servant,

AUBREY LEIGH DEVERÉLL.

Evelyn refolded the letter, and consigned it to her pocket, convinced that she had misinterpreted Deveréll's protracted silence, and with her recent bitterness toward him fully exorcised. Presently she looked up, and encountered her mother's questioning gaze. The unwonted color of her daughter's cheek, the happy light in her eye, were now noticed by Mrs. Weldon; and Evelyn felt her face burn still hotter. Her eyes drooped under the earnest look.

"You and Monsieur Deveréll are strangers, I know, mamma; but as he is one of Aunt Lydia's intimate acquaintances, and my *friend*, I am certain you will welcome him."

"I believe he is the young Frenchman who paid you such constant and — as Sister Lydia wrote — significant attention in New Orleans last winter?" said Mrs. Weldon evasively.

"True, Monsieur Deveréll *was* courteous to me while I was there," returned Evelyn; and she spoke almost curtly.

Mrs. Weldon, feeling more perturbed through this curtness, continued, gently: "Owing to papa's absence from home, your friend's sojourn here will prove somewhat dull, I fear, for want of the customary hunting and fishing. Monsieur Deveréll will certainly be welcome. But Evelyn," she added with growing anxiety, "let me entreat you, do not let his stay lead you to neglect your duty toward Wilford Hylton."

"Wilford Hylton!" echoed the daughter, every drop of color forsaking cheek and lip. Then, with a futile attempt to regain composure, she said with a forced laugh: "Why, you dear silly mamma! You take a very sentimental view of Wilford's addresses to me. This has been no love-affair,—at least, not on my part! Reassure yourself!"

She would have laughed again, had not Mrs. Weldon arrested her by a tone of unwonted severity.

"Evelyn!" she cried, and her eyes were pained as they rested on her child's face. "Evelyn, it can not be that you have been trifling with this man! Your father went to Memphis last week, believing his heart's dearest wish had been realized, —believing you were Wilford's promised wife. It can not be that you have heartlessly deceived one so good, so noble, so true as Wilford Hylton! It can not be that you have been thus false to us all!"

"I was weary of this monotonous life, with being exiled from the world. It was with this desperate craving for change, that I promised Wilford my hand; but I have bitterly repented my folly more than once, during the short weeks of our engagement. Wilford bores me inexpressibly! I believe I actually like him less than any other gentleman of my acquaintance. With visions of a gay and fashionable life in New Orleans, however, wherein was centred my ambition, I believed I could be happy, even with him, after a fashion, — happy with an insipid *blond* constantly in my train. I detest blond men! They are sentimental, prosy, — everything but agreeable to me, and I shall never marry one!"

"You have cancelled your engagement with him, then?" Mrs. Weldon questioned, or rather sobbed.

"No; but we are to take a canter over to Fairacre this morning, and it will be a good opportunity," returned the other, with almost stolid indifference.

"Poor Wilford! poor, poor boy!" sobbed Mrs. Weldon; and her head sank lower and lower until it rested sorrowfully on the table.

"I should think," pursued Evelyn, with a growing sense of vexation over her mother's depression, "you would consider my happiness before Wilford's."

"But, daughter, after all these years of what he considered vain worship, you at least gave him encouragement. More, you gave him a happiness he never dared dream of. Now you would deliberately nip that new-budded happiness, and thus despoil a life that would otherwise be fruitful in all that is bright and worthy. You would trample on a true heart, only that your own may be again put to the test of disappointment."

Evelyn started at these words, but her mother went on in the same wounded tone: "Lydia has insinuated that Monsieur Deverell is considered somewhat of a flirt, — an admirer of the ladies in general. Though his proposed visit may be incited by friendship only, it is this visit, evidently, which prompts you to a revocation of your engagement with the best young man in our circle."

Evelyn flushed and paled under these true-aimed words. Had her mother then read the secret she had tried to guard from all the world! Her tone certainly signified as much.

The girl felt her position to be very trying. She saw that to prolong the subject would be awkward as well as impolitic. She wished her mother would leave the room, or that something would occur to break the awkward silence which ensued. She did not care, just at that moment, how terrible that something might be, if it would only offer her an opportunity to run away to her own room, where she might be alone with her unutterable joy, — the joy which was convulsive from long suffocation.

The minutes seemed hours; but at length footsteps were heard along the hallway outside the breakfast-room. Another moment, and the door was thrown open by the butler, who announced: "Massa Hylton! Missy Eb'lyn, Alcides am saddled at de block."

CHAPTER III.

I HATE the crowded town;
I can not breathe shut up within its walls.
Air, I want air, and sunshine, and blue sky!
LONGFELLOW.

WELDON GRANGE, one of the oldest and richest estates in Florida, stood picturesquely in the midst of vast orange-groves, which, in this summer month, gleamed with richest dark-green foliage, the yellow globes thick-hanging in delicious contrast.

Almost castle-like appeared the massive stone structure, with its stately wings jutting abruptly toward the north, east, and west. Its many oriel windows and gabled roofs were parched and blackened by the suns of at least five decades, and guarded by several silvern spires, reared like sentinels against the vaulted sky. Quaint carvings about the eaves, and surmounting the pillars which supported the verandas, frowned savagely down upon a lawn smooth as velvet. This lawn swept along to the wide driveway on one side; while on the other it engirdled artistic flower-beds, and formed a striking background to the bevy of marble cherubs around the fountain, and to the fair Naiad who peered gracefully through the veil of

(21)

water. This fountain was the chief feature of the grounds, the water being thrown up from a mammoth seashell, supported by the nymph. Rising into the air in divided and scintillant columns, to the height of many feet, the water was abruptly shivered into a myriad of gem-like drops, and then fell musically back into the basin-lake below, which contained a multitude of goldfish, and where floated the large-leafed Ethiopian lily, and other aquatic plants. A thick and even-clipped hedge of cedar skirted the orchards, except at the southern extremity, where a lake gleamed through a high and tangled wall of weeping-willow and cypress-pine.

Outside this hedge, look in whatever direction one might, naught but an endless stretch of forest met the eye, with occasional sunny openings, through which the white road could be discerned, as it trailed along beneath interlaced branches of hemlock, pine, and cypress, making its way, like a huge serpent, toward Jasper, the neighboring town, in one direction, — toward Cypress Dell, the Weldon burying-ground, in another direction; and in yet another, toward the gentle Suwanee, near whose banks was situated Gerald Weldon's vast rice plantation, known as Fairacre.

How far removed seemed the Grange and its beautiful surroundings from the noisy world, — how remote, indeed, from the tinkling cymbals for which Evelyn's heart so languished! The Grange

seemed like a little world distinct unto itself this
evening, with the blue-arched dome above, the air
so hushed, — with no voice of a living or breathing
thing, no sigh of leaflet, no whisper from the furred
pines, lifting their dark arms high against the sky.

It was almost sunset. Already the flake-white
clouds above were tinged with amethyst and gold,
and flowers were breathing out their sweetest
incense. Magnolia blossoms made the atmosphere
almost stifling with their fragrance, — so oppressive,
indeed, that Hazel Verne — who was sauntering
along the avenue beneath their cloistering arms,
and had reached up a rounded arm to take one
of the waxen chalices — concluded suddenly that
she did not want it, and plucked a bright green
leaf instead.

Then away she tripped down the avenue, with
Bijou at her side, — her heart so full of happiness
that low, sweet notes burst from her lips, despite
her desire to repress them, so sacred did she hold
the quiet which reigned throughout. It seemed to
her like silent evening prayer, in which even the
birds had united; and what was her song but
prayer, — the prayer which the guileless of heart
all sing, in which even the angels join! The
murmured song died away gradually, as the young
girl came deeper and deeper into the orchard;
and when it had ceased altogether, the air was the
more solemnly still. Toward an aperture in the
high hedgerow Hazel made her way, and then

stood, with hands clasped absently behind her, her fair hair kissed by the gentlest breeze, and her eyes fixed, expectantly, upon a certain clearing in the forest, through which a glimpse of the road to Jasper, six miles distant, was visible.

She was watching for Evelyn's return, the latter having driven to the station to meet her expected friend and guest, from whom she had received a despatch that morning, stating that he would reach Jasper by the evening train.

At length Hazel perceived a thick cloud of dust curling upward, which signaled the vehicle's approach. When this cleared away she saw that two persons were seated in the wagon. Fully convinced that her cousin had not been disappointed, she called to Bijou, who had been sitting near, — his soft black eyes fixed upon her face, with that expression of affection so peculiar to his breed. Linking her hand lovingly within his collar, they went together beyond the hedge in search of wood-violets, which, at this season of the year, grew luxuriantly in shady nooks throughout the forest. It was some time before the cart, drawn by Alcides, — Evelyn's riding pony, a beautiful iron-gray, with sweeping, jet-black tail and mane,— advanced through the gate into the driveway. Here Evelyn gave the reins into the hands of the hostler, suggesting to her companion that they walk through the grounds to the house.

Monsieur Deveréll was somewhat above the

medium height, finely proportioned, with broad shoulders and a knightly bearing, which made his presence commanding. From beneath somewhat heavy but perfectly-arched brows, a pair of dark-brown eyes looked out, clear and steadfast. In their depths the spirit of wit reposed, which spoke volumes, even when the lips were mute beneath the shadow of the drooping brown mustache.

His hair, of a shade darker brown, was worn close-clipped, thus defining a high, olive brow, — his noblest feature, indicative, like his eyes, of intellectuality, befitting the forehead of some olden bard. His hands were decidedly masculine in shape, but white and soft, — unmistakably, hands whose touch could speak eloquently enough to excite woman's love. His voice was never monotonous; and every syllable was a note suggestive of its rich tenor. What a voice! What power to thrill a sensitive heart! There was rapture in listening to it, even in ordinary conversation.

As Evelyn and her visitor sauntered on, he surveyed, with a true connoisseur's eye, the magnificent picture which the Grange presented in the twilight, with the oriel windows ablaze in the sun's parting rays, and the spires, like fairy-wands, gleaming against the sky, — a sky where sprites might dwell in love, a home where happiness should reign supreme; and so thought Deveréll, as he gazed silently, almost breathlessly, upon the picture.

"What a perfect background!" he at length

remarked to Evelyn, who had been watching, with
eyes full of a pleased light, his charmed contemplation of her home; for she was proud of Weldon
Grange.

"The lake glistening yonder through the dark
foliage, together with this gorgeous sunset, confer
such a magic effect that I am inclined to believe all
this to be but a scene of enchantment, and shall
expect, presently, to see water-nymphs take full
possession. Truly dear mademoiselle," he added
seriously, "you should be content and happy,
beyond a desire, in such a home. It is heavenly!"

"Happy!" and Evelyn challenged him with a
coquettish glance from beneath her long lashes.
"Ah yes!" with a sigh, which (in justice to her,
let it be said) was not feigned. "I know I *should*
be happy here; but, monsieur, even Paradise itself
would in time grow tedious if, day after day, the
same humdrum routine beset you. My conception
of true happiness involves life in town, where one
is offered constant diversion. I am not idyllic
enough to circumscribe my existence within orange-
groves and rice-fields."

Aubrey laughed. "Ah, Mademoiselle Evelyn,
how our opinions differ! To me the air is stifling
in the crowded town. I would never become bored
with such joy as could be extracted from a home
like this. With all this pure, sweet air to breathe,
these endless forests to explore, I should find
continual diversion. And you have a companion,"

he added. "Mrs. Seymour has mentioned to me
a foster-sister, — your cousin, I believe."

"Oh, Hazel is but a mere child. Being under
the tuition of a governess, of course she proves a
very poor companion for me," returned Evelyn;
"but come, monsieur," she continued, — discom-
fited, she knew not why, at this inadvertent,
though direct reference to Hazel Verne,—"what a
neglectful hostess you must think me, for suffering
you to loiter here, when I should remember your
fatigue, and that you are almost starved. Come !
I see mamma is waiting, on the veranda, to be
presented."

Introductions being over, and a few compliments
exchanged between Mrs. Weldon and her daughter's visitor, he was conducted to his apartment,
and Evelyn hurried away to dress for dinner.

As she reached the head of the stairs she came
abruptly face to face with her foster-sister. Hazel
was dressed in white lawn, her bright curls caught
into a careless cluster at the back of her shapely
head, and there confined by a knot of pale-blue
ribbon. Lovely and pure she appeared, like the
tiny bunch of wood-violets which she held in one
hand ; but the smile which lingered about her
sensitive mouth lost something of its brightness as
she met her frowning cousin thus suddenly, and her
eyes fell beneath the glance which always expressed
so much disapprobation when fixed upon *her ;*
yet she asked, half-hesitatingly : ".Will I do,
Cousin Evelyn ?"

"Will you do for what?" Miss Weldon let her eyes wander from the bronze hair to the faultlessly clad feet of the younger girl, and a palpable change crossed her features.

"To be presented to your friend, Monsieur Deverèll," replied Hazel confused, and then deeply flushing under this close inspection.

"I presume you are presentable," returned Evelyn at length; "but," added she loftily, "you could well have spared your toilet this unusual consideration, as Monsieur Deverèll will probably not give you a second glance.— What are you going to do with those violets?" she asked abruptly, as her eyes fell upon the delicate petals in Hazel's hand.

"I have brought them from the dell, and thought to wear them at my throat," said Hazel.

"Give them to me!" said the other imperatively. "You are much too young for superfluous adornment! Such a thought means vanity; and vanity in a child is more than absurd, — it is ridiculous! Besides, plain and neat attire, without embellishments of any sort, would be more befitting a girl in your position."

Thus speaking she took the flowers from the hesitating hand. Paying no heed to the tear-laden eyes she continued: "And I must enjoin you, Hazel, do not make yourself conspicuous tonight in the drawing-room,—as you generally manage to do before strangers,—by introducing your book of

sketches; and do not tell monsieur that you delight
in rowing, and will take him for a sail on the lake
sometime. All this is child's play and bores one
exceedingly, as I have before told you. Monsieur
Deveréll is *my* guest, remember, and his entertainment rests with me alone."

With these words she turned and swept down
the corridor toward her room, leaving Hazel to
descend the stairs slowly, with lips quivering and
eyes suffused with tears, — tears so often forced
from their secret wells by the stinging tongue of her
cousin.

In the hall below Hazel encountered her aunt,
who was on her way to the dining-room. Impulsively she threw her arms about Mrs. Weldon's
waist, crying as she did so: "Aunty, I would like
to take my dinner with Arline tonight! May n't
I? Do please say I may!"

Wondering at the girl's vehement manner, Mrs.
Weldon gently disengaged the clinging hands, and
drew her pet around in front of her.

"Why this new caprice, my darling?" asked
she tenderly; and then the troubled face was
uplifted to her own.

"Because — because — oh aunty, I had rather
— I had rather not." Here she faltered, sobbing
softly.

"Why, what can have happened to you, child?
But an hour ago I looked into the garden, and saw
you with a face as glad as the flowers," said her

aunt in alarm; "but there, there!" she added, — stooping to imprint a hasty kiss upon the bright hair, as she suddenly remembered that her daughter had gone upstairs just before, and was perhaps accountable for Hazel's grief, — "you may go to Arline's room if you prefer. I will see that Sarah sends up a cosy dinner which you may enjoy together. I shall miss you at table, darling; but go, if you would be happier away."

"Not happier away from you, dear aunty," whispered Hazel. Then with a grateful kiss she bounded upstairs, and away to the governess's room, where, upon Arline's kindly bosom, she sobbed away her grief, and was soon all sunshine again.

CHAPTER IV.

LADY OF THE LAKE.

SWEET is the breath of morn; her rising sweet
With charm of earliest birds. MILTON.

THE following morning, when, as the poet sings,

Earliest day
Dappled with gold the eastern ray,

Hazel arose. She was Nature's true offspring, and in her bosom throbbed the power of sentimentality. Hence, during the season of perfume and roses, she could never think of allowing Baby Morn to glide away, without lingering with her awhile in some favorite resort.

To Hazel the flowers smelled far sweeter when empearled with dew, and the wild birds' earliest song-notes were rife with clearer melody than when the day had grown older. Then, too, at sunrise the butterflies came, in great families, wearing their most gorgeous colors, to enjoy, with her, the sweets of the garden. They seemed more numerous than ever this morning, as Hazel entered their fragrant retreat, — looking a queen among them, as she hovered over a tea-rosebush, drinking in the fresh aroma of the flowers.

She presented a picture of youthful loveliness,

(31)

to which, if portrayed on canvas, a Titian might have given pre-eminence in his studies. A spirituelle face was hers, with a skin whose texture corresponded with the delicate heart of the rose she had plucked, and which she now devoured with azure eyes, brimful of thoughtful pathos. Her lips, slightly parted, glowed a rich carmine, over teeth as perfect as pearls. Crowning all was her glorious hair, the sort that artists rave over, — now pure gold, now a true chestnut or bronze, as the lights and shadows played upon it.

She wore a light-blue merino dress this morning, of the Mother Hubbard design, — destitute of all trimming, save for narrow frills of white lace at throat and wrist. This modern-antique frock, falling in loose folds from the breast, kept one in ignorance as to her form; yet, if her contour was undefined, her every movement was toned with unconscious grace, which the very naiveté of her dress made the more irresistible; and the large rustic hat, which she' suffered to hang carelessly over her shoulders, rather than rest on her head, was, like her other apparel, *en rapport* with her youthful loveliness.

Our young heroine had not long to tarry in the garden this morning; as, before leaving her room, she had resolved upon going down to the lake, from one point of which she desired to sketch a patch of water-lilies, whose development she had been watching for several days past. In her eyes they had now attained the height of perfection, and rocked on the clear breast of waters, a beauteous commingling of buds and blossoms, — their hues, of the daintiest pink mingled with waxenwhite, their whole effect softened by a background of dark, broad, heart-shaped leaves.

Under one arm Hazel carried her sketchbook; and soon, with a last wistful look at the garden, she hastened away, taking her course, with the fleetness of a fawn, through a narrow path which divided the orchard, leading down to the willows.

The happiest hours Hazel could remember since her advent at Weldon Grange had been passed on the placid bosom of the lake. Here she was wont to sit or lie by the hour in her little boat, reading, drawing, or idly dreaming, and allowing the gentle current to drift her hither and thither at will.

Sometimes she would not loosen the boat from its fastening, but would lie therein, beneath the sheltering willows. Rocked by the motion of the water, and charmed by the notes of some wild bird overhead, she would fall asleep, and dream, — her head pillowed upon Bijou, her one inseparable companion.

This morning, on gaining the margin of the water, Hazel untied her boat. Calling the dog, who had found the scent and followed in pursuit of his mistress, they both jumped aboard, and Hazel took the paddles and rowed out, making a circuit around her tuft of lilies. There was hardly a dimple on the lake, and not enough breeze astir to render the boat unsteady. So, having chosen a favorable point of view, she abandoned the oars, opened her sketchbook, and commenced tracing delicate lines therein. Deftly her white fingers strayed over the leaf, as with rapid glances she interpreted the living flowers before her. So absorbed did she become in her work, that a sudden sharp growl from the dog caused her to start with such violence as nearly to upset the boat.

The pencil fell from her hand as she directed her glance toward the bank, whereon Bijou's eyes were fixed with such savage interest, while he growled continuously. What Hazel saw on the edge of the water was nothing to arouse the dog's protective instincts. It was only a tall young man, apparently on the sunny side of thirty, with deep-hazel eyes, half-laughingly and half-seriously bent upon her, and a white hand indolently twisting the corners of a heavy, brown mustache, while he leaned in graceful abandonment against a sapling.

As Hazel met his steady gaze, across the short distance intervening, she acknowledged his deferential, if unduly confident bow, with the slightest inclination of her head. The next moment, however, she felt the hot blood rush into her face and throat; for she suddenly remembered the indiscretion involved in speaking to a perfect stranger. Thereupon she averted her face, and at once resumed pencil and sketchbook; but all was now confusion. She had forgotten where she had left off drawing, and could not direct her eyes toward her study with any deliberation, being conscious, the while, of the fixed gaze of those masculine eyes. To sit idly in the boat would, she knew, be extremely awkward; so putting aside her portfolio, she resumed her oars, with the thought of rowing toward the opposite embankment.

" There," she resolved, " I will secure my boat, and take a quiet ramble with Bijou in search of wild flowers." With this thought she glided onward, with the adroitness of one who had long been used to the water, and was rapidly widening the distance between them, when there came an abrupt shout from the bank behind her.

" Mademoiselle! Mademoiselle! " called the voice; and, fully confident of its being directed toward herself, Hazel cast a quick glance over her shoulder, to see the strange gentleman gesticulating, and beckoning her to return.

More confused than surprised, and more vexed than pleased at this new freak of familiarity, she rested on her oars irresolutely, watching the crystalline beads drip from their blades. Should she return? She debated this question hurriedly in her mind for a moment. Until now she had not given the gentleman's identity a thought; but suddenly it flashed upon her that he must be

Evelyn's visitor from New Orleans; whereupon she deemed it her duty to at least pay him due respect.   At once she turned her graceful head and looked at him again, this time with a faint smile beaming from her eyes, rather than lips.

" You were calling me, monsieur? " she cried out half-timidly; and her voice floated like a silvery lute to Aubrey Deveréll — for he it indeed was — across the tranquil water, breaking in upon the birdsong over his head, like a silvery lute.

" I merely desired to express sincere regrets to mademoiselle for having disturbed her at her drawing.   Pray resume it, and I·will leave forthwith."   Saying this, Aubrey touched his hat and bowed with profound reverence, as Hazel began rowing toward him.

" Oh, I dare say the lilies will remain unmolested until tomorrow morning, when I shall finish sketching them," she returned laughingly; and then she added half-shyly, as she drew very near the embankment where he stood: " I presume you are Monsieur Deveréll, my cousin's guest, who arrived yesterday from New Orleans? "

" I have that honor, mademoiselle," he assented, again bowing low, with one hand upon his breast ; " and in return I must ask," he added, "who may be this fay in fairyland?"   He bent his handsome eyes upon her with a look of deep admiration as he spoke, — a look which sent the crimson into her cheeks, and caused the long lashes to veil a pair of

eyes which monsieur thought the loveliest he had
ever beheld.

"Oh, I supposed you knew, monsieur! I am only
Hazel," she replied, trying to dispel her unwonted
diffidence. She had now touched the shore, and
was on the point of following Bijou, who had
bounded from the boat and was sniffing suspiciously
around monsieur's heels; but suddenly thinking
that her new-formed acquaintance might enjoy a
short sail, as it was still quite early, instead of
accepting the hand proffered to assist her out she
asked: "Do you enjoy rowing, Monsieur Deveréll? If so, I will take you over and show you
my beautiful water-lilies."

The words had no sooner been spoken than he
was beside her with one light bound. "And will
mademoiselle permit me?" asked he, placing his
white hands upon the oars, and mentally remarking
upon the rare loveliness of this wee Lady of the
Lake, who freely surrendered them to him, and her
seat also, herself taking the place in front.

"Now," resumed Monsieur Aubrey, as, with two
deep strokes, he cleared the bank by a dozen yards,
"you tell me you are Hazel; but is not this a little
vague? Will you not say Hazel who?"

His companion was laughing gayly, her amusement being provoked by Bijou, whom they had
left on the bank, but who had plunged in after
them, and was now making frantic efforts to gain
the side of the boat. Being questioned thus, her

countenance instantly lost its mirth. As she looked into his face, he saw the deep-blue eyes were full of hurt surprise and disappointment.

"Why!" she exclaimed, "has neither my aunt nor my cousin mentioned me in your presence? I am Hazel Verne! Mrs. Weldon is my aunty."

Her heart grew heavy at the thought that her foster-mother could have so far forgotten her existence as not to name her to Evelyn's guest. "After all, what does it signify?" she continued. "A mere child like myself can be of little interest to you. Doubtless they had more important things to talk about."

"A mere child!" repeated Aubrey, amused at her words. "I beg to venture," he added, "that mademoiselle has seen her fourteenth summer."

"I was fifteen last March," returned the young girl. "Cousin Evelyn, though, looks upon me as an infant."

"But," continued the young Frenchman, with a merry twinkle in his eye, "infants do not sketch, and row themselves about on the water, except in fairy tales. Your cousin's idea of infancy is truly inconsistent." At this they both laughed heartily.

"But do not allow yourself to think for a moment, my wee Lady of the Lake, — may I so call you?" he added playfully, — "that Madame Weldon has been so unmindful of you. She mentioned her little niece to me several times last evening, — a niece who, I believe, excused herself from dinner through some caprice, but to whom I should be presented today. I have heard of this same niece through others also; but, strange to say, I never heard her name, in full, until within the past twenty minutes. Now, you see, we have escaped the formality of an introduction, and thus stolen a march on Madame Weldon and your cou — ”

“ Monsieur Deveréll ! Monsieur Deveréll ! ” called a voice from an unknown quarter, in not altogether placid accents. Looking toward the bank, they both saw a white-clad form standing amidst the tufted growth of ferns and grass bordering the water.

“Ah Mademoiselle Evelyn, *bon jour!* ” exclaimed Deveréll, gaily. “ You see,” continued he, “ I have made myself quite a hero this morning, — in fact a second Knight of Snowdoun ; ” and he laughingly turned to his fair companion, though failing to note the change which had come over her face, giving it a half-terrified look.

Not until this moment had Hazel recalled Evelyn’s words to her on the previous evening: “ Do not invite Monsieur Deveréll for a sail on the lake ! ” These words now were blazoned in memory with letters of flame. The startled look deepened in her eyes, while her heart suddenly grew numb. Hers was not the grayish pallor which had settled upon Miss Weldon’s countenance, as she encountered the pretty picture on the lake; for Evelyn clenched her hands in the fury that seized her, and the feeling of antipathy toward her foster-sister deepened into scalding gall, which seemed to rise in her throat and strangle her. She grew dizzy, and mistily heard Deverell's jocular words, as she would have heard them in a dream.

She soon mastered her outward perturbation, however. She had exerted all her skill, this morning, to render herself doubly fascinating in the eyes of her visitor, and she would not suffer a mere chit, like Hazel, to undo her artistic work; for she was fully conscious of her own success at the toilet. Evelyn wore a close-fitting robe of pearl-white texture, graced with endless falls of foamy lace, with white satin bows interspersed. A cluster of white rosebuds were half-buried in the jabot of lace at her throat, while a single bud nestled amid the luxuriant meshes of her hair. She looked a very goddess of purity, but in truth she was like the flower which bears a gnawing canker at its heart, threatening its destruction.

By the time Aubrey and Hazel had come ashore, Evelyn appeared an utter stranger to anger. She extended a lily hand to the gentleman, with one of her most benignant smiles, — and with just enough color in her cheeks to render her perfect, in attractiveness.

"Breakfast is served, monsieur, and I have been scouring the premises in search of you," said she, as he deliberately secured the boat to a willow bough. "We will go to the house at once, as mamma is waiting." Then, as she accepted his proffered arm, she laughingly added: "So you have proven a second James Fitz-James!"

"And my little Lady of the Lake, — how fair a fay is she!" returned Aubrey, in a tone which, despite its playfulness, had a shade of seriousness in it. He failed to see the sidelong glance directed from the accusing black eyes toward Hazel, — a glance which flustered the young girl's heart, and buried itself therein like a poisoned arrow.

CHAPTER V.

THINK naught a trifle, though it small appear;
Small sands, the mountain; moments make the year;
And trifles, life. YOUNG.

WELDON GRANGE boasted of many apartments; but few were so bright and alluring
as the spacious morning-room, with its lofty ceiling
of polished oak, and its elaborately carved wainscot,
with alternate oak and walnut panelling. A broad
and deep-set oriel window at the east end admitted
golden floods of sunlight, while another, its vis-a-
vis, overlooked the garden, and the tennis-lawn
beyond.

The appointments of this room were very
tasteful. The furniture was of carved walnut,
upholstered with vermilion and gold damask, and
the graceful window drapings bore the same warm
colors. Through the plate-glass doors of a massive
sideboard an endless array of crystal, silver, and
Sèvres china glittered and flashed; and all the
minor details, the pictures and bricabrac, were in
keeping with the luxury which reigned throughout
the room.

Breakfast was served. Buttered toast, fried

chicken, steaming coffee, were sending forth an
aroma so delicious as to tempt the palate of an
epicure.

"Though I have already trespassed upon your
orchard this morning, Madame Weldon," said
Deverell, falling a ready victim to the charms of
snowy damask, and leisurely peeling an orange, "I
can yet enjoy another of these delightful Navals.
They are unparalleled in flavor."

As neither of the ladies offered to join him, he
added: "I fear you natives of this floral land
fail to fully appreciate the luxuries about you. —
Ah! *Ma petite* Ellen Douglas will have one,
surely," he continued to Hazel, who murmured a
low, "Thanks, yes, monsieur;" and then she
turned alternately white and red, as he prepared
the fruit, for she was conscious, the while, of her
cousin's burning eyes fixed upon her, and secretly
wondering if she had been guilty of another misdemeanor, in accepting this little attention.

Mrs. Weldon's smile reassured her, however, and
the orange lost none of its sweet flavor because of
that acrid glance.

Breakfast passed off merrily. At its conclusion
Evelyn proposed a horseback ride, to which
Monsieur Aubrey, being a modern centaur, readily
assented.

"We will take a canter over to Fairacre,"
continued Miss Weldon. "That is papa's rice
plantation, and lies about six miles northward in

the river valley. The road leads through alternate woods and dells, and is considered one of the prettiest in the country. You shall ride Don Carlos, monsieur. He is a spirited stepper, and father's pet. He has not been saddled since his master went away, but you will find him docile and manageable."

The proper order was forthwith despatched to Noel, the hostler, to saddle Alcides and Don Carlos with all possible speed.

"The morning is simply perfect, and should be made the most of, you know," Evelyn added, with one of her most alluring smiles, as they arose from table. "You may take a turn about the grounds, monsieur, while I don my habit; or, if you would prefer reading, you will find the late Tallahassee and Jacksonville papers in the library."

Waving him a temporary adieu with her jewelled hand, as they turned into the wide hall, she said something softly to her mother, and the two ascended the stairs together, Mrs. Weldon first stopping to take leave of Hazel, before the girl went to the schoolroom for her daily studies.

As Mrs. Weldon followed to her daughter's room, she was full of secret wonder as to what Evelyn might wish to say to her so privately. She was not kept long in suspense. No sooner had the door closed behind them than Evelyn abruptly faced her mother, and said, with the fierceness of one who has long restrained her anger: "Why

do you permit that girl to stray about the grounds
so early in the morning, without her governess ?"

Mrs. Weldon stood utterly confounded. She
suffered her daughter to talk on with no attempt
at stopping her tongue.

"You are blind to her insolence and cunning!
She was up at daybreak this morning, and went
down to the lake, under pretence of sketching.
Really her design was to risk a romantic meeting
with Monsieur Deverell. It was only last night
that I charged her not to invite my guest to row.
She did not even wait for an opportunity to defy
me, but deliberately sought one. How successfully
her mischievous scheme has resulted, you can see
for yourself!" She paused, panting, her angry
eyes riveted on her mother's face, which was
undergoing a convulsion of pain.

"My daughter, — Evelyn dear!" she faltered at
length, "I fear you are a snapper up of unconsid-
ered trifles, as the poet puts it."

"Trifles indeed! This is no trifle!" retorted
the daughter, her temper increasing with every
word. "On the contrary, it is a matter of material
concern to me. That child shall be made to
answer for her impertinent conduct. The little
wretch!" Evelyn ended her speech with an
emphatic stamp of her foot upon the carpet.

It was something extraordinary for even this
arrogant girl to give vent to such violent words,
and Mrs. Weldon heard this epithet applied to her

beloved foster-child with wounded surprise, which
revealed itself in every line of her countenance.
She winced with inward pain, and compressed her
lips in order to stay the severe rebuke which rose in
her thoughts; for she believed calm reasoning to
be best.

Presently she said, at the same time passing one
gentle arm about her daughter's waist: "Dear
one, you do Hazel great injustice. I am confident
her meeting with Monsieur Deveréll was purely
accidental. It is her custom to be out these
fine mornings, running about the grounds before
the rest of us are awake. From such innocent
pleasures I would be the very last to restrain her;
for in her sentimental appreciation of the gifts of
Nature she but inherits the healthful constitution
of the Vernes. I remember the golden days of my
own youth, when Sister Lydia and myself were
happy in roaming the dewy pastures, ere the sun
had warmed the sleeping flowers into life. We
tried to outshine each other in the number of
butterflies we could count, fluttering in the space
about us, or balancing themselves to sip the sweet
drops from the blossoms. I heartily wish that
you, my daughter, had been endowed with a sunny
nature similiar to that which made my own childhood and girlhood so golden. Then there would
be the link of harmony between yourself and your
orphaned cousin, which is now sadly lacking."

There was no softening in the impassioned face

turned toward the open window, through which stole the gentle morning breeze, fanning the soft lace curtains, and breathing sweet odors from the garden below.

During a few moments of silence Evelyn tugged nervously at one of the satin bows on her dress, until finally the little ornament became detached from its resting-place amidst the lace, and fell to the floor. She looked at it, and then planted her foot upon it contemptuously, — for all the world as if it had been one of those fragile insects referred to by her mother, which she would gladly crush in wanton cruelty, because she must have something to vent her spite upon.

"Am I to be held responsible for my disposition, which, doubtless, is to be deplored for its barbaric common-sense?" Evelyn asked abruptly, and with strong irony. She added, a bitter smile curving her lips, "Had I inherited your romantic and perfect characteristics, thus gratifying your motherly ambition, even then I might have found it difficult to consort daily with one who has usurped my place in my father's affections, — an impostor!"

Evelyn articulated the last words with malicious emphasis. Mrs. Weldon's face blanched, and her lips were purple with the intensity of the pain she suffered, as she dropped into the nearest chair.

"Evelyn," she wailed piteously, as tears filled her eyes, "this is merciless in you! It is disrespectful to me, and cruelly unjust to your absent father, who loves you completely, unselfishly. Such viciousness amounts almost to crime toward an innocent and defenceless child! I used to think, Evy," she sobbed brokenly, " I used to think, when you were a little girl on my knee, that naught but the noblest of traits were wrapped up in the heart of my loving and tender rosebud-idol. I watched that bud expand from day to day, guarding it, dwelling upon its perfectness, as only a mother can dote upon her only child; but beneath my very eyes, the flower of my bosom has developed a moral cancer. In some mysterious way my treasure has been transformed into a rude cactus, prickly toward the parent who gave her birth, ready to crush the hearts which love and trust her implicitly, ready to defile her own lips with odious sentences! Oh God, I am so disappointed in my child!"

Her frame shook tumultuously. Her face was in her hands. Through the fingers tears rained thick and fast, falling upon the light fabric of her dress, and moistening it.

The cause of this sorrow stood by with mute lips, her tall form erect in statuesque severity. She stood thus for some time; but at length, as if her stony pride were gradually overruled by better feeling, a new flush overspread her fair skin, while the angry and defiant look in her eyes gave place to a softening moisture. Her proud lips quivered perceptibly, as she took first one step and then another toward her weeping parent.

"Mother!" she whispered, falling softly upon her knees beside the bent form, and twining repentant arms about her mother's neck. "Forgive me, dear! I did not mean, — I have never been intentionally cruel to you, darling. I love you devotedly. There, there, don't weep!"

Evelyn took her own handkerchief, a tiny square of filmy lace, and dried the wet cheeks and lashes with tenderest care. Then pressing a kiss upon the nervous lips, — a lingering kiss, teeming with the warmth of filial affection, — she continued, as she laid her head upon the heaving bosom, in which a new happiness was kindling: "If you have been disappointed in me, mamma, if I have fallen short of your parental ambitions, pray do not hold me altogether responsible for my shortcomings, which are legion; I know, dear, and you know, we do not have the shaping of our own characters or lives. They are the work of Destiny, — at least in part."

How many years had intervened since that queenly head had been laid in love's abandonment upon the maternal bosom, as it now lay? How many years since heart had thus been pressed to heart? It seemed a century to Mrs. Weldon, as her tears of happy thanksgiving fell upon the bands of dark hair which she smoothed so tenderly, whispering: "My darling, my only love! You are dearer to me than the whole world beside!"

The interval had seemed long; but in truth it was only four years. The day which brought Hazel Verne to the Grange had marked the change in Evelyn. It was then that the evil had been born in the heart of the flower, — the flower in which centred so many parental hopes and prayers.

CHAPTER VI.

BENEATH THE PINES.

Songs shall be heard as long as fields are green,
And skies are blue, and woman's face is fair.
                                                SMITH.

A S Aubrey paced slowly down the magnolia
avenue, mounted upon the beautiful black
steed, Don Carlos, Evelyn tripped jauntily down
the front steps, equipped for her morning canter.
The long folds of her olive-green skirt were
thrown with careless grace over one arm; and a
perfect-fitting basque of rich velvet, a shade or
two darker than the skirt, outlined her exquisite
figure; while a pearl-handled whip completed the
outfit, and gave her a Di Vernon air, which her
mirror had told her would prove irresistible to her
waiting knight. A long ostrich plume, corre-
sponding in shade with her habit, caught up her
wide-brimmed hat on the left side, curled backward over the heavy coils of her hair, and then
gave a capricious sweep downward to the shoulder,
thus lending to Evelyn's face a sort of gypsy
beauty, which rendered her doubly fascinating.

As Deveréll paced up to the mounting-block she
saw the look of undeniable admiration in his eyes,
and her heart beat with a thrill of triumph. He

(51)

alighted in order to assist her to the saddle, paying her a softly spoken compliment as he did so, to which Evelyn replied blushing, — not with diffidence, but with increase of joy: "Thanks, monsieur! I am so glad you are pleased."

The folds of her skirt being properly adjusted Aubrey remounted Don Carlos, and away the handsome pair rode, each happy, as only the spirit of youth can be, which has known naught of the world's deeper sorrows.

Evelyn had forgotten her recent annoyance, — had forgotten even that moment of confidence with her mother. For this seeming callousness let no one censure her too severely, insomuch as some day, in the dim, dim past, — a day perhaps forgotten, — the reader may have had one thought, one joyful anticipation, which shut out all others from the heart, as the picture of a golden day, spent in the society of this young Frenchman, barred Evelyn's memory to all else on earth.

She mastered her peerless Alcides with such adroitness as to win repeated compliments from her companion ; and Monsieur Deverell well knew how to frame a pretty compliment, albeit he had no flattering tongue, and owed his manner of doing homage to the fair sex wholly to heredity.

With him Evelyn manifested no likeness to the ice-plant. On the contrary, she was one perpetual torrent of life and animation. Though his admiring speeches acted like wine upon her, making the

blood come into her cheeks and rapture sparkle in
her eye, — though they thrilled her inmost soul with
ecstacy unspeakable,— she neither grew sentimental
nor stupidly serious, as the lovelorn are apt to do,
but almost matched Aubrey himself in brilliancy of
repartee.

It was indeed a perfect morning. The sky was
"deeply, darkly, exquisitely blue," without the
faintest cloud-drift visible. The air was sweet
with the elixir of ripening fruit, and vibrated with
the wild bird's joyous notes. There was just
enough breeze afloat to fan Evelyn's plumes into
coquettish play, and make the horses move with its
exhilaration.

Leaving the estate, and entering the open country
road, the animals broke away into a spirited gallop,
as they emerged abruptly from a shady amphitheatre
into an open and sunlit glade. Evelyn indicated
the different points of interest as they rode on, but
secretly wondered if her companion would never
take up the thread of their acquaintance where it
had been dropped in New Orleans, a few months
before, and tell her how he had treasured the rosebud he had taken from her hair ; but the rosebud
was not destined that day to be resurrected by
Aubrey from the grave of the past. The briefly
happy winter they had passed together in the
Crescent City, though once or twice alluded to by
monsieur, was mentioned casually, and in tones
strangely at variance with a lover's.

Once, after they had gained the river-valley, and were trotting leisurely through a section of pine-land, the young Frenchman drew his rein abruptly, and looked up at the bough-entangled roof above, — so dense that only a golden lance of sunlight shot through it here and there. What a secluded home of Nature was this! Here fair Flora smiled apace, and Evelyn's heart throbbed jubilantly. At their feet grew ox-eyed daisies, pale forget-me-nots, and wood-violets in luxuriance, amid thick-tufted green. Massive clusters of fern nestled against sturdy pine-trunks, while graceful bluebells stood guard, and nodded gleefully at each other. In another spot flourished the frail maiden-hair, and within the embrasure of its delicate shadow the gentle anemone looked coyly up, and breathed sweet incense on the air; while overhead unceasingly warbled the birds, as if especially engaged by Flora to furnish music for her festival.

Into monsieur's brown eyes there crept a light of reverence; and his heart beat appreciatively, as he gazed speechless upon this celestial scene. Those who knew Aubrey best assured him that he was designed for an artist. If so, he had evaded his calling; not wholly, however, for, though he could not have delineated the simplest leaf or bud upon canvas, his heart vibrated with boundless love for every tribute of Nature's hand. He could see character in the flowers, poetry in the cloven sea of foliage; and he could have fallen devoutly to his knees then and there, worshipping the great Creator in a song of praise.

All the gladness of Aubrey's being found voice in music. His whole soul was the sleeping-place of mystic chords, which lay ready to awaken at a moment's bidding. They awoke now. On the fragrant air his voice rose trembling, first in low, sweet strains, as if deft fingers were straying over invisible harp-strings. Then the sound increased, swelling into clarion tones, which woke the distant hills into a grand chorus of echoes. Presently his voice fell again, and finally died into a whisper, like the murmuring wind.

This was not the first time his singing had electrified the soul of Evelyn Weldon; and now she sat like one spellbound, with a face on which was written a whole page of adoration for the man beside her.

Monsieur had chosen an air from Schubert, and the words were an offering to the Queen of Nature. The composer could not have felt more keenly in writing than did Deverell in singing these strains, which echoed his heart's truest sentiment; and when he had finished the song there were tears in his eyes.

With a smile, born of the unutterable happiness he experienced, he bent a look upon his companion, and noticed that her eyes also were dim with tears. Evelyn averted her face. With a quick and impulsive gesture she brushed the drops away, as if ashamed of such weakness.

The air was now solemnly hushed and still. Even the birdnotes had ceased at the warning of that new voice.

"Monsieur," said Evelyn presently, "you have even put the birds to shame. Truly you ought to prize such power! You could move the hardest heart, I believe!"

Aubrey slightly bowed his head, with the deference due to this plain-spoken praise; but the voice of praise having been so long familiar to his ear, he did not feel flattered, and replied, with that quiet gravity which became him so well: "If mademoiselle appreciates my song, it is enough. My heart would burst, it seems to me at times, could I not breathe out in song some of the sentiment which pulsates within. Such beautiful scenes as the one now stretching out before us never fail to snatch me into the lyric mood. — How lovely are those wood-violets!" he added abruptly. They remind me of your Cousin Hazel's eyes! What a sweet, sunny character is hers! As they commenced to ride on again at a slow pace, he quoted those words from Longfellow's poem on Maidenhood:

> Standing with reluctant feet,
> Where the brook and river meet.

Miss Weldon gave her bridle a sudden and impetuous jerk, causing Alcides to prick up his ears

and quicken his trot to a canter. Aubrey, hardly
remarking her silence, — or her action, small in
itself, yet eloquent of secret disquiet, — continued,
in the same subdued but ardent tone: " She
reminds me, not a little, of your mother. Indeed,
I would sooner take her for madame's daughter
than yourself."

With the inward conflict waxing stronger, yet
with a successful attempt at outward calm, Evelyn
rejoined : " It is singular that people should fancy
a likeness between mamma and her foster-child,
when, in truth, there is no family—" She
abruptly checked herself, biting her lips until the
blood almost started from them. Aubrey gazed at
her in silent wonder ; and Evelyn, feeling this,
flushed and paled beneath his glance ; while at the
same moment a nefarious resolve formed itself in
her bosom.

At length she turned towards him. Meeting his
gaze boldly she said, in tones wherein there was no
shrinking : " What I was about to say, monsieur,
is strictly confidential."

The young Frenchman bowed assent, as a look
of deepening interest settled on his handsome
face.

" Hazel Verne," continued his companion, " is
only mamma's niece by adoption." A flutter of
suppressed triumph pervaded her words; but this
monsieur failed to notice. " A niece by adoption !" he ejaculated. " Mademoiselle, I think, — I
hardly understand,—"

" It is easily explained," remarked the other, with
a laugh which sounded like an evil omen under
that green canopy, and in contrast with the sweet
perfume of blossoms and the happy song of birds
about them, — a laugh which struck undefined
dread to the Frenchman's soul. " What does that
laugh portend ?" was his unspoken query.

This laugh was followed by these words, uttered
in the same half-exultant tone : " Hazel was my
Uncle Henry Verne's adopted child. As a dying
charge he gave her into the keeping of my
mother."

A deep frown knit itself in Aubrey's brows.
" Has this young girl been kept in ignorance as
to her birth?" he questioned gravely. " If so, it
has been a grievous wrong toward her, which is
certain to end in bitterness."

" Your question calls for a lengthy story, Monsieur Deveréll, — which I had rather not narrate,
when there is so much pleasant diversion for us."

This she said with feigned regret, for thus to
relate Hazel Verne's history had become all at once
a fixed resolve; yet in doing this, how unconscious
was Evelyn that she was deliberately setting fire to
the sweetest air-castle woman's fancy ever builded!
Little did she know that she was about to seal her
own bitter doom! Thus it was; though with no
forecast of the fatal result she went on desperately:
" You shall hear the story, — under a pledge of
secrecy however, as, outside our immediate family,

you are the first to whom the truth has been confided. Even Aunt Lydia Seymour is ignorant of it."

"Then I must insist," began the gentleman deprecatingly,— for the Deverell sense of honor was genuine, and Aubrey recoiled from words not designed for his ear; yet at Evelyn's imperative words, "Yes, monsieur, I have already unveiled the main truth; and now you shall hear the related facts," he sat like one under a spell, and hearkened to the story.

CHAPTER VII.

BETRAYAL.

EVERY true woman's breast yearns for the caress of baby fingers, just as surely as the true woman's heart holds the priceless jewel of mother-love.

"FOUR years ago," began Miss Weldon, "mamma received a telegram from her only brother, Henry Verne, summoning her to his deathbed, in Memphis, Tennessee. The startling news nearly cost dear mamma her own life, as she was devotedly attached to her brother; and though several years had passed since she had received special news of him, she was totally unprepared for the shock.

"She rallied, however, and went North immediately, to Memphis, reaching there only in time to hear a dying statement from Uncle Henry's lips.

"He was not, strictly speaking, an affectionate brother. Hence the protracted silence which he had maintained towards his sister. Meanwhile he had married a young Memphis lady,—heiress to nothing but a beautiful face. Being a successful financier, uncle did not allow her want of dower to interfere with their domestic felicity, which was complete, until the lapse of several years found them still childless. Then the young wife fell into a decline, rendering change of climate necessary. They travelled extensively, visiting all parts of Europe and America, but without gain to Mrs. Verne's health. Despairingly my uncle returned to Memphis, with his slowly but surely dying wife.

"It was about midnight, on the evening of their return, when they were both startled from sleep by a strange cry, repeated again and again. Going to the front part of the house, whence the noise seemed to come, Uncle Henry opened the door and looked out.

"It was a wild winter's night, and snow lay thickly on the steps; but there, against the gleaming white, he saw something dark, which proved to be a bundle. This he lifted and carried to his wife. Imagine her surprise when, putting back the thick folds of a shawl, a baby-girl opened its blue eyes into her face and smiled.

"The craving of her mother-heart was at last satisfied. Pressing the infant to her bosom in grateful thanksgiving, she doubtless believed she might live to nurture it. Indeed she did recover strength at once; but it was only artificial strength, poor thing! After a few days of strained excitement, her old symptoms reasserted themselves, and she grew rapidly worse.

"The babe, which she had learned to love with all the fondness of parental affection, had to be surrendered entirely to a nurse; and on her dying bed my aunty gave the child as a sacred legacy to her husband, begging that he would love and rear it as she would have done, had life been spared her, begging that Hazel should never know that he was not her own father. Uncle promised all that his wife asked. Through bankruptcy and poverty he remained true to his trust, and grew to love his foster-daughter as though she were indeed his own flesh and blood.

"But then came a tidal wave of affliction. He was struck with paralysis, and, while suffering this infirmity, his very roof was sold, by assignees, over his head. This proved to be his deathblow. Knowing this he telegraphed for mamma, as I have before said, wishing to transfer his sacred legacy into her keeping.

"Hazel was then eleven years old. Mamma accepted the charge; but she urged, in justice to my father, that to him also should be confided the secret of the child's birth. Uncle readily assented to this. Immediately after the funeral mother returned home, bringing her foster-child with her.

"Monsieur, this is Hazel Verne's mysterious history. It was never intended that I should be informed of it; but on the morning of their arrival mamma entered the library, accompanied by papa, and as I chanced to be standing at the window behind the curtains, which concealed me entirely from view, I overheard every word that passed between them.

"Father, though at first ill-pleased with the idea of fostering a child whose pedigree was shrouded in mystery, finally put aside prejudice, and promised, should Hazel prove herself worthy, to make her joint heiress with me to the Weldon estates."

Here Evelyn paused. Her heart beat tumultuously, while her eyes and cheeks glowed with volcanic fire.

"Monsieur," she resumed presently, "imagine yourself in my place at that moment, listening to a father, as he planned such a division of his wealth, between his only and beloved child and — another, who may have been born in the slums of Memphis, for aught he knew, — for aught he knows unto this day!"

Monsieur Deveréll sat, while Evelyn was speaking, with his eyes fixed upon Don Carlos's jetty mane; but now, as he lifted them to her face, she saw in them a look of profound pity, mingled with another look she could not so well interpret, but in which there seemed to be little of the sympathy she had anticipated.

At last he said : "The child's history is singularly sad and interesting, — a history which doubtless would have led me to agree with those interested in her behalf, had I accidently overheard their opinions."

Overwhelming indignation arose within Evelyn at his words. Had she then fallen so short of her mark? Had she, in confiding to him a secret her parents guarded so religiously, — a secret which, for four long years, had embittered her very existence, — in doing this had she awakened sympathy in Deverell's bosom for this nameless foundling, instead of for herself? After these many years of suppressed torture, had she cried aloud, only to have redoubled misery heaped upon her, instead of the condolence she had so trustingly believed would be forthcoming from the lips of him whom she loved better than the whole world beside, and who had given her encouragement to believe that love fully returned?

With such thoughts Evelyn looked again at the young Frenchman, and with ashen lips said bitterly: "Believe me, monsieur, the consciousness of being wronged by my parents overruled every other feeling, or else pity for this young girl might have prompted me to affection."

"But Monsieur Weldon has ample fortune for you both, mademoiselle! His estate is reckoned among the very wealthiest in the South," said Aubrey, feeling himself by no means equal to the occasion.

Evelyn grated her teeth in contempt of his words. Then, forcing a little laugh, she said, with a futile attempt to dissipate further thoughts about Hazel from the mind of her guest: "Oh well, the subject is certainly not worth the loitering away of a whole forenoon! Come, monsieur, we have

actually squandered half of it already. A race,
and a new whip if Alcides wins!" With this she
dashed ahead, challenging him with another peal
of painful laughter, which jarred upon our hero's
ear; but he spurred his horse, and in a moment
had gained on Alcides by several yards.

"The whip is mine!" cried he, facing about and
waiting for Evelyn to come up; but while his voice
sounded cheerful enough, there was a weight upon
his heart which would not lift itself. He saw in
his mind's eye a little blue-robed form, with hair of
mingled gold and bronze; and a pair of pathetic
blue eyes looked up into his own, while a sweet
voice said, "I am only Hazel." *Only Hazel! Only
Hazel!* he kept repeating to himself. Hazel who?

It seemed to Aubrey that he would willingly
surrender ten years of his life, if by so doing he
could purchase the right to ferret out the mystery
surrounding this orphan, whose image had so
recently entered his life.

On the return ride these two, whose spirits had so
recently been bubbling over with youthful gayety,
— whose clear voices had rung out on the July air,
making the woods reverberate with joyous laughter
and song, — felt very little like lovers. Though
the conversation seldom flagged between them,
there were no more pretty compliments, no more
answering blushes, none of these fond glances
which had constituted Evelyn's heaven. Aubrey
scarcely glanced toward her; or if by chance

he looked at her, it was in a manner utterly
devoid of the tenderness Evelyn had so often seen
in his telltale eyes, glances which had conveyed a
world of promise to her heart. The very absence
of these silent speeches threw Evelyn into a
despairing mood.

Only the night before — which now seemed to
her an age ago — she had sought her room, after
bidding her guest good-night in the hall, where
repeated hand-pressures, and passionate looks from
his dark orbs, made her very happy; and as she
beheld her own beautiful lovelit face in the mirror,
she felt, beyond the shadow of doubt, that she was
destined to become Madame Deveréll. Now a
change came o'er the spirit of her dream, and she
told herself that Hazel Verne was the evil genius
who wrought the transformation.

"Is it not enough that she should come into my
life and infringe my rights, without dooming me
to utter misery?"

They were turning an abrupt curve in the road,
as she questioned herself thus bitterly, when all
at once she became conscious of an advancing
horseman. She needed only one look to recognize
in the rider none other than the young barrister to
whom she had given a claim upon her hand, a
claim she now saw fit to revoke, believing the
future held for her a far happier fate.

It was not however the remembrance of that
promise, neither was it the remembrance of her

recent coldly written revocation of that promise, which caused her hand to close convulsively over the handle of her riding-whip, and her face to turn from white to red. Her disquiet was prompted by the belief that she discerned unmistakable evidence of intoxication in the bearing of her old suitor, whose horse was bearing directly upon them. What should she do, — recognize him in such a disgraceful condition ? — Never!

Only a few rods now intervened between herself and the unsteady horseman, and Evelyn abruptly commenced a very animated historical sketch of an ancient mill, near which they were passing, and to which were attached several blood-curdling legends; the substance of one being, that the rusty machinery was known to revolve on certain midnights during the year, its blazing furnace tended by ghostly and grotesque skeletons, who danced around it, as witches waltz about their caldrons, chanting weird dirges, to which the rattle of their bones kept time.

Evelyn plunged into a rapid narration of this absurd story, hoping thus to avoid any acknowledgment of Wilford Hylton's presence. Imagine her astonishment at hearing a sudden exclamation from her companion, in the very midst of her tale: "Hylton! Well, by all that's righteous, it's the old boy himself!"

Did she hear the words in a dream? No, there was certainly nothing more real than those two

riders meeting, and engaging in a prolonged and
jubilant hand-wringing. Seeing that matters had
now developed into so dramatic a situation, and that
some action on her part was inevitable, Evelyn
rode slowly forward. As Wilford lifted his hat
she saw immediately that her conclusion as to the
young barrister's condition had been erroneous.
No sign of dissipation was apparent in the lines of
that noble countenance. No red demon looked out
from those clear blue eyes. There was no stain on
the fair mustache, nor did the pale lips falter in
their speech. Though all these signs of intoxication were happily absent, there was that in his
shrunken and pale face, and in his unsteadiness in
the saddle, which spoke plainly of protracted
illness, — such illness as seldom comes to a man
A broken heart! Alas, who can describe the pain
thereof, save one who has endured it ?

Evelyn extended an icy hand to Wilford, saying
briefly, and with her old reserve : " Good-day, Mr.
Hylton ! "

What more was there to say ? How could she
meet those honest eyes, filled with mute reproach
and living misery, and say, " I am glad to see
you, my friend." No wonder she averted her face
to conceal a burning flush roused by consciousness
of her cruelty.

She experienced unspeakable relief when Aubrey
explained presently : " We were at the university
together, mademoiselle, Mr. Hylton and I. This

sudden and unexpected meeting is a pleasure one
does not often experience in a lifetime. I believed
him in Jacksonville, and fully intended hunting him
up before I left the country."

Other remarks followed; but Wilford was burning to free himself from the presence of a woman
whose heartlessness had wellnigh given him a
deathblow, and so he took advantage of the first
opportunity to say: "I am stopping with an
uncle, half-a-mile north, on the left of the road,
Deverell, you can't miss the gothic house of gray
stone, with two vicious lions guarding the entrance.
Come and dine with me on Monday, and we will
chat over our old college days. Adieu until then,
old boy, and fail me at your peril. I shall expect
you at five, sharp." Then away the fair-haired
fellow galloped, more miserable than ever.

Tired and disappointed with the world in general,
Evelyn hurried to her rooms, after her return to
the house. Throwing herself upon a divan, she
gave herself up to abusing the fates which had
ushered into her sphere of existence two such superfluities as Hazel Verne and Wilford Hylton.

What would be the sequel of this meeting
between her guest and the barrister? The more
she debated this question in her mind, the more
convinced she became that nothing would ever
reach Aubrey's ear from Wilford, regarding their
past *affaire.* Her knowledge of the barrister's
noble nature was in itself proof positive that he

would never allow one syllable to pass his lips in condemnation of her.   At last, with all her present doubts set at rest, her old ambition reasserted itself; and with reviving hope came Phebe, to assist her in dressing for dinner.

"Get out my pale-mauve silk, with the lace drapery," she said to the mulatto maid, "and arrange my hair in high puffs, with the sapphire dagger ornament.   Now Phebe, do your very best. I rely on you as an expert, you know."

"An' it's berry little sprusin' up as you acquire to look hansome as a prince, Missy Eb'lyn," returned Phebe, much elated by her mistress's flattery.

CHAPTER VIII.

THE MAGICIAN.

Music can noble hints impart,
Engender fury, kindle love. ADDISON.

"ARLINE," said Hazel the next day, after study-hours, "Who was the Lady of the Lake? Was she some noted heroine?"

The French governess, wondering at her pupil's question, looked down smilingly into the pathetic eyes.

"Why, *ma chère*," she replied, "she was Ellen Douglas, the heroine of Sir Walter Scott's beautiful poem, Lady of the Lake. Have you never read it? No? And have you not seen the portrait of the Douglas's Daughter, which hangs in my room? *Allons*, I will show you."

Hazel pressed one of the woman's hands to her lips with unwonted fervor. "Oh my Arline," she exclaimed, "I know of nothing that would give me more pleasure than to see the portrait of Ellen Douglas!"

Puzzled more and more, though refraining from further questions, Arline led the way to her own private apartment, which was located in a retired part of the house, adjoining the study-room. Here she opened the shutters to admit more light, and then led Hazel up to the hearth. Pointing above

(71)

the mantel, where hung a small frame of ancient workmanship, she said: "That is the Lady of the Lake. I brought the picture with me from France, and prize it much, as it once hung in the studio of my grandfather. It is strange mademoiselle has never taken notice of it before, having so often been in my room. "   ,

"Oh yes, Arline," said Hazel quickly, "I have noticed the picture before, but never thought to ask the subject.—And this is Ellen Douglas!"

With red lips slightly apart, and hands clasped loosely before her, Hazel stood long in a rapt posture, suffering her eyes to dwell upon the classic features of the Douglas's Daughter, who stood leaning upon one frail oar in her little shallop,

> With head upraised and look intent,
> And eye and ear attentive bent.

Ellen's supple figure was clad in clinging plaid. Jetty ringlets rippled from beneath a silken snood, and covered her shoulders like a mantle. Each feature of the little painting charmed Hazel, as nothing of the kind had ever done before. Almost unconsciously she murmured, — so very softly that Arline, who had already busied herself with a piece of needlework, did not catch the sound of the girl's voice: "Beautiful, *beautiful* Ellen Douglas! I wonder if James Fitz-James was your lover!"

She turned at length with a suppressed sigh, and slowly approached her governess.

"Is the character not beautiful, *ma chère?*"

asked the Frenchwoman, looking up from her work as Hazel drew near.

"Beautiful!" echoed the young girl passionately. "I have never seen so lovely a face as hers in my life; but Arline,"—pausing with clasped hands, and eyes full of thoughtful pathos,—"I wish I knew something about her, about the poem. Will you not some day tell it me?"

"Perhaps mademoiselle would like to read for herself. I have all Scott's poetical works, and there are other poems among them of equal interest. You may take them to your room, if you like, and read to your heart's content."

Going to her bookcase Arline took therefrom a handsome green and gold volume, which she handed to Hazel. "Madame also has Scott's poems in the library downstairs," she resumed, "but they are in one large volume, complete, with illustrations, which would not be as convenient for you to handle. In my set every poem is separately bound. When you have finished Lady of the Lake I will give you Marmion, or the Lay of the Last Minstrel."

Hazel could find no words to express her delight, but she lifted herself on tiptoe and imprinted a warm kiss upon either cheek of the kind Frenchwoman, whispering as she did so: "Dear Arline, you are always doing something to make me happy, and I do so love you!"

Then Hazel ran out of the room, her young

heart fluttering with gladness at the thought that she was to learn all about Ellen Douglas, and perhaps James Fitz-James; for the two names had been uppermost in her mind since yestermorn. With the dainty green and gold volume pressed tight to her breast she sped along the corridor to her own pretty chamber, and locked herself in to read.

Dinner over, Evelyn threw a zephyr shawl about her shoulders, and went, in company with her guest, for a stroll about the grounds. They lingered in the garden till the dew began to fall, and spangled scarfs were spread aloft in the sky. Then Deveréll suggested re-entering the house, because of the gathering dampness.

"It seems like a penalty to be compelled to spend so lovely an evening indoors," said Evelyn ruefully; "but mamma is so anxious to hear you sing! You certainly," pressing his arm faintly, and speaking in a persuasive tone, "will be kinder to us than you were last evening."

On the occasion referred to our hero had politely declined to exercise his vocal powers, but to his companion's entreaty he now replied: "What a pity there is no moon! We might then spend the evening on the lake, and I would tire you out with singing. To me there is something unspeakably delightful in music on the moonlit water. As we are denied the ruling of the firmament, however,

I shall with pleasure contribute to mademoiselle's entertainment in the drawing-room.—Hazel, your cousin, does she enjoy music? Does she sing?"

Hitherto he had been speaking with an absent-mindedness which wellnigh maddened the maiden at his side; but as he questioned her thus, his handsome face was lighted with a sudden animation, which Evelyn noted with the acute eye of jealousy, despite the deepening gloom.

With her accustomed self-possession, however she replied briefly: "Hazel, I dare say, enjoys music in a childish fashion. She is little more than a child, you know. As for singing, her talent that way is, like my own, grievously at fault."

Evelyn did not trust her eyes to meet his as she spoke; but the basilisk lurking in their depths would no longer have perplexed Deveréll. He had guessed that little affection existed in Evelyn's heart toward the young girl whose life was so tangled in a web of mystery, and who aroused such a different feeling within his own bosom.

Five months earlier Aubrey believed he had seen Evelyn Weldon in every phase of her character, and she had seemed to him the embodiment of purity and generosity. Now he had detected flaws in this queenly being, of whom he had brought himself to think as the probable mistress of the home of his ancestors, believing she would sustain and grace the position creditably to those who had formerly reigned there—flaws that must never be found in a Lady of Deveréll Hall.

Deceit, disloyalty! These were defects which made woman, however fascinating otherwise, a disfigured gem. Though a hundred beautiful traits might shine in her character, they could not redeem this blur.

How little did Evelyn Weldon imagine that morning when narrating Hazel's history, under the cloistered pines, that she was wilfully shattering her dream-castle, on the very eve of its assuming substantial reality. All that now remained of the castle was an unsightly ruin. She had wantonly betrayed her dead uncle's trust; nor was it alone a death-trust broken, for the living had been impiously deceived.

Monsieur was not a little disappointed and chagrined at the untoward turn taken by an *affaire* which he had deemed the most important of his life; yet he inwardly congratulated himself, inasmuch as he had been brought face to face with the perilous truth, ere the fatal leap had been taken. Better awake from a happy dream in time to save himself from impending flames!

Though he had turned a reluctant ear to the story of the interesting foundling, though he had felt himself almost a traitor as the words fell from Evelyn's lips and buried themselves like lead in his bosom, yet he nourished them there. Appealing blue eyes and sunny hair, above a frock that matched the eyes in hue and clung about a slender and immature form, were elements of a picture graven upon his heart, — a picture which haunted him every hour, and would not fade away.

"Hazel, Hazel! but Hazel who?" This was the revolving question. If he appeared preoccupied this evening, it was little wonder.

Evelyn ushered him along the shadowy veranda, through the long French window, into the spacious parlor, and conducted him at once to the open piano. "I remember, monsieur," said she archly, "that you always prefer playing your own accompaniments; so pray be seated, and do not think of abandoning this stool until that mysterious warbler in your throat has quite exhausted himself. — Here is a portfolio containing songs by many composers. Doubtless your favorites are among them." But Monsieur Deveréll sang altogether from memory, and left the handsome brown and silvern music-case unopened.

Evelyn ensconced herself in the corner of a luxurious armchair, near the piano, while Mrs. Weldon sat, busy with some delicate needlework, by a small inlaid stand, where the light from a rose-tinted shade fell upon her countenance, flooding it with holy loveliness.

With masterful power our hero's fingers touched the keys, awakening a seductive prelude. His chest expanded, his lips parted, and out poured a strain from Donizetti's Lucia, — a strain subdued and searching, which throbbed through the house. Measure after measure rosè and fell, floating through the halls, reaching even the kitchen, where it broke in upon an animated negro chorus.

One by one the sable dependents stole out and moved stealthily down the side veranda, toward the drawing-room windows, which were open to admit the fragrant atmosphere from the garden; and soon the silhouettes which revealed themselves in the deep frames would have been sufficient to encourage any singer, had he chanced to glance that way.

Through one window could be seen Aunt Sally, the cook, with a bright yellow bandanna twisted about her head, while in each of her strong bare arms was held a spellbound pickanniny, whose big black eyes glistened like emeralds in ebony settings. At another point stood Phebe, together with the butler, their heads bent close together as they whispered with hushed voices, and now and then suffered their eyes to meet in glances eloquent with more than musical appreciation. In a third aperture, unopened, from which the heavy portières were looped aside, there were other visages, each aglow with pleasure at this unusual treat.

Meanwhile where was Hazel Verne? Let us steal to her window and glance in upon her, as she bends with flushed cheeks and thirsty eyes over her poem, The Lady of the Lake. Not once had she stirred from her chair since dinner. Her rapt posture, the light that came and went in her beautiful face, the smiles and tears which by turns took possession of her eyes, the sighs that fluttered half-smothered from her lips, all declared that Ellen Douglas's joys and sorrows had become Hazel's own. So completely lost was the child to all her surroundings, that even when she came to these words of the minstrel to the Douglas's Daughter,

> Yet, oh loved maid, thy mirth refrain,
> Thy hand is on a lion's mane!

and the music from below, like notes from a silver flute, fell round about her, she did not come fully to herself, for the song resounded much like music she had oft heard in her dreams. Thus she read her poem, line after line, and the song-notes lingered, until it seemed as if sob after sob were poured from a broken heart into her ear.

Suddenly the book fell from her hands to the carpet. With bated breath she sprang to her feet, each nerve strained to listen. The room was now alive with those magic strains, and words from The Bohemian Girl (Deverell was singing " When other lips and other hearts ") thrilled her soul. She had once been taken to Tallahassee to hear this tuneful opera, and had been so affected by the tribulations of the abducted Arline, that her violent weeping had been a source of direst mortification to her arrogant foster-sister; and she had often recalled certain passages of the plot, and renewed her sympathetic tears.

Mechanically Hazel approached the door, and glided like one enchanted down the hall. As she approached the foot of the staircase, and turned toward the drawing-room, whose doors were wide open, someone grasped her arm tightly, and whispered: " Ah Mademoiselle Hazel, what music, what grand music! It is monsieur, my country-man, who sings!"

"Yes, Arline," returned the young girl in a low voice, " it is he. Did you ever hear anything half so beautiful? But I must go in, I must be nearer! Won't you come too?"

The governess shook her head dissentingly. " I prefer to remain here," she added; whereupon Hazel moved toward the drawing-room alone.

No-one observed the white-robed figure, standing with clasped hands upon the threshold, her head bent forward, and her eyes, with ineffable sadness and longing in them, riveted upon the singer. No-one noticed her as she glided noiselessly over the soft carpet toward the piano, where she mutely stood, close behind Evelyn.—Nobody observed her until the singer paused and, glancing up suddenly, cried joyously, " Hazel!"

CHAPTER IX.

THE GREEN-EYED MONSTER.

Oh stay, oh stay!
Joy so seldom weaves a chain
Like this tonight, that oh, 't is pain
To break its links so soon. MOORE.

IF there was not something akin to joy in
Aubrey's tones as he uttered this name, there
was certainly something which prompted Evelyn
to start as if she had been stung. She let her eyes
range several times up and down the form near
her, — taking in every detail, from the excited
posture to the vivid crimson that had mantled the
face, as Hazel found herself thus suddenly awakened
from the spell which had bound her.

Instead of sadness, there was now a startled
expression in her eyes, as she slowly raised them
to the Frenchman's countenance, and murmured
brokenly, as she put back the hair nervously from
her temples: "Oh monsieur, I pray you will
pardon me! I was sitting in my room, reading,
when I heard your voice, and — and I came! — I
wished to be nearer. I love music dearly, and
have heard that opera once in my life, and so I
recognized your song. It was heavenly."

Monsieur's eyes glanced from Hazel's face to

Miss Weldon's, and he could not help noting Evelyn's pallor, though her fierce anger was cautiously hidden beneath the heavy lashes, as she bent her gaze upon a spray of delicate orchids, which had fallen from her belt into her lap. With this she toyed nervously, as she felt his eyes upon her, while her bosom was aglow with perturbation.

"Is this a *child's appreciation* of music?" Aubrey questioned within himself, as Evelyn's words came back to him. "This little maid enjoys music in no *childish* fashion!"

"You are not going to run away so soon!" he exclaimed, as Hazel began a retreat from the piano.

She felt aggrieved. She wondered at his silence, and tried to convince herself that he, as well as Evelyn, was displeased at her coming; but she paused, with a glad light in her visage, as monsieur continued, in earnest tones: "Stay Hazel! I will sing for you until midnight, if you enjoy hearing me."

"Yes, darling," interposed Mrs. Weldon, "by all means stay. I would have called you before, but I knew you were reading, and did not like to disturb you."

Thereupon Hazel nestled into a large chair beside her foster-mother, forgetting all save the one thought that she was to hear more of that wonderful voice. Yes, even the memory of Ellen Douglas was banished for the time, as once more

Monsieur Deveréll held his listeners spellbound, —
all save Evelyn, who never allowed her glance to
wander from the illumined face of her foster-sister.

At length, as the singer lost himself in his chosen
melodies, Evelyn arose, and noiselessly crossed the
room to her mother. " Tell monsieur," said she,
bending over the elder lady's chair and whispering
hurriedly, " to please accept my compliments, and
excuse me for the rest of the evening. One of
those odious headaches has seized me suddenly,
and I must retire at once. I must be where there
is quiet."

" I will go with you, dear, and see that you are
made comfortable," returned Mrs. Weldon, rising
anxiously from her chair.

" No, no, I shall not permit it ! " said her
daughter with a deprecating gesture. " Phebe can
do all that is required."

The proud beauty swept down the wide apartment ; but on gaining the doorway she paused long
enough to cast one backward and reproachful look
at Hazel, whose gaze followed her unconsciously.
The dart must have hit its mark, for Hazel trembled
visibly. Her face was pained and bloodless, but
still turned toward her cousin.

Afterward, when Evelyn had disappeared, Hazel
sat with great orbs riveted upon the floor, in a half-
bewildered, half-frightened way, with only the
memory of that unkind look before her mind's eye.
She tried, oh how vainly ! to find some interpreta-

tion of Evelyn's behavior. Even the sound of Aubrey's voice, which had charmed her soul into ecstacy, was now drowned in the one supplicating cry of her heart: "What could Evelyn mean by such a look?"

Reaching her apartment Evelyn tore from her throat a necklace of rubies and sapphires, which had suddenly become unbearably tight. Flinging the gems rudely upon her dressing-table she commenced a feverish pace up and down the room, her desperate thoughts finding vent in hot, rustling words.

"Dared I but breathe a word or two in that girl's ear, she would be glad enough to court obscurity in the future! Oh, but I dare not! To do this would be to condemn myself forever in *his* eyes. Then where would be my triumph? Levelled to the dust! And she — ? No, no! I must needs choke back the words that rush so often to my lips, and go on in silence, letting a child of infamy eat out my heart's sweetest hope. Oh the nameless torture that has filled my life since yestermorn! Jealousy? Jealous of a child whom he knows to be branded with mystery and shame? Bah! I must be mad! — Yet, why does n't Aubrey broach the subject of — the subject that fills my heart to suffocation? He has palpably changed since his arrival at the Grange. That evening his every word, every glance, was eloquent with — his purpose in coming; but now he is almost cold toward me. It may be this preoccupation is but the forerunner of a proposal! Yes, for much is involved in such a step. I shall try to bide my time patiently, till he sees fit to speak,—which may be even tomorrow! Ah yes, even by another sunset I may be able to recall my wretchedness of tonight with secret amusement."

With this hopeful yet subdued thought the girl began to consider the impropriety of her sudden disappearance from the drawing-room; and poor Hazel's innocent head became the target of censure for this breach of hospitality on Evelyn's part. Why did that girl make her cousin — yes, she must still say *cousin* — feel so terribly? Would my lord suspect the true cause of Evelyn's absence? She believed this impossible. Nevertheless, after a moment's debate, she resolved upon the advisability of a speedy return. She applied a light wash of French enamel to her face, that it might appear paler, in accordance with her pretence of sick-headache. Then she saturated her handkerchief with cologne, took a vinaigrette, and was ready to appear before monsieur in the role of invalid.

As she softly opened the door, voices came echoing up the staircase, in an exchange of goodnights; and by this she concluded that the little party had disbanded. She inwardly congratulated herself that her going down would yet be in season to bid her guest goodnight. She would doubtless find him alone in the hall. Oh sweet thought!

She heard her mother going about the house, on her usual nightly missions. Now, fully assured that she should find monsieur alone, Evelyn glided down the corridor, whispering to her heart that even tonight all doubts might be exiled forever by the coveted confession. At least she would hear from him sympathetic words, which alone would be as balm to her restless soul.

She reached the heavy oaken balustrade, and was on the point of descending, when a subdued murmur of voices floated upward, like the hum of night. With palpitating breath she paused, one jewelled hand resting on the railing, the other pressed close against her heart. Her now anxious face was bent eagerly forward.

"Tell me, little one, are you happy here?"

These words came to Evelyn in the familiar voice, whose tones had such power to rouse each fibre of her being.

"Yes, oh yes, monsieur. I am happy, quite happy, since I heard your singing."

"It is not that! I do not mean that! Tell me! Is your life, your home, a happy one? Do not be afraid to trust me, Hazel. I wish to be your true friend."

This time the Frenchman's suppressed yet agitated voice was met by the reply: "Oh monsieur, never could one be blessed with a happier home than mine. I have all one could wish."

The listener peered over the banister, but with a deathly face, her eyes glittering with a greenish hue. She drew herself back the next instant; for there, just beneath her gaze, under the vivid glare of the chandelier, stood Deveréll, bending over one of Hazel Verne's little hands, — even touching it with his lips, and murmuring: "Goodnight, my little friend! Be thine the fairest dreams that angels bestow upon the pure, and be thy future life ever as thou sayest it is at the present, — very happy! Goodnight, child, and God bless thee!"

Like a restless spirit Evelyn sought her chamber again. Flinging herself upon a divan, she remained there through long hours of the night, striving with the nettle which had crept into her life. Not once did the thought come to her that, as she had brewed her own bitter cup, she must perforce drink it.

CHAPTER X.

HE gave to misery (all he had) a tear,
He gained from Heaven ('t was all he wished) a friend.
GRAY.

AUBREY, with his quick perceptions, was keenly alive to the fact that his old and endeared college-friend, Wilford Hylton, was the victim of some serious trouble, bodily or mental. Often, since their recent meeting, he had recalled the young barrister's woe-begone visage with painful regret, wondering what could have wrought so deplorable a change in the hopeful and vivacious youth of college-days. Possibly his ambition had been thwarted by unkind Fate!

At the university Wilford and the young Frenchman had been close friends; but during an interval of years the chain of communication between them had been severed by the drift of circumstances. After a limited vacation Wilford had entered the office of his uncle, a prominent lawyer in Jacksonville; while Deveréll had travelled extensively, abroad and at home, thus rendering his address too uncertain for continuous correspondence.

More than three years had elapsed since either

(88)

had received definite news of the other. Naturally
the thought suggested itself to Deverél, that
Wilford's impaired health must be due to business
reverses. Riding alone and at an idle pace
through the forest, on his way to Hylton's abode,
our hero recalled his friend's beautiful character,
as it was associated with bygone days, — his unselfish nature, the almost womanly tenderness of
his affection, the rich cadence of his voice, as it
resounded in eloquent debate, the fair hair, brushed
back from a noble brow, the luminous eyes, so true
and expressive. Aubrey remembered the tall and
well-built form, with its manly bearing and its
graceful movement.

He could not forbear a smile, as he called to
mind a certain occasion when, as the two were
walking, with interlocked arms, about the recrea-
tion-ground, Deverél declared, that if the Fates
had only created his companion of the opposite sex,
his heart would have been laid at his — or rather
at her — feet.

How Hylton laughed as he retorted : "In such
a case, *mon ami*, college discipline would prove an
insurmountable barrier between us."

Arriving at the specified brown house, with its
ferocious stone lions, Deverél saw Wilford seated
within the embrasure of a bay-window, apparently
on the lookout for his visitor.

"My suspense had wellnigh reached madness,"
exclaimed Wilford, bounding down the steps.

"You might have spared yourself undue anxiety, *bon ami !*" returned monsieur, with a warm hand-pressure. "I would not miss this meeting for a fortune."

It seemed to Wilford at that moment that the sun had risen again over his benighted world — the sun which he believed had set forevermore. Under the firm pressure of that true hand, with a soul's steadfast friendship beaming from those eloquent eyes, how could he doubt the fidelity of man. Surely it was good to feel the sunlight beating upon the frozen heart, after these days of wintry desolation!

For a whole fortnight Wilford had walked, drank, ate, and slept like one under the spell of somnambulism. The sun had shone and warmed the earth into a flood of glory, but not for him. Roses had bloomed and intoxicated the air with their aroma. Birds had vainly sung and fountains had vainly sprayed in the garden, where each day had found him walking with hanging head and sluggish step, oblivious to everything save the thought that the one woman of his heart had proved herself a traitress.

Evelyn had proffered him the ecstatic cup of love. In the bottom he found poison; but he found it too late! The cup had been drained, and Wilford was a doomed man.

It must have been full sixty seconds that the two men stood gazing straight at each other. Each silently wondered what the other's experiences had been during the years of separation. At length, as if he had interpreted something of Deveréll's mind, Wilford spoke : " We both have our stories, old boy ; but these we must reserve until after we have dined. Uncle Allan and his wife have gone to the city. Concluding the dining-room would seem barn-like, with only us two, I have ordered dinner in my sanctum, where I am sure we shall be more cosy."

"Good!" exclaimed the other. "It will seem like the old days, when we used to smuggle champagne and goodies into our dens, and thus manage our private feasts."

Deveréll laughed, slapping his companion's shoulder. Encouraged by seeing the pale face brighten at this reference to past escapades, Aubrey followed his host upstairs.

The sanctum was a spacious room, and presented a most inviting appearance, with its gray carpet and substantial furniture, not to mention the luxuries which make up a man's comfort, as well as the superfluities which show a woman's taste and (despite their utter uselessness) delight the eye of refinement. The most attractive feature of the room was the neatly laid table, with its array of crystal and china, and its promise of Epicurean delights.

When all was in readiness the man-servant assumed a statuesque attitude near the door, with the good-natured expression of "At your service, gentlemen," on his face; but this look was exchanged for one of amazement as the young host said kindly: "You may go now, Peter. I shall ring when you are wanted."

"De champagne, Mars Wi'ford! Sha'n't I open it afo' I goes?" asked the colored boy, hesitating, but with his hand on the door-knob.

"All right!" assented Wilford; whereupon a little popping act followed. Then the friends were left to themselves.

Deveréll was determined to cheer the spirit of his host, if such a thing were possible; and his incessant flow of humor certainly had the desired effect. As the ghosts of old college jokes were resurrected one by one, Wilford's cheeks began to flush with new animation, while through his smiles shone the illumined soul.

Genuine mirth burst from his lips; and such a marked transformation was wrought, that when our ebony friend Peter reappeared, to arrange the cloth for dessert, he could do nothing for a moment but stand looking at his young master's face.

With the termination of dinner, however, their wit seemed nearly spent. Each young man tilted back his chair, after lighting a cigar, conscious that more serious matters than strawberries and wine were next in order. Heretofore not one syllable had been uttered between them about the personal matters which had filled the years of separation.

For some moments a strained silence reigned between them, such as many have experienced, when brought upon the "anxious seat" for grave confession. Neither sought the other's glance, but rather avoided it. As Deveréll puffed dainty whiffs from his Havana, watching the delicate blue smoke curl upward, Hylton sat motionless, gazing steadfastly through the window, and restlessly twisting his smouldering cigar.

To all things there is an end. At length this constraint was broken by Wilford. Turning slowly from the window, he remarked: "I hoped to run across you two years ago, when I was abroad. In Paris one day I followed a young Frenchman into a café, mistaking him for yourself. I was not convinced of my error until I spoke to him. This was in October. Were you in Europe at that time?"

After a moment's reflection the other replied: "At the time you mention, two years ago, I was visiting my sister in Genoa. A month later I was in Paris! And you?"

"In Vienna, where my business was concentrated. I remained in that city two months. The time was consumed in the discussion of my case. At its conclusion I returned home."

"And your mission abroad? I trust it proved fruitful?" said monsieur interrogatively.

It was with no small degree of suspense that he awaited Hylton's response; for, as he covertly studied the pale face opposite, he believed he saw the unmistakable stamp of financial disappointment written thereon.

This was a false interpretation, however. After a moment's pause Wilford looked up. Meeting his friend's anxious gaze he began, in a voice which conveyed little triumph, but much bitter irony: "Yes, after protracted argument. I established our client's title, against a Hungarian competitor, to an inheritance of fifteen-hundred-thousand florins, and returned home with flying colors. It was the first important case in which I had figured, having been admitted to the bar only a few months before. Since then I have advised effectually in many noted cases in our own State, and my professional career has been one of marked success. I remained for two years junior partner with Uncle Allan. Failing in health, he concluded to retire from business to his country-seat here. I desired to keep up the firm in Jacksonville; but uncle is childish in his enfeebled state, and urged me to establish an office in Jasper, where I can be near, to act as his private adviser, as well as to share the comforts of his home. At the same time, he felt sure of my success in these parts. His was a correct prophecy. Fortune has followed me. I have been continually fighting and conquering, and for the wealthiest people in this section."

"But," continued Wilford with a sarcastic air, as he tossed his neglected cigar through the

window, "after all, where is my triumph? What
is one ambition fulfilled, if in a far sweeter way
we are exalted to Heaven, only to be hurled
mercilessly down? What is victory? Through
eloquence we win laurels. We think to win roses
of love, through months of prayerful perseverance,
only to have them abruptly transformed into
thorns that sting like adders? What is Fame, if
Fortune guides us to the topmost rung of the
ladder only to mock us, — to open our eyes to the
terrible conviction that there is no such thing as
truth?"

Wilford's voice became husky. Every muscle
of his face twitched with agitation, while his blue
eyes remained fixed upon Deverell, whose own
eyes now were dim.

Aubrey remained silent. His heart prompted
no fit response to an utterance so unexpected as
this. Indeed, Wilford's words were somewhat
enigmatical, and Aubrey could only revolve them
in his mind, trying to define them. In this state
of mental perturbation the young barrister left
Aubrey for some moments, and commenced a
restless pace to-and-fro, with his hands clasped
behind him.

When he at length resumed his seat his voice
betrayed less agitation, but was still tremulous.

"Do not put too hasty a meaning on my words,
my friend. I spoke madly! At sight of your
countenance, some of my lost faith in human honor

was roused. A few days ago all became darkness to me. I had forgotten your very existence, and was too utterly cast down to care for it. Now the sky has changed. I glory once more in the light of a friendly face!"

"*Mon Dieu!* What great sorrow is this of yours, Hylton? Confide in me!" exclaimed the young Frenchman, deeply moved.

"Why should I suffer my wound to bleed afresh?" said the other sadly.

After a brief silence he added: "Yet to you I *will* confide this much, — I have loved, — loved with a fool's mad devotion! In return I have been betrayed, ruthlessly, heartlessly betrayed, by an enchantress, an accomplished deceiver. This is the skeleton in my closet! What now is your prescription? I am stifled with this air, and long for new fields and pastures green."

Moved by some impulse (we may guess what!) Devérell moved abruptly forward. Grasping one of Wilford's hands he pressed it convulsively, as he exclaimed fervently: "Come with me, Hylton! I am about to make a trip West, and you shall be my companion. — Afterward, — but no matter! Let the future care for itself. Remember the proverb: Wisely improve the present; it is thine. Oh my friend, look not mournfully into the past! Let those who have sown woeful seed reap their own bitter harvest. For you there is a noble life ahead. — Live that life!"

We shall think none the less of our fair-haired barrister that a big tear stole slowly down his cheek, as he silently heeded that exhortation; though he walked toward the window ashamed of such weakness, for this was the first tear he had ever given to this misery.

" And *your* story! What has been your experience during these years?" Wilford asked, when they were both calmer.

" I have never realized the insignificance of my experience so acutely as now, when one so noble portrays to me his own. My life has been one continuous *dolce far niente.* I have been one of Byron's wanderers. My bark has drifted down the winding Rhine, sped over the blue Mediterranean, and plowed the waters of two oceans. I have viewed the wondrous land of my ancestors, travelled from the Pyrenees to the Ural Mountains on that side, — from the Alleghanies to the Rockies on the other; yet I am restless as a schoolboy, and feel that I should have been thrice happier with five-hundred a year, a fixed purpose in life, and the conviction that I had furthered someone's welfare in the world besides my own."

" But you will marry? You have a splendid estate, and in your home will be centred the sweetest ambitions of life," ventured Wilford. He dared not look up, and waited with palpitating heart for Deverell's response, in which he felt much would be involved. The blood mantled his brow. Something swelled in his throat, and seemed to choke him, when at length that answer came.

"It may be years before Deveréll Hall sees a new mistress. As yet I have but vague plans in that direction."

His words contained electric power, which brought every drop of blood in Hylton's veins to a standstill. For a moment the latter's heart almost ceased beating. Then it thumped madly. It seemed to him that Deveréll must certainly hear the impatient thuds, and unconsciously he thrust one hand beneath his waistcoat and clutched it over his heart, as if to muffle the sound.

By a supreme effort Hylton spoke, with an ill-assumed smile: "I thought it not unlikely that the dark-eyed Siren at the Grange, — that, — that our Land of Flowers offered you some strong attraction." He forced a light laugh as he thus concluded.

"The relation between Mademoiselle Weldon and myself is by no means serious, be assured. We met in New Orleans last winter; and as I was an old and favored acquaintance of Madame Seymour, the young lady's aunt, we 'took a friendly interest in each other, — that is all."

He spoke hurriedly; and this precipitance was sufficient proof to Wilford that much within his friend's bosom was left unsaid.

Soon after, Deveréll took his leave, with a

promise to call once more before he left the neighborhood; then they would discuss arrangements for their Western tour.

"He does not suspect the truth!" said Wilford, returning alone to his room. "He dreams not of her treachery, and I pray Heaven he never may! If she reap bitter fruit from her own nefarious planting, mine shall not be the tongue to sting her, nor mine the hand to slay that happiness which she would fain purchase at the price of truth."

CHAPTER XI.

A PROMISE.

If there should come a time, as well there might,
When sudden tribulation smite thine heart,
And thou dost come to me for help and stay,
Fear not! — Thy trial-hour shall be
The dearest bond between my heart and thee.

WORDS THAT BURN.

OVER a week had elapsed since Deveréll's advent at Weldon, and since the night on which he spoke those few hurried words to Hazel in the hallway, which Evelyn overheard, he had never caught a glimpse of the child, except at table, when she usually occupied her accustomed place.

Yes, — once he had seen her, walking with her governess along the forest-road, close by a large gateway, through which Evelyn and he passed in the pony phaeton; but then he could only exchange a bow and friendly smile with Hazel, much as he longed to speak. Did this lonely orphan purposely avoid him? and wherefore? These questions oppressed him.

The end of his visit was approaching. He felt that taking his departure without having again spoken to the young girl would be like going away with the fiercest craving of his heart unsatisfied.

(100)

Perhaps it was a blessed craving, actuated as it was by undefined dread for her future, and a wish to assure her of his undying friendship, which she might claim in time of need.

A month ago — nay, only a week — Aubrey would have laughed to scorn the very idea of suffering the image of a child of fifteen summers to take such complete possession of his thoughts, — he, the observed of all observers, free to woo among the wealth and beauty of the land!

Perhaps he had imagined himself in love more than threescore times; for he was of true French blood, never contented when away from the light of woman's eyes. He had basked in that light many seasons and in various climes; yet to the charge of *trifling*, which some of the fair ones entered against him, he could reply, Not guilty! His integrity had always drawn a line between frivolous gallantry and reverence for woman. Not once had he overstepped that line.

His recent infatuation for Miss Weldon had never been put into words; yet if his eyes had betrayed passionate sentiments, if his hand-clasps had been eloquent of more than friendship, what then? Truly the long months of his silence toward Evelyn had been months of severe contest between heart and reason. His visit to the Grange had been impelled by the resolution to ask her hand, a proof of the profoundest devotion his heart had ever known.

Alas! Of this devotion, nothing now remained. His idol was shattered. With the assurance of Evelyn's falseness of character, her outward charms, previously so seductive, faded into nothingness. There was naught but deception in the face where he once saw incarnate beauty and purity.

Monsieur Deverél now viewed as in the "hollow mirror of remorse" his coming thither. He marked the sad change which had come over Evelyn, with a pain which made him suffer somewhat as she did.

Her face was now wan, and dark semicircles lay beneath the eyes which had shone with the lustre of woman's pent-up love. Formerly her bosom was in tumult when he was near, and her hand became tremulous when his own came into accidental contact with it. This change he noted with heartfelt dismay, and he pitied, oh how he pitied her! Well he knew that her strongest love had been dedicated to himself; and conscience told him he had deliberately encouraged that love, by seeking her companionship in her own home.

Giant shadows of self-reproach haunted him through the day. With Evelyn's sad features rising before him in the dead of night, banishing sleep from his pillow, he wondered if it were not best to sacrifice his own happiness for the protection of hers, — if it would not be best to speak words that would make him her liege forever; but with a new day his self-interested reason would return. He told himself that if a woman were capable of betraying the parents, the treason within her must be hard to overcome, and she might be faithless to him. He remembered Brabantio's words to Othello:

> Look to her, Moor! Have a quick eye to see!
> She has deceived her father, and may thee!

This fatal germ might spread within her nature, until she became a very demon!

Meanwhile Evelyn's mind became less tranquil with each passing hour. Night after night she lay with arid eyes riveted on the impenetrable gloom, her misplaced faith creating sprites who whispered: "On the morrow he will speak! Be comforted! Yes, on the morrow!"

As day succeeded day, and Aubrey's visit lengthened into almost another week, — a week which seemed a year in Evelyn's life, — and still he was silent, she began to relinquish her trust in the nameless phantoms which hovered about her pillow, and to accept the truth in its bare horror.

"He does not love me!" Despite her mad desire to crush this thought, it raged like a crested reptile from morn till night, from night till morn again, until at length Evelyn found herself crouching before this disappointment like a leopardess at bay.

How endlessly the years stretched out before her, as she began to look the future in the face, and to imagine some other woman in Deveréll

Hall! Now it was that the beautiful face of her foster-sister rose in jealous thought, as if to incite Evelyn to mental wickedness, amounting almost to crime; for she believed that in that pretty face alone lay the barrier between herself and supreme happiness.

It was Friday evening. The following day Aubrey had fixed for leave-taking. He was to join his friend Hylton in Tallahassee on Sunday, whence they would go to New Orleans, there to perfect arrangements for their travels on the Pacific Coast.

These plans were really of recent contemplation with Aubrey; for on leaving New Orleans, less than a month before, his mind had pictured scenes in which only a lovely bride and ardent groom figured; but these scenes had vanished into thin air. Instead of the same aspiring young Frenchman, he was now as grave and preoccupied as some savant, who has become such an enigma to himself, as to wonder if it would not be well for him to enter some disciplinary convent.

It was seeing his college friend so cast down, that brought the first idea of going West to Aubrey; but the proposal having grown into a rooted project between them, he hoped the diversion would prove a means of reviving their depressed spirits, so that both would gradually forget their respective heart-affairs, so very closely related, though neither of the two friends knew the main-spring of the other's story.

A warm rain had been falling in intermittent showers since morning. On this Friday Evelyn and her guest had therefore been confined indoors all day; but as evening came on, the rain abated, and only a few silver-faced clouds remained. Fleet-winged birds scurried home to their mates, and the day died with a sunset startling in its grandeur. Such a rainbow as is only seen in southern skies had spanned the horizon; but the clouds were transformed into mingled amethyst and gold, spreading themselves over the western border, and gradually absorbing that beautiful scarf of promise, until it seemed as if the Judgment Day was harbingered by a sea of fire.

Deveréll had been standing alone on the front veranda, watching this gorgeous spectacle with breathless delight. He liked to watch the vivid coloring fade, even as he had liked to watch its beginning; and it was only when a few opal flecks alone remained that, with a deep-drawn sigh, he descended the steps, and sauntered slowly up and down the garden walk.

Having lit a cigar he clasped his hands absently behind him, and gave himself up to meditation about his journey. In less than twenty-four hours he must say adieu to little Hazel! Would this be a final farewell between them? Would the mystery surrounding her young life ever be solved? If so, by whom?

Was there a person in existence who could or would assume the right to fathom her past, and bring the secret of her origin to light? Oh, that he himself might claim so gracious a mission! But to do so would be to forfeit that which he held dearer than life itself, his honor! This was involved in his pledge of silence to Evelyn. If some day Hazel should be brought to give up the worthy friends she enjoyed in the Weldons, what then? Would her foster-sister then tell her all, and in so doing condemn her own soul to torment?

With this thought a vague terror seized the thinker; and this was accompanied by the fierce craving to see and speak with Hazel, — to beseech her to rely upon him in any time of tribulation.

So overmastering was this desire that his pulse began to flutter passionately, and he could distinctly hear his own heartthrobs. Could his surmise be a forecast of some disastrous cloud drifting close upon Weldon Grange?

Where was Hazel? In what direction could he turn to find her? Was it in answer to this cry of his inmost soul that, as he passed beneath a window, he heard the sob of someone in distress?

Involuntarily he paused. Above these half-stifled throes he heard another voice, speaking in hot impassioned tones: " So you have suddenly developed a liking for poetry! " Something like a hiss followed. " I would to God the waters of that pool yonder had closed over you *forever*,

before that fatal morning! *Impostor! Snake!* —
There! How I. should love to serve you like
that!'"

Something came whirring through the open
window, beneath which Aubrey stood, — a book
in dainty green and gold, which fell upon the wet
grass almost at his feet. He caught it up and
pressed his lips passionately upon the cover,
whereon his quick eye saw the title, Lady of the
Lake.

"Hazel has been reading this!" The thought
sent a glad thrill through him. Placing the volume in his breast-pocket he once more inclined his
ear to listen, feeling no twinge of conscience as he
did so, but telling himself rather that some good
angel must have guided his footsteps.

The voice, which he of course recognized as
Evelyn's, could be heard no longer; but the piteous sobs grew louder and more convulsive, as did
also the tumult of his Gallic heart. How he longed
to leap through that window, and avow himself to
Hazel Verne as her sworn defender!

Scarce had this longing been formed, when suddenly a face appeared at the window, — Hazel's!
She retreated swiftly on seeing him, for according
to the maxim, "the heart waits not the guidance
of the senses." Aubrey, instead of moving out of
her sight, stood looking up now with sympathetic
eyes.

Hazel was in deshabille, having just begun her

toilet for dinner when Evelyn entered her room, and this cruel scene followed. Her gold-brown hair was unbound, and rippled about her shoulders like a halo, and she wore a loose dressing-gown of palish-tinted blue. She stood with her small hands clasped appealingly, her sweet lips quivering slightly apart, while unspeakable anguish and fear shone through her tears.

Never until this moment had Deverell cherished an unmanly feeling toward womankind. If in his inmost heart he cursed the woman who had inflicted such pain upon a young innocent, who can censure him?

Taking a quick step forward he climbed the strong trellis to the low piazza-roof, laid one hand upon the window-ledge, and whispered as he saw her shrink away: "Do not turn from me, Hazel! I have heard all. I have been listening, though I did not mean it, believe me! Oh *petite amie*, I entreat you, do not let such words grieve you! They are unworthy your tears. They were unwomanly, cruel, unjust; but she did not mean them, I am sure she did not! So dry your tears and come nearer me."

"That is right," he added, as the girl obeyed him, with something of the confidence of a startled fawn. "Now tell me, little one," he continued, "where you have been hiding all these days?" He spoke hurriedly, hoping to divert her thoughts from her present grief; and this he did for a moment.

"Hiding?" repeated Hazel, as a faint smile broke through her tears, like the sun through a mist-veil. "Why, monsieur, I have not been hiding! Arline, my governess, will go to the seashore next month, to take her summer's vacation, and I have been busy preparing my French review; but monsieur, please,—my hair,—I had just begun my toilet,—"

"I like to see you like this," he interrupted quickly, noting her swift discomfiture and vivid blush, as she raised one half-bared arm to her head, where, amidst the meshes of bronze, a white comb clung caressingly. "You remind me now of a picture that hangs in the gallery at Deveréll Hall. It is called the Sunshine of Saint Eulalie. Some day you shall see it.

"But see!" he added abruptly, "I saved your book from being ruined utterly. It fell upon the damp grass, but it is damaged very little." Smilingly he handed the volume toward her.

"Oh monsieur, how shall I thank you! The book is Arline's, and I feared it would be hurt," cried Hazel, gladly extending her hand to grasp the treasure.

Before relinquishing it Aubrey caught her hand, clasping it within both his own, he did not know how closely. He felt that the time had come when he might speak the words he so longed to speak. Conscious how the precious moments were flying he began, with a voice wherein agitation revealed itself all too plainly.

"Hazel, I have wished for this moment! To-morrow I must say adieu to you; but before going I want to win a little promise from your lips, — so little, indeed, that I know you can not refuse to grant it. You are so young, Hazel, and without parental love. You have kind and loving friends in your aunt and uncle; but, little one, the future is so uncertain! These fond relatives may be snatched from you. Should such a thing happen, there will be need of other friends to take their places. Then will you think of me, Hazel? Will you turn to me as to a brother, who would serve you, even at the peril of his life?"

Hazel hesitated, trembling perceptibly, as a terrified look crept into her face.

"Aunty and uncle taken from me! Oh monsieur!" she cried huskily; whereupon Monsieur Aubrey released her hand, filled with grief at having caused her a moment's sorrow.

Realizing that the import of his words was too weighty for a mind so inexperienced, he hastened to modify them, saying with gentle ardor: "Forgive me if I have distressed you! Do not think again of my words. I do not think there is a likelihood of your ever having to sacrifice those whom you love so dearly. I wish merely to impress you with the warmth of my interest in your future welfare. Now," seeing the tear-stained face begin to brighten again, "will you not repeat after me these words, simple in themselves, yet significant of much, — will you not say, *I will trust you, mon ami?*"

"Oh *mon cher ami!* You are all that is noble and good! I feel that you are, and I *do*, — I shall *always* trust you!"

Her face was bright with the fervor of her words, and her eyes met his with filial confidence.

He held them with his glance for one brief moment. Then he bowed low over her little hand outstretched to him, merely touching the delicate finger-tips with his lips, and murmuring: "God bless you!" after which he turned and walked quickly away, to hide the emotion which her words had called forth. He had gained far more than he had hoped for!

CHAPTER XII.

ADIEUX.

He shall find no fiend in hell can match the fury
  of a disappointed woman! —
Scorned! slighted! .dismissed without a parting pang!
                                          CIBBER.

BEAUTIFUL as a siren looked Evelyn Weldon as she drove her guest to the station on Saturday afternoon. Her perfect-fitting dress of gray camel's-hair was enlivened by a huge cluster of scarlet poppies, worn at the belt; while her large Gainsborough, also gray, was trimmed with ostrich plumes, which swept over her shoulder, lending a soft radiance to her face, otherwise colorless as ivory.

No spark of the old lovelight shone from Aubrey's eyes, as he turned them passively upon her, saying that he had passed a most enjoyable week, and was deeply indebted to mademoiselle and madame for their hospitality, — that sometime in the future he hoped to reciprocate by entertaining them in New Orleans, while Deveréll Hall was open to them at any time they might choose to make themselves his guests.

He meant no cruel thrust. His feeling was one of contempt, not cruelty. His visit to the Grange had been most informal. He had even presumed to offer himself as a guest, after a protracted silence between himself and the daughter of the house, — the only inmate thereof whom he had ever met. What then, seeing that his past attentions had been suggestive of something deeper than friendship, could this visit have portended to Evelyn, if not, a continuation, perhaps a culmination, of their tenderness?

He now felt that he had virtually proven himself a craven in Evelyn's eyes; and that in this clumsy attempt to extricate himself from a dilemma so embarrassing to both, he must appear a double deceiver.

How *could* he be so sacrilegious as to invite her to Deveréll Hall, after what had transpired! It was as though a mighty chasm yawned between them, — he safe-footed on one side, she unsteady on the other, looking to him for succor which he refused to grant, while with folded arms he dared her to leap the abyss, though well aware that she would die rather than attempt it.

Truly Evelyn was to be pitied. She lowered her head, in order to hide the misery aroused by his words, and her soul writhed in bitterness.

"He has deliberately sought my heart as a toy, to be picked up and discarded at his pleasure!" This thought compelled an audible groan as they came in sight of the railway.

Monsieur Deveréll saw her hands tremble, like

the fibres of her plumes, as she tightened her
hold upon the reins, and guided Alcides around
the last corner. In after years he never forgot
the agony depicted on her countenance, when the
moment came for their exchange of farewells.
Taking her hand, whose coldness he felt even
through its thick gauntlet, he saw her lips tremble,
as they faltered, " Adieu monsieur ! "

For a moment remorse and compassion nearly
overmastered him. His hand closed convulsively
around hers. Rapidly he formed a fierce resolution, a sacrificial determination. The irrevocable
question was on the verge of utterance: " Evelyn,
will you become my wife ? " when, like a flash, a
face with tearful eyes rose between them, making
him exclaim aloud in his agitation, " *Mon Dieu !* "
The blue veins about his temples swelled almost
to bursting, and drops of perspiration started from
his brow, as once again he heard the cruel words
Evelyn had used toward poor Hazel: " I would
the waters of that pool yonder had closed over
you *forever !* "

At this instant there was a scream from the
locomotive, and the cry of *All aboard!*

"Adieu, adieu, Mademoiselle Evelyn ! " he said
huskily, as with another spasmodic hand-pressure
he hurried forward.and swung himself upon the
last platform of the moving train.

Then he glanced back, waving his hand toward
her; but she made no answering gesture. She

might have been a carved statue sitting upright in the phaeton, though her face was turned toward him, and her eyes glittered vindictively.

When Aubrey was seated in the smoking-car he threw open the window and looked back over the road, hoping to catch a last glimpse of Evelyn, that he might wave yet another signal of farewell. No trace of phaeton or driver was at first visible; yet, as he continued to gaze, suddenly, through an abrupt opening in the woods, he saw Alcides flying over the dusty road, urged to this speed by frequent applications of the lash. Deveréll gazed spellbound, until all sight of Alcides was lost, and also of the red plumes of his mistress.

Settling into his seat, Aubrey bought a late Tallahassee Journal; and he opened it, but not to read. His eyes rested vacantly upon the same unread paragraph until the sun had set. Twilight, so brief in southern skies, closed in, and at length the brakeman passed through to light the lamps; but Aubrey remained oblivious of all save his thoughts of the "child of mystery."

CHAPTER XIII.

A TELEGRAM.

FATE leads us blindfold at nightfall to the edge of the abyss of the morrow, and we know not what one step may bring to pass.

POOR Alcides! Rarely before had this beautiful creature known a sting of the lash, and his gentle flesh quivered under cruel blows, which left welts on his silvery coat, with here and there a bloodstain. Foamy flakes issued from his nostrils, and fell behind to mingle with the dust.

On, on, madly on, Evelyn urged him, seemingly to inevitable death. Pardon this inhumanity! She was mad, drunk with the fury of disappointment, and hardly responsible for her deed. For years she had fondled and humored Alcides, as she might a child, and would have fought with one who dared maltreat him; but now a wicked determination was kindled within her, whose fierceness involved moral blindness. Not until she reached the Grange did Evelyn take note of her horse's deplorable condition.

She was then met by Noel. Attracted by the sound of rapidly approaching wheels he came from the stable yard to see who it might be, little dreaming his young mistress was returning so soon. With a loud exclamation of astonishment he opened the gate; and as Evelyn drove through, a cry of horror escaped him. "Lo'd o' my soul, Missy Eb'lyn, dat ah hoss done ben *his* las' trip! Ye heahs me?"

As his young lady mechanically handed him whip and reins, and jumped out unassisted, he resumed, with growing anger: "Chile, has n't yer got no feelin', 't yer lashes a poo' animole, un' makes him sweat un' foam un' breed at de mouf, like as him's made o' wood? Un' yer alluz makes fight as when I currys him down a leetle too rough like! Now look ee yah, if dat would 'n bring de teahs to Marsa Wel'on's eyes, den dis yah coon do n't know wat's brack nor wat's wite, dat's all!"

If this semi-insolence had been provoked by any other incentive, Evelyn would have loftily checked the hostler's words, and perhaps ordered some severe punishment for the bold negro; but when she saw her beloved horse panting, foaming, bleeding at the mouth, — where the bit had made ugly gashes, — she was mute with remorse. Perhaps she had killed her favorite!

"Into the stables, Noel, and attend him well," she said anxiously, as he took Alcides from the shafts. "Be sure and attend him well!" she repeated, "and you shall receive extra silver this month."

"If 'tendin' 'll do any good!" returned the man

dubiously; "but if you ain't had yo' las' ride on Alcides, den I's missed my reckin', dat's all." He spoke doggedly, realizing his present importance, and quick to take advantage of it; but Evelyn did not heed his last remark, for she was on her way into the house.

She at once went to the family sitting-room, where her mother was almost sure to be found at this hour. Mrs. Weldon looked up in amazement as her daughter entered. "Why dear, back so soon? You have scarce been gone two hours. You must have driven fast."

"The roads are in fine order, and I enjoy swift driving," said Evelyn evasively; and not until she removed her large hat did her mother observe the paleness of her face. "Why Evelyn," she then cried, "are you ill?"

Evelyn tossed aside her gauntlets, dropped languidly into a chair near Mrs. Weldon, and repeated sarcastically, "Am I ill!" Her words were followed by a laugh so wild as to evoke an involuntary gasp from the anxious mother, who gazed for a moment into the hard face before her, ere she could bring herself to speak again.

"Evelyn, my dear, you are disappointed!" she at last ventured to say, in a sympathetic voice. "Oh," she went on tremulously, "I am so grieved to see you thus! — I warned you!"

Although these last words were spoken in that tone of gentle reasoning which only comes from a true mother, they called a quick flush to Evelyn's face.

"You are prejudiced, mamma, and *have* been, from the first. I shall not listen! You *warned* me? Yes, you warned me, through your biased views of Aubrey's past attentions to me; but of these you were absolutely ignorant! You really know nothing about our past relations. Your ideas are gleaned from Aunt Lydia's letters, and she merely stated her conclusions, not the facts. To me Monsieur Deveréll's recent visit to Weldon Grange bore but one interpretation, which was palpable enough on the evening of his arrival; and this purpose would have been carried out, but for a little episode down by the lake the next morning. Hazel Verne's face in an instant divided our lives, his and mine. If you failed to see the change in him from that hour, you must have been blind. Perhaps you closed your eyes to the pathetic picture of your foster-child on a certain night, when she crept so stealthily into the parlor as monsieur was singing; or, if you saw it, you would doubtless explain her emotion by her great love of music! I claim, on the other hand, that this very emotion was conjured up, as a silent but eloquent appeal to his heart. Oh, her scheme succeeded, — how well it succeeded!"

Another hard laugh followed, as Evelyn recalled the little scene she had witnessed in the hall between Aubrey and Hazel.

"Evelyn, you are mad! Such intrigue would be inconsistent with the child's years! She is little more than a child, and has no thought of such a sentiment! You are heartlessly unfair in your censure!"

Mrs. Weldon spoke with quiet severity, but she felt a dull pain at her heart, and compressed her lips firmly, to suppress the rising sobs.

"So you contend that Hazel's trip to the lake that morning was devoid of any motive inconsistent with her age," went on the other remorselessly; "but I am doubly convinced of your error. Wondering why Hazel kept her room so closely after study-hours, I questioned Arline, and learned that her pupil had suddenly become very much absorbed in Scott's poems. I went straight to Hazel's room. As I expected, I found her pouring over The Lady of the Lake, which seems to have received an irresistible charm since her first meeting with Aubrey, when he applied to her the very romantic title of *Ma petite Lady of the Lake!* Very charming, I admit. So you see, mamma, it is useless asking me to agree with you about your guileless foster-child. She is a precocious actress,— one peculiarly well qualified to execute the role of enchantress!"

"Evelyn, I implore you, —"

"She has wilfully undermined my happiness, — the one ambition of my heart. But for this I might have brought myself at last to tolerate her.

Now, even to live under the same roof with her will be unbearable. My chief motive in speaking now is to say that either she or I must leave the Grange, and at once."

"Dear Heaven, that it should come to this!" wailed the mother, pressing one hand against her heart, while the other was uplifted beseechingly.

Mrs. Weldon would have said more, had not Evelyn interposed: "Spare yourself undue pain, mother! My own is enough. It is deeper than you will ever know. I *love* Aubrey Deveréll! Only Heaven knows the fulness of my love for him! Long ago I gave him my heart. After a secret struggle, when I believed my love unrequited, I succeeded in living it down. I called myself a fool, for nurturing so deep a regard toward one whom I had known but a brief season, and finally I conquered myself. I brought myself to see the world almost as I had seen it before I ever met Aubrey. Then came his letter, to raise again my buried hopes! You know what followed, mother. Aubrey came next day; and on the evening of his arrival he told me, in all but words, that mine had been the correct interpretation of his coming, — that he loved me! My eyes would not close themselves that night, for the joy this confession brought to me. The darkness was alive with glowing pictures of happiness in store for me. — The morrow was scarcely born when the wrecker came, — the mermaid with blue eyes and

fair hair, the Lorelei of my destruction. From
the hour he looked into Hazel's face, Aubrey
was changed. He began treating me with studied
politeness, and then with a coldness that almost
killed me."

Here Evelyn stifled a sob, and then added:
"Now, mamma, I have uncovered my heart to
you, and I am done. My soul's bitterness towards
that girl, no words can fathom. Let your own
heart decide which of us shall go. You might
place her in a convent until she comes of age." .

Mrs. Weldon was weeping, weeping unrestrain-
edly,— partly through compassion for her wayward
daughter, partly from love for her foster-child.
She could not for a moment believe to be true the
words applied to Hazel. She knew they were the
imagery of a jealous brain. This thought soon
became a vigorous protest.

The tears were dried in Mrs. Weldon's eyes at
length, and she looked up, saying with a new
sternness: "Evelyn, your love has been defeated,
and consequently you think you must blame somebody besides yourself. Your feelings toward my
niece are wicked. They grow from such trifles
as create in me no distrust of Hazel. I can not
consider seriously your wish for a separation.
Yours is a wild proposition, and redounds to your
discredit. How could you imagine me capable
of conceding so much to your demand? Your
wish to have me send Hazel from the Grange is a
direct insult to me."

" Your concession will signify little after another month," returned Evelyn, grasping the rod more firmly at her mother's words. "On the twenty-fifth of July I shall attain my twenty-first birthday, and then I shall no longer be amenable to parental discipline, nor doomed to a life of seclusion. I can choose my own pathway!"

"Your reasoning is just, Evelyn. Nevertheless, parental authority must be respected, or else a child is liable to the penalty of a worse exile than you name. Your father has been a true parent; but his heart, if once hardened, would be as unforgiving towards disloyalty, as it is now tender towards the only living issue of our marriage."

Mrs. Weldon was pained; for speaking such words to her beloved child was like a distressing dream.

The agony in the mother's heart was growing unbearable, yet Evelyn persisted: "Beggary would be preferable to daily contact with one I loathe, a reptile. I had rather work for bread, than eat at the same table with *her* day after day. My father will doubtless give her half his fortune! Why not make her his sole heiress, and let me take what ought to be her place in the world, — what would be, but for charity! — walking the streets, a nameless, homeless, hungry girl. The object of your benevolence has found a warmer place in my father's heart than I ever held there, and I am certain what election *he* would make between us."

She paused, her gaze fixed on the grief-blanched face before her, — a face which suffering seemed to have furrowed deeper during the last half-hour.

Did this poor mother hear aright? Were the words *nameless, homeless, hungry* heard in a dream? No, no! They were real; but surely they were spoken at random. They were merely the outburst of a fevered brain, like all Evelyn's speeches that day. How could it be otherwise? How could Evelyn know aught concerning the doubtfulness of Hazel's birth? This was the religious secret of Mrs. Weldon and her dear husband. During four long years they had guarded in their bosoms the death-trust of Henry Verne. Not once had they debated that trust between them. Even when alone in their chamber they rarely alluded to it; for they held it as too sacred for careless reference.

Thus Mrs. Weldon argued with herself amidst the strained silence which ensued, and she half-resolved to let Evelyn's words pass unnoticed.

But those later words: "The object of your benevolence has found a warmer place in my father's heart than any I ever held there."

Ah! Mrs. Weldon felt doubly assured as to her daughter's delirium, and the mother's wonted sweetness returned. No harshness revealed itself in her voice, as she slipped down upon her knees beside Evelyn, whose features were rigid while her hands were firmly clasped.

With a mother's gentleness Mrs, Weldon placed her arms about the slender waist of her daughter, and said: "Evelyn, be calm, my dear. Do not use such words again, I beseech you. They pierce my heart to its core. You wrong your gray-haired father in his absence. You *must* know, my darling, his unselfish love. You have been cold and restrained toward him. Perhaps you have spurned the first place in his bosom; but it has been yours always. True, my brother's orphan girl holds a dear place there; but his big heart has room for you both, though you, his very own, have always been first."

"If brought to the test he would send Hazel away, rather than see me go?" persisted the girl, a hopeful gleam in her look.

"Oh my child, why will you persevere in this folly? Every such word is a sharp dagger in my heart!" Hereupon Mrs. Weldon burst again into convulsive sobbing, letting her head fall hopelessly upon Evelyn's lap.

For some moments nothing was heard save the measured ticking of the clock, broken by half-smothered sobs from the distressed mother; but presently there came the sound of light footsteps speeding through the corridor. The door was opened, and Hazel crossed the threshold, bearing in her hand a sealed envelop.

It was now twilight, and the new-comer did not at first notice Evelyn, half-concealed behind a

Japanese screen; but Mrs. Weldon, hastily arising, advanced toward Hazel, as the latter cried excitedly: "Aunty, a telegram for you! The boy rode over with it from Jasper. He said it required immediate attention."

Mrs. Weldon grasped the envelop wonderingly, while Evelyn pressed forward, possessed with a lingering hope that here was a message from Deveréll.

Again and again Mrs. Weldon turned the buff cover about in her hands, ere she could bring herself to open it. In her younger days this method of correspondence was seldom used, except in times of calamity; and as she had received several such despatches during her life, her extreme agitation was natural.

Bijou, the large Saint Bernard dog, had followed Hazel, and thrown himself on a huge bearskin rug. With noble head erect he abruptly set up a dismal howl, like the ill-omened moan of the north wind. The sound was unlike any that they had ever heard from Bijou before, and for a moment they looked at each other, and at the dog, with anxious faces.

"Put Bijou out, Hazel! Oh, *do* put him out! What can such actions mean? Has he some instinctive knowledge of coming trouble?" said Mrs. Weldon in awestruck tones.

By no persuasion could Bijou be induced to stir from his position; though as if comprehending the annoyance of his demonstration, he gave one deep sigh, rested his head against Hazel's skirts, and riveted his knowing eyes upon Mrs. Weldon, now and then beating his shaggy tail against the floor, as was his wont when impatient.

"Don't close about me so, girls! — Heaven bless my Gerald! I trust he is safe!" added Mrs. Weldon, almost inaudibly. Then, as the words recurred to her, *It requires immediate attention*, she impulsively thrust the message into Evelyn's hands, almost gasping as she did so: "Read it for me, daughter! I do not think I have the courage. Hurry!" she added breathlessly, as she nervously thrust her hand inside her bosom, clutching it tightly over her heart.

As Evelyn tore open the envelop the mother impulsively walked to the open window. The next instant she was arrested by the agonized exclamation: "Father, oh my father!" There was a faint echo, of *father, father*. How heartless seemed this mimicry! How it turned a heart-wail into sport.

With unnatural calm Mrs. Weldon gently unclasped her daughter's fingers from the paper, and these words danced before her in flaming letters:

To Mrs. Julia Weldon, at Jasper:

Disastrous wreck near Eufala; am one of its victims, wounded unto death. Come immediately.

GERALD WELDON.

There was no shriek, only a low, broken cry of "Gerald! Oh, my best-beloved, I am coming!" Like a lily no longer young, yet with the essence of loveliness and purity still enshrining it, Julia Weldon fell prostrate, white and still as marble.

CHAPTER XIV.

ORPHANED.

So softly death succeeded life in her,
She did but dream of Heaven, and she was there.
DRYDEN'S *Leonora.*

TELL me, my soul, can this be death? POPE.

IN a moment Evelyn and Hazel, the latter having divined the purport of the telegram,. were on their knees beside the stricken wife. Loud were the lamentations of both girls, as they chafed the cold hands, and bathed the rigid features, the mask of death. Was ever death itself more ghastly?

The servants gently forced the girls away, and then bore the form of their beloved mistress to the sofa, where they unloosed her garments. What was the terror which stole over their dusky faces, when fifteen minutes elapsed, and their efforts to recall her to life proved futile?

Evelyn sat looking on, half-stunned but dry-eyed, the natural tears scorched away by the unutterable suspense of her soul; but when she saw Chrissie, the housekeeper, and the other attendants, pause in their vigorous work, Evelyn rose abruptly, and threw herself upon her knees beside the couch.

"Mamma, oh mamma darling!" she almost shrieked, "why do n't you open your eyes? Why do n't you speak to me, your Evelyn? Oh my darling, speak! This silence will kill me!"

Snatching one of the slender hands, she covered it with kisses. Finding it cold as ice, she held it in her bosom, hoping to bring it back to life and warmth. A smile, with the peace of Heaven in it, seemed to enliven the blue lips which Evelyn kissed so often, and each moment seemed an hour, as this perverse daughter knelt by her mother's side.

Why the terrible stillness of the room? Why was not everyone stirring, and helping to awaken her loved one? Evelyn looked searchingly into each face. Why were the servants wearing such tearful countenances? Had they heard of her *father's* dread condition? Where had Hazel gone? Had she abandoned her benefactress in this trying hour?

Presently Evelyn became conscious of someone sobbing bitterly at the foot of the couch. Looking around she saw Hazel crouching there, her head bent low in grief. "Go to your room, Hazel!" said Evelyn, almost gruffly. "Go to your room! Your agitation will excite mamma all the more, when she awakes from her swoon."

"Oh Evelyn, do n't, please do n't send me away from her! I could n't, indeed I could n't bear to go!" sobbed Hazel piteously.

"Well, move farther off, then. You must n't stay near her, crying in such a way. Chrissie," turning to the housekeeper, as Hazel moved slowly apart, "get more hot mustard-water! No, stay! Lay your hand over her heart for a moment! Is n't there a faint fluttering? Surely there is!"

Chrissie thrust her hand beneath the clothes, pressing it close against the silent heart, where Evelyn's had been lying.

"Do n't you detect the slightest — just the slightest fluttering, Chrissie?" repeated eagerly the unsuspecting daughter.

The housekeeper suffered her hand to remain there long enough to make "assurance doubly sure" that no pulsation, however faint, made itself known. Slowly withdrawing it she shook her head deprecatingly, while great tears dropped from her lashes, wetting the satin cushion upon which Mrs. Weldon's head rested.

Noting this, Evelyn began to experience a terrible fear. She essayed to speak, but the question which involuntarily rose to her lips froze there. For one moment she stood with stony face turned toward the housekeeper, but a mist slowly gathered before her eyes. Then she began to sway like a wind-tossed reed; and the next moment she would have fallen, but for the timely aid of Arline, who had just returned from an accustomed walk, and hurried to the sitting-room to learn the cause of the evident commotion, and see if anything was seriously amiss. She had hardly learned the true state of affairs when she caught the fainting girl in her arms, and, with the assistance of Chrissie, bore her to a chamber.

Here Evelyn recovered consciousness, after the application of a restorative. "Arline, Chrissie, what has happened? Tell me the truth! Is she — is she — no, *no!* it can not be! Tell me that I have been dreaming! Tell me that I have been the victim of a horrible illusion, or else I shall go mad."

At first she raved wildly, but soon spoke more quietly. "Only arouse me from this faintness, and let me go back to poor mamma. Ah, bless her! I left her weeping. I was so cruel; but *she* — that girl — goaded me to wickedness. My darling said that my words were like daggers! I must go to her and beg forgiveness! I *must*, I MUST!"

She sprang toward the door, but Arline detained her before her hand touched the knob. "No, no, mademoiselle! You can not·go now, — not yet, *ma chère*, — but presently, when you are better, and able to see your mamma, I will lead you to her. Soon the doctor will come, and do what he can for her."

"Then she is sick, but *not* dead?" whispered Evelyn huskily. "I knew it was only a wretched dream. I remember now, it was that awful news of my father which crushed her to the floor. —

Arline," grasping the governess's arm appealingly, "only think! My own dear father is dying,— dying alone, away off in Alabama! What can be done, Arline? Mamma can not go to him, nor can I leave her."

Arline looked about her hopelessly. The house-keeper had returned to her mistress's bedside, for by this time they had taken the lifeless form to Mrs. Weldon's chamber, so there was nobody to corroborate Evelyn's words.

"Mademoiselle's mind is not quite right as yet," she observed mentally; and then added aloud, with gentle confidence: "It can not be, *chère amie!* Monsieur Weldon is in Memphis, and *certainly* well."

Evelyn gazed at Arline mutely, a momentary gladness dawning upon her thoughts. "In Memphis, and well?" she repeated slowly; but this was followed by a deprecatory shake of the head, and a return to hopeless misery of face and voice.

"You do not know, you do not understand, Arline! It was that which caused my mother to fall. My father was on his journey home. The train was wrecked near Eufala, and he was left a hapless victim. He is dying now! Only think, how terrible! He who left us less than three weeks ago, the very picture of health, is lying alone, wounded unto death. Perhaps he *is* dead! Merciful Heaven!"

Evelyn was almost screaming now, and wringing

her hands like one bereft of reason. "I never knew until now, when too late, the depth of my love for him! Oh father, my best of fathers, come back to me!" As she threw herself prostrate across the bed, sobbing as though her form would be rent in twain, Arline turned away to weep in sympathy.

"Can this be true?" she whispered. "Oh *mon Dieu*, have pity, have pity!" and she raised her eyes to Heaven in tearful supplication, before softly stealing from the room.

Seven o'clock! The moon's silvery light was bathing the white road, over which two horsemen rode on their way to the Grange. One was the bearer of a second message. The other was Doctor Weaver, the family physician. He rode in advance; but the messenger, spurring his horse hotly, gained rapidly on the doctor. Two or three mad dashes, and the riders were neck and neck.

"Doctor Weaver," said the breathless messenger, "I made quite sure it was nobody else, for your saddlebags were quite visible in the moonlight. To the Grange?" The doctor nodded assent.

"A sudden affliction this in the family?"

Doctor Weaver looked puzzled. "Ah, you have heard, then?" he rejoined presently, naturally concluding that his companion referred to Mrs. Weldon's illness. "I trust, however, it is not serious."

"I carry news of its fatality, sir!"

"What do you mean, man? I — I do n't follow you," exclaimed the other, with some touch of impatience.

"You know about the accident, the wreck? — Weldon is dead."

"My God!" groaned the other, as he checked his horse with a sudden jerk. "*Wreck?* What wreck? Who did you say was dead?"

"Gerald Weldon!"

"Impossible!"

"Your pardon, doctor. We have just received news direct from Eufala, the scene of the disaster. The Squire was returning from Memphis, and was one of the victims."

"If this be true," said the doctor strongly agitated, and touching his companion's arm as he spoke, "then I implore you, in the name of Heaven, keep the news to yourself until I have ascertained the condition of my patient, Mrs. Weldon. She has heart-trouble, and such a shock might prove fatal, especially if thrust upon her without warning."

"But she was apprised of the accident this afternoon, and also of her husband's dangerous condition."

"Then I fear the worst! Poor woman! However, you will gratify me by waiting in the yard until I give you a signal."

By this time they had passed through the gate, to the graveled sweep. Doctor Weaver took off

his saddlebags, and was hurrying on, when, much
to his annoyance, the messenger called after him:
"I say, Doc, would you mind delivering the telegram yourself? There is no answer, and my work
won't let me idle away much time."

The doctor grasped the despatch, thrust it into
his vest pocket, and strode rapidly toward the
house, where he found Chrissie awaiting him on
the front veranda.

"She'm dead. You too late, Marsa Doctah!
My good deah mist'is am done ben dead two
hours!" sobbed the faithful colored woman.

Solemnly they entered the sad death-chamber
together.

CHAPTER XV.

ALONE.

LEAVES have their time to fall,
And flowers to wither at the north wind's breath,
And stars to set; but all,
Thou hast *all* seasons for thine own, oh Death!
HEMANS.

THE dead leaves fall. We love them in their verdure, as sweet diversions from our daily cares; but we watch them flutter in beauty to the ground, and we trample upon their ashes, oh how ruthlessly!

We pluck a half-blown rose, with which to adorn the bosom. We prize and love it, in its fresh, pure beauty, when its petals breathe sweet incense. For a little time we are the flower's glad possessor and friend; but when its brief life begins to wane, when its head droops low on the stem's exhausted strength, and the fragrant breath is gone forever, then we snatch the rose from its resting-place, and fling it to the winds, — thus proving our ingratitude. Yet if thankless, we are often unconsciously so.

We pursue our separate paths through life, thoughtless of our Heaven-sent joys, regardless of the great Destroyer's presence, until he rises grimly to assert his claim upon our own dear flesh and blood, — until he creeps stealthily in and breaks the golden links which bind the household band. Then we are brought to realize all that death's sphinxlike presence involves! We are no longer selfish. As we look upon the impassive forms of our loved ones, — his prey, — the tenderness in our erring natures awakens.

. Goaded by the remembrance of our coldness to the dear ones when in life and health, we fall upon our knees, and lavish contrite tears and kisses upon marble hands and lips, squandering love upon ears that are deaf to it forever! When dust has been consigned to dust, we wrap ourselves in sable robes, and hide us away from the world for a season. We weep, we wrestle with our hearts, because they remind us so inopportunely of the debts we owed to those who have left us.

Thus was it with Evelyn Weldon. A week ago, and she was calmly happy in the possession of both father and mother. Today she is desolate, in the thought that not to her will come again the touch of father's hand, the sound of mother's voice.

Evelyn was at first stunned, and then wild, with grief over her double bereavement. The two lives most dear to her had gone out almost simultaneously, leaving her an orphan. She crept softly from the chamber where Arline left her, and entered the sitting-room unobserved, but just in time to hear Doctor Weaver pronounce the sentence which seemed her own doom: "She has been dead for quite two hours!"

Drop the curtain of silence over the terrible scene which ensued. We read of a Greek statue which immortalized sorrow. They called it Veiled Grief. It represented a father about to sacrifice his child, his face shrouded in a mantle. No mantle could shroud the grief which reigned throughout the beautiful home of the Weldons on this memorable summer night. Never did death render silence more sacred.

Evelyn and Hazel knelt, or rather crouched, all night beside the bed whereon rested what was yesterday the hopeful mistress of the Grange. The girls did not exchange a single word. The first rays which peeped through the shutters — mocking the feeble light of the candles, burning low in their sconces — fell athwart the snowy sheet, above which both heads were bowed, mute as the dead.

Evelyn's grief was no longer audible. Her lamentations had spent themselves at midnight, and only an occasional quiver betokened that she was still alive to her sorrow. At intervals Hazel wailed aloud for the dead to return, and her sobs were frequent.

The cuckoo lifted himself from the roof of his ormolu home, and proclaimed in shrill accents, which seemed to deride the holy quiet, that it was six o'clock. As his last note was sounded, Hazel arose from her kneeling posture, and went to the opposite side of the bed. All night her stricken heart had been crying, but so silently that only angels might hear: "Evelyn, let me love you! Let me love you, or I too must die!"

Now Hazel stood for a moment beside her cousin's bent form, ere she could bring her lips to frame the words. Suddenly Evelyn felt an arm steal softly about her neck. She looked up listlessly, but let her head fall heavily upon her arm again, when she saw who stood beside her.

Nevertheless she could not deafen her ear to the mournful words: "They are both gone from me, Evelyn, and I have none left but you! Oh Evelyn, Cousin Evelyn, let me love you now!" Her arm tightened its clasp about the neck of her foster-sister, while tears fell upon the bands of dark hair.

Evelyn disengaged the clinging arm and arose hastily. "Hazel, this is no fit place for a scene," she said coolly. "We will speak of ourselves when all this trouble is over. I am desolate, — oh God, how desolate!" Thereupon she covered her face with both hands and groaned miserably; but after a moment she added: "I can think of nothing now but my cruel bereavement. You have Arline! Go to her!"

"But," faltered the other, "Arline, though so kind and good, can not comfort me now, Evelyn; but you are of my own flesh and bl ——"

She was abruptly checked. The secret rose again treacherously to Evelyn's lips, even in this awful hour. "You are not," she began, as a sudden fire leaped into her eyes; but her tongue clave to the roof of her mouth, and she found herself powerless to proceed with the unholy words. There came a face before her, — a face with gray eyes full of wounded reproach, — her mother's eyes!

With an effort Evelyn averted her eyes from the child's pathetic face, and turned them slowly toward the dead; and now that wicked light died out of them, and the hard lines disappeared from her mouth. "Go! Leave me alone with my dead darling!" she cried, with a wild gesture, but without turning again toward Hazel. "They will bring my father home — and — and — place him beside her. I *must* be left alone with them! They are *my* dead, *mine* only! Leave me to my bitterness! Has not every heart its own?"

Slowly and silently Hazel quitted the room. "Yes, they are *her* dead, not *mine*," she whispered to herself. "I have no claim upon them; but oh, how they loved me! They both loved me, as I loved them. Oh Evelyn, if you knew how. my heart is breaking, you could not send me away! I am so utterly alone!"

Hazel stumbled through the wide halls and out of doors, her tears falling like rain. She took no heed of the flowers, as fragrant and bright-hued

today as yesterday. The birds skimmed the air in
sweet freedom, flinging their joyous notes at each
other as they did yestermorn; yet Hazel took
small note of them, as with dilatory step she wandered, — she knew not, cared not, whither.

Mechanically she followed the garden path,
reached the wicket, lifted the latch, and continued
on through the orange grove, toward the lake.
Suddenly, as she reached the skirt of willows, she
noticed a sound of labored breathing close behind
her, and saw Bijou in full chase. With a glad cry
she waited for him, and then knelt beside him,
clasping her arms about his neck.

"Bijou, dear old friend! I still have you!" As
she felt his sympathetic tongue lapping her face,
her grief became so vehement that the dog also
moaned piteously; but presently she arose, linked
her hand within his collar, and together they passed
through the willows down to the edge of the
water, where her boat was tied.

Two hours later Arline, worried by the long
absence of her charge, went down to the lake,
which she knew was Hazel's favorite resort; and
there she found her, fast asleep in the hollow of
the boat, her head pillowed upon Bijou's neck.

CHAPTER XVI.

WEDDED IN DEATH.

My love, my blessing while on earth;
Then over the river we two shall go,
And stand in the light of God's great smile;
In life, in death, and in after-death,
My love, my blessing, all the while.

THE day appointed for the funeral was ushered
in clear and cool, with only the low rustle of
zephyrs to disturb the quiet which brooded over
the Weldon home. Scarlet geraniums flamed
beneath the windows of the death-sanctuary; but
just above this bold flower the pale jessamine
trailed, its meek eyes open toward heaven, yet with
here and there a filmy veil, as if cast by some con-
dolent spirit-hand.

There was no visible sign of life about the
Grange. The shutters were closed. Even the
shades in the servants' quarters were closely drawn.
Long streamers of crape on the door-knobs
prophesied the dreary months which must elapse
ere happiness would again pervade that stately
home.

Was ever such sorrow known before? In the
same lofty and magnificently appointed parlors
where, thirty years before, Julia Weldon had stood

(143)

decked in bridal white, a happy and trustful girl-wife, she now rested in her funeral casket, beside the form of her husband. Wedded in death! As loyal to each other as when they knelt at God's altar, and took the solemn vows of wedlock, they now stood before their King on his great white throne, blessed forever, through almighty love, with happiness immortal. Such is fidelity's reward!

The two caskets were wreathed in jessamine, for that delicate flower falls to the ground in the full beauty of life, and is therefore the fittest emblem of sudden death.

Mrs. Seymour, accompanied by her only daughter, Myrtle, — a beautiful girl of about Hazel's age, — arrived from New Orleans the preceding evening; while other relatives, including a younger brother of Mr. Weldon, with his family, came from Jacksonville, Tallahassee, and other parts of Florida.

Together with many other sympathetic friends, the visitors were congregated in the parlors to listen to the solemn rites of burial. Mrs. Seymour stood at the head of the casket which held the form of her dear twin-sister, and gazed upon that beautiful countenance, bright with the halo of Heaven.

By her side stood Myrtle, one arm consolingly encircling her mother's waist. Her dark eyes were fixed pityingly, not upon either dead face, but upon Hazel, who stood with her slender hands clasped, while her white face gleamed through the sable veil which fell over it. Myrtle's heart went out in

sympathy toward this frail girl! How she longed
to entwine comforting arms about her neck, and
whisper the deep love of her heart!

Myrtle had been told that Hazel regarded her
aunt and uncle with deep and filial love, and that
this affection was returned tenfold by the foster-
parents; and Myrtle wondered who would now
take their place toward this lone child. Would
Evelyn love and care for her? Myrtle's eyes
turned from Hazel's face to Evelyn's, who also
stood on the opposite side, leaning heavily upon
the arm of her uncle.

The New Orleans girl had noticed that no
open sympathy had been exchanged between the
cousins, though heretofore she had given the matter no reflection. She marvelled now why Hazel
was left standing alone; why Evelyn did not
encircle her with a comforting arm, as she herself
yearned to do; why they did not weep together,
like sisters.

Suddenly Myrtle burst into passionate weeping.
Though she had moaned continuously, her grief
had heretofore been subdued; but now her lamentations, breaking thus abruptly upon the ears of
the other mourners, caused them all to look on in
surprise. Mrs. Seymour drew her darling closer
to her side, and pressed her there tenderly.

"Do n't, my love! Do n't weep like that!
Aunty is happy. See how peacefully she is resting beside dear uncle. — Oh — Julia, Julia! It

seems as if part of my own life had gone out with yours!"

"But mamma," whispered Myrtle, "it — it — isn't alone for aunty and uncle that I cry; it is for her — my Cousin Hazel. She looks so lonely over there, and I love her so! Oh mamma, I love her more than I can tell. There is a feeling here" — pressing one hand close to her heart — "I can not describe, but it is full of longing for her!"

Incoherent as were these words, they were intelligible to Mrs. Seymour, and each syllable went direct to her heart. She directed her troubled eyes toward Hazel, and a moan escaped her. Then she leaned heavily upon the arm of her husband, and Mr. Seymour bent his head to catch the words she whispered in a choked voice: "Papa, take Myrtle around to Hazel. She stands there all alone, and our darling wishes to go to her."

Mr. Seymour gravely did his wife's bidding, to Myrtle's almost irrepressible satisfaction. As he resumed his place beside his wife, and gently placed her hand within his own, he was startled at its coldness, and looked down anxiously into her face, believing she might be ill. He would have asked her, but the expression in her face held him spellbound. Her eyes were fastened upon the two young girls, and instinctively his own followed them. Strong though he was, he felt his breath quicken, and he drew his wife closer to his side, keenly alive to the feelings that nearly overcame her.

The two young girls were of the same height. Both were slight and supple, both were fair. One had golden-brown hair, and eyes like sapphires; the other had tresses bright as the purest topaz, and her brown eyes were large and liquid, with a soft and tender expression, such as we see in the eyes of a fallow deer. They stood with entwined arms. Their heads were bent together, and together their tears fell. There was a likeness between them, — nay, it was almost startling.

During these occurrences the service had been delayed, in expectation of the arrival of a few distant relatives; but now the folding doors were swung wide open, and the minister moved toward the casket.

"I am the resurrection and the life, saith the Lord."

In a beautiful spot in Cypress Dell we leave Evelyn's parents, at rest in the family cemetery. Over them the plumed trees whisper their low requiems, while jessamines lovingly entwine the monument, which bears the simple inscription :

SACRED TO THE MEMORY

OF

GERALD AND JULIA WELDON

———

WEDDED IN DEATH.

CHAPTER XVII.

SIXTEEN YEARS AGO.

ALONE, yet I am not alone. **JESUS.**

"GENTL'UM t' see Missy Eb'lyn!"

Evelyn and Mrs. Seymour were closeted in the younger lady's boudoir, and engaged in earnest conversation when this announcement was made by a servant.

Weeks had passed since the funeral, but Mrs. Seymour still remained with her bereaved niece.

Evelyn took the card nervously from the silver tray, while a sudden hopeful color leaped into her worn face; but this died out, leaving it paler than before, as she read the name, *J. Oglesby, Esq.*, with these words hastily pencilled below: "Solicitor to the late Gerald Weldon."

Evelyn arose languidly. "It is papa's lawyer," she explained to her aunt. "I will go down and learn his errand. I hope he does not come to discuss my legal affairs. I do n't feel equal to the ordeal. There are times," she added, moving listlessly toward the mirror to adjust a black lace mantle about her shoulders, "when I almost wish I had been left penniless. I can hardly hope for a moment's peace in future, with these properties

(148)

all staring me in the face. They are added burdens!"

" Ah, dear child, you have yet to learn the true value of riches," returned her aunt quietly. " The day will come when you will bear proudly your title of the wealthiest woman in the State."

" Wealth, wealth! A future gilded with such a reputation, yet devoid of happiness!" sighed the young lady. " Aunt," she added, turning wearily from the mirror, " those words of Shakespeare so often recur to me of late:

> How weary, stale, flat, and unprofitable,
> Seem to me all the uses of this world!"

" Poor dear!" sighed Mrs Seymour, as the door closed behind her niece. " She is right! All the gold and jewels in the land can not gild a bitter sorrow, or render it an ounce lighter; but I fear there is some deeper grief than loss of her parents! How she started at the sight of that card! Can Aubrey Deverell have anything to do with her misery? Did his visit bring bitterness? How significant were her words about *wealth* and *happiness!*"

The elder lady was still meditating thus when the younger returned. " It is as I anticipated, aunty! Mr. Oglesby called about papa's will!"

" Well?"

" He has one in his possession, drawn up six or eight years ago. He says, however, that another will was drawn up, not long before poor papa's departure for Memphis. He thinks this last one must be in papa's secretary, together with other private papers. If you will come with me, we will look through the desk together."

Mrs. Seymour arose at once, and they went downstairs. After a patient search Evelyn found the document in question; and Mrs. Seymour's countenance underwent an expression of unspeakable pleasure, as she read the clearly written lines with her niece, and saw that the vast rice-plantation, called Fairacre, was bequeathed to Hazel Verne, his own and his wife's adopted child.

With this exception the whole of Gerald Weldon's property was willed to his beloved wife, with a large yearly income reserved for their " only lawful issue, Evelyn Stanhope Weldon." After Mrs. Weldon's death, the whole estate was to descend to Evelyn, Fairacre only excepted. Of course when Mr. Weldon made this will he did not dream that his wife would precede himself by a few hours into the undiscovered country of shadows, or that his own earthly career would meet so untimely an end.

Evelyn at length replaced this precious paper in its pigeonhole. " You see, aunt," said she, and with a bitter curl of the lip, " my father has left this *charity* child independently rich! Some waifs are truly fortunate! "

Her sarcasm seldom missed its mark, and Mrs. Seymour was plainly wounded. She could not find it in her heart to resent Evelyn's words; but she replied proudly, though in her usual gentle tones: " Hazel is a most worthy object for his generosity. That he has shown deep affection for her does not surprise me."

Evelyn vouchsafed no reply, but looked with a marble face out of the window, into the autumn sunlight.

Stung to the quick by what she believed extreme selfishness in her niece, Mrs. Seymour adopted a line of quiet reasoning.

" My dear niece," motioning toward the beautiful view commanded by the library window, " this estate alone will net you a revenue adequate to the maintenance of a handsome establishment in town, — to say nothing of your other property, your grazing-land, stock, houses, bonds. Surely you can not grudge my dead brother's orphan the comparatively small share allotted her ! Had your father omitted this provision, how freely would I have taken Hazel to my heart and home; and in the end I would have treated her as my own daughter. To have her with Myrtle always, would make it seem as if God had given me back my —— " She could say no more, for choking tears forbade.

Something in this grief touched a chord of sympathy in the unforgiving Evelyn. She moved restlessly in her chair, and presently ventured to lay her hand upon her aunt's arm.

"Aunt Lydia," with a touch of real tenderness in her voice, "try and forget the past! Have we not enough present grief, without calling back that of so many years ago?"

"Oh girl, girl!" cried Mrs. Seymour passionately, leaving her seat and pacing the room, "can I forget the sorrow which haunts me every waking hour, making me often a stranger to sleep, and besetting me with unreasonable anticipations every day? With hoping, I have grown old and gray, — hoping, hoping, hoping — for sixteen weary years! Not one day but a mother's supplication has gone up to Heaven, that the lost might be found; but no answer has been granted! At last, with despair closing about me, and with my burden of grief made heavier by the loss of my only sister, I find my soul crying out for a release from its torture, even by death."

She paused nervously and then faltered: "Evelyn, my dear, I am faint!" and groped her way to the nearest chair.

In a moment Evelyn had brought a glass of wine, which she held to the bloodless lips.

Presently her aunt spoke again: "I should repress my feelings. To give way to them, as I did just now, is sure to make me ill; but oh Evelyn, pity me! Sympathize with me as your mother did, and give your Cousin Hazel some of the affection you would have bestowed upon — upon Myrtle's little sister. The feeling has often come to me of late, that this poor orphan might have been given to our branch of the family to fill the vacancy left by my lost darling. Julia wrote me once that this thought came to her also. Won't you try and find room for Hazel in your heart, Evelyn? Oh try to love her, for the sake of her dead parents!"

She paused, awaiting some reply; but as none came, she went on eagerly: "I have feared that you and Hazel are not quite happy together! Last winter, while you were with me in New Orleans, I hoped, day after day, to hear you speak of her; but the name scarcely passed your lips, and so I was led to believe that you were not in friendly relations with her. I see that mine was a correct reading of your heart; but now that you are brought to realize her position in the world, as doubly orphaned, you will surely be more lenient. Not only by ties of blood are you near of kin, but you are sisters in grief. Promise me, Evelyn!— What is it, dear? Are you ill?"

She asked this question, as her niece turned her ghastly face from the window, and clutched at her throat, as if suffocated.

"It is nothing,—nothing but the closeness of the room!" Evelyn faltered huskily; but after a moment she went on more calmly: "Aunt Lydia, I wish you would talk no more of Hazel. I can never bring myself to regard that girl with anything like affection. I have my reasons for this,..

reasons which I can not impart even to you, whom I love dearly, and would confide in above all others."

The determination of Evelyn's utterance baffled Mrs. Seymour. She tried to fathom the meaning of such bitter words; but the more she thought about Evelyn's dislike of the young girl, — who, in Mrs. Seymour's eyes, seemed the embodiment of the pure and lovable, — the more she wondered what could be its unrevealed cause."

Suddenly a happy thought occurred to her, and she voiced it eagerly: "Then, dear, if you think you can not soften your heart toward my brother Henry's child, I shall deem it a privilege, a sweet privilege, to take her home with us. She and Myrtle can find happiness in one another's companionship. Myrtle pleads in every letter for me to bring her little cousin with me; but never until now have I ventured to speak to you on the subject, for I feared you would regard the proposal as selfish. I did not for a moment think you would care to part with Hazel indefinitely. She and Myrtle have made about equal progress in their studies, and — "

"Impossible! I will not suffer my mother's orphan to quit Weldon Grange under any circumstances," said Evelyn abruptly, obstinacy revealing itself both in face and voice. "It would be an injustice to the dead. In another year, perhaps," she went on with forced calmness, — for the very thought of Hazel Verne's going to New Orleans roused the devil within her, — " after she has completed her studies, — Hazel may make Myrtle a visit; but she will certainly continue to make this her home, until she attains her majority. After that she will be mistress of her own actions, and can choose for herself."

" Meanwhile, what will life be to her here at Weldon Grange, without the presence of love to brighten it?" asked the other, the ready tears again filling her eyes. " Promise me that you will not try to make Hazel unhappy! You will at least promise me this, Evelyn!"

" I shall see but little of Hazel during the next year," returned her niece, still unmoved. " She will be continuously under the charge of her governess; but if my promise will give you any satisfaction, you have it! I will not seek to make the girl more miserable than she is."

There was that in Evelyn's tone which restrained the words of gratitude on Mrs. Seymour's lips. She sadly left the room, after touching her niece's brow with a formal kiss.

" What, take *her* to New Orleans, where she would be in daily contact with *him?* — Never! Sooner would I place her behind the walls of a nunnery!" This Evelyn muttered to herself when alone.

For more than an hour she sat buried in thought. Almost unnoticed the afternoon waned, and every

object in the library took upon itself a shadowy
form.

At length the girl lifted her head from the
cushion on which it rested, and looked about her.
Why was it that two girlish faces seemed to stare
from every pedestal, every frame, from every nook
and corner of the room, — Hazel's and Myrtle's?
Here she would encounter sapphire eyes, and there
a pair of brown ones. Two bisque images on the
India cabinet suddenly assumed the features of
these two girls. How like, yet how unlike each
other!

It can not be! The thought is absurd, when
Memphis and New Orleans are so far apart! Yet,
oh God, the thought haunts me like a demon!"
Shudderingly Evelyn arose, and then hastily fled
upstairs.

CHAPTER XVIII.

TROUBLED FACES.

BUT thou art here. Thou fill'st
The solitude. Thou art in the soft winds
That run along the summit of these trees
In music. Thou art in the cooler breath
That, from the inmost darkness of the place,
Comes, scarcely felt. BRYANT.

ALTHOUGH the day was wellnigh spent, Evelyn had yet to make her accustomed visit to Cypress Dell. She preferred to make these visits to the dead unattended, though the distance was more than a mile, and the unfrequented road ran through a dense wood. Indeed she courted rather than feared this solitude.

This evening her step was slow and careless. The birds and squirrels, which hastened into ambush at her approach, afforded all the society she desired. In this aromatic forest she felt that sense of freedom which seldom came to her at the Grange, where the rooms, though bright and lofty, seemed like prison cells, and the atmosphere, though pure, and fragrant with the breath of flowers, was often stifling and unbearable.

There was always a weight upon her mind. It made her restless, and a stranger to the peaceful comfort which pervaded her home, and which she so much enjoyed in the old days.

Her grief over her double bereavement was deep and heartfelt; but even such affliction must in time reach a reconciliation with the inevitable. Outward lamentations must sooner or later cease, giving place to calm endurance.

This change had come to Evelyn. She began to look her position in the face, and to accept it as right, as well as unavoidable. She seldom reflected upon her great possessions, however. What was wealth? Could it replace what she had loved and lost irrevocably? Could it purchase back her parents? Could it redeem her alienated lover?

Awhile ago Evelyn was ambitious and gay, with joy in each today, and a longing for the "golden dawn-glow" of each tomorrow. Now she was a miserable and disappointed woman, looking hopelessly forward to the grim future, and wondering how many years of desolation she must needs endure.

Her thoughts this evening, as she walked toward Cypress Dell, were centred upon one whom she regarded as lost to her, — Aubrey Deverell. She told herself that if he should return to her and say: "Evelyn, I am beggared! I am worse, — lost to every sense of honor! Will you accept me in my degradation? Will you relinquish Weldon Grange, and your vast possessions, for a wretch so unworthy?" she would cry out, from the depths of her idolatrous heart. "Yes, Aubrey, my love! Every farthing will I renounce for you! Without you, the world is but an empty void. Beside you, even in beggary, I should be tenfold happy!"

Such was Evelyn Weldon's devotion. Unconsciously she spoke her thought aloud, and the passionate words echoed down the vine-tangled ravine below: *Happy, tenfold!* Terrified she stood still, for the sentence sounded like fiendish mockery.

"Happy!" she cried again, with hands upraised in defiance. Then, as the tears coursed down her cheeks: "Merciful Heaven! Is there no light for me? Am I always to be thus miserable?"

Miserable! murmured the pines. *Miserable!* came the weird and dismal echo from the hollow.

Evelyn looked timidly about her. "Surely the evil spirit is in pursuit of me! Who else could mock me thus cruelly?"

With a suppressed cry she involuntarily quick-ened her steps, experiencing for the first time an unspeakable dread of the dark woods. Soon the white monuments in the cemetery came into view. With a feeling of relief she hurried forward, and commenced to twine fresh jessamine about the stone which marked the resting-place of her parents. She had strewn the mound with fresh flowers, and stooped to rearrange a vase toppling under a weight of white roses, when she heard a faint rustle behind her.

She glanced around, the forest terror reviving, and making her pulse beat fiercely. Nothing was visible, however; so she attributed the noise to some bird or squirrel, and renewed her pious attention to the graves.

When all was in order she sat down on a rustic bench, and surrendered herself to memories of the departed, remembering all their good and generous traits only, and recalling the selfish thoughts she had cherished and the cruel words she too oft had spoken.

Then her mind wandered, from those with whom she had forever closed all earthly accounts, to the living, whose image was ever uppermost. She recalled Aubrey as he had once been, and as he was and must be, — forever be, — estranged from herself.

With this came creeping back her bitter feeling toward Hazel, an emotion which had lain partially dormant during her recent trouble.

Once she had been nearly overmastered by it, — that morning in the chamber of death, when she would have betrayed her mother's trust, but for the memory of her whose spirit had taken flight, yet whose influence lingered to shield the child of mystery from such pain as would have been born of the words Evelyn was tempted to utter, — tempted by the beautiful face which Evelyn believed to be the evil genius of her life.

She saw it now, with the stamp of suffering

thereon, — the eyes swollen with weeping, the lips quivering, the cheeks hot and tear-stained. She saw the slight form and the clasped hands. She heard again the plaintive cry, that would have softened a heart of adamant: "Evelyn, let me love you!" Nay, she laughed bitterly at the memory of Hazel's words.

"Let her love me, — *me*, from whose lips she has snatched the sweetest nectar! The pale-faced sorceress! I will live to be revenged on her! I will make her suffer a hundredfold for every pang. She has cursed my life, and I hate her!"

When Evelyn was ready to return home, it was close upon sunset. Kneeling she pressed her lips to the sacred dust which held her parents' ashes, and then walked hurriedly down the knoll, out through the wicket, into the open road.

Already the sky had assumed faint tints of rosy gold. Shadows had lengthened beneath the pines, until only an occasional streak of light signified that it was still day. Evelyn had never been alone in the forest so late. Though by nature intrepid, she now looked forward to her homeward walk with a feeling of undefined solicitude.

Little did she dream, as she hastened onward, that a pair of glittering black eyes, set in a pinched and yellow visage, were watching her through a clump of cypress shrubs, which grew a few feet from the roadside.

When she had gone some distance from the spot,

a mulatto woman, bent with infirmity, emerged cautiously from her hiding-place, and followed Evelyn with catlike tread.

At length reaching that section of the forest she most dreaded, Evelyn paused and peered anxiously about her, as if to reassure herself of safety. Imagine her terror! A short distance behind she saw a dusky object shrink suddenly into the shadows of a pinetree, as if to avoid discovery. For a moment the girl stood like one paralyzed. The next instant she would have shrieked aloud in sheer fright, had not her better reason forbade.

What should she do, — run, walk on as though nothing extraordinary had happened, or go bravely back and confront her foe, — if foe indeed it was?

Presently the thought occurred to her that her aunt, becoming anxious at her prolonged absence, had sent out one of the servants to escort her safely home. Stimulated by this thought she resolved to make assurance doubly sure by investigation, and began retracing her steps toward the dark form, which she still saw crouching among the shadows.

She had almost gained the spot, when suddenly she recoiled with a cry. In that figure she recognized nothing familiar, but saw a shrunken face, with eyes which flashed ominously in the twilight. The hair, which might once have been a slavegirl's pride, was now unkempt, and straggled about her face and neck in coarse uneven wisps, giving her a witchlike appearance.

"Who are you? What do you want? Why are you dogging my footsteps?" gasped Evelyn in one breath, as she strove against the awful fear that possessed her. Then, encouraged by the sound of her own voice, she repeated: "Why are you following me, I say? Speak!"

The mysterious creature, frightened by her assailant's threatening attitude, rather than her words, gradually drew herself up to her full height, and asked, in a voice quavering and indistinct: "You lib at de great house yondah?" pointing toward the Grange with a motion of her long, bony hand.

"Yes," said Evelyn haughtily, "but what of it? How does that concern you?"

For a moment the woman maintained silence; but she clutched nervously at her threadbare shawl, and breathed with apparent effort. At length she placed her hand over her chest, from whence issued a rattling sound, suggestive of consumption, and articulated brokenly: "De chile, oh missy, — de chile, — Hazel! How am de bressed lamb?"

"The child Hazel!" repeated Evelyn excitedly. Then, struck with a sudden idea, she grasped one of the mulatto's arms fiercely, and said, in that imperative tone which she knew so well how to command: "Tell me why you ask about Hazel Verne! What do you know about her?"

For answer the mulatto groaned miserably, as she lifted guilty eyes to Evelyn's searching looks.

"You are silent," continued the girl. "I charge you, speak at once, or it will be the worse for you!" As she spoke Evelyn drew a tiny metallic tube from her pocket, placed it to her lips, and sent a shrill whistle reverberating through the forest.

The woman's obstinate silence maddened her. Though knowing that the whistle could not be heard at the Grange, she believed it might startle the witch into communicativeness, and so repeated the sound three or four times.

"Ah," cried Evelyn exultingly, for the old woman trembled until her teeth chattered audibly, "that frightens you, I see! Well, it need not, as I did not call loud enough to be heard at the house; but, if I have occasion, I can summon every one of my servants. Shall I do this, or will you speak? Why do you prowl about the premises at nightfall? Why do you ask for my, — for Hazel?"

The mulatto dropped upon her knees and bent her head, so that her straggling wisps of hair mingled with the dust at Evelyn's feet. Then she commenced an incoherent muttering, of which Evelyn could distinguish only the words, "My poo' brack soul," and, "I's a sinnah, wat de good Lawd 'll soon call to de jedgment-seat."

A suspicion was slowly awakening in Evelyn, —

a suspicion which transfixed her. She waited
for the woman's babble to cease, — scarcely allowing herself to breathe, lest the spell should be
broken.

The mulatto was silent at length, but she re-
tained her contrite posture at Evelyn's feet till
the silence was insupportable. Then Evelyn said,
with less severity: "Come, get up! I am patiently
waiting your confession." A slight motion in the
bent. form was the only indication that these words
were heard.

A sound suddenly broke the stillness, a sound
which caused Evelyn herself to start as if shot, —
the sound of approaching footsteps.

She stooped, and almost shrieked in the mulatto's
ear: "I have been heard! Hark! Someone is
coming! You have not another moment to lose,
if you wish to escape. Tell me if I have guessed
the truth! That red scar, below your eye, leads
me to believe you the woman who stole Myrine
Seymour from her cradle sixteen years ago, —
Philias Ward!"

At these words, and with the agility peculiar to
her blood, the woman sprang to her feet. "Oh
massy, have massy, miss!" she entreated wildly.
"I *is* dat wicked wretch! I come all de way f'om
Memphis t' make de 'knowledgment, for I's gwine
soon t' die, and couldn't go afo' de good Lawd
wid such a load o' sin. See!" reaching under
her worn shawl, and bringing from thence a small

bundle, tightly wrapped in oilskin. "Dar's de bressed gal's close, as she wored 'em wen I carr'd her away f'om her fam'ly. My honey chile! Fo' more'n dese fibteen yeah I's done kep' track ob her, an' now I knowed my days was so nigh done for, I come way down heah to Floridy t' make dis 'fession, an' t' see de lamb resto'ed to de bosom ob her fam'ly. Oh p'omise me, miss, p'omise me — "

"To the forest yonder! Hide yourself!" cried Evelyn, thrusting the other's trembling hand aside violently, as she extended it in a gesture of entreaty. "Trust all to me, and fly! My aunt, Mrs. Seymour, is coming! I hear her voice! She will recognize you!"

A startled cry rang out upon the calm air, and the next moment the mulatto darted into the woods with the speed of an adder.

CHAPTER XIX.

DARKSOME DEEDS.

'T WAS strange, 't was passing strange;
'T was pitiful, 't was wondrous pitiful.
OTHELLO.

ALONE stood Evelyn, like one awakened suddenly from a dream. The deathlike solitude about her was interrupted ever and anon by the plaintive murmuring of the pines, and by the sound of those steadily approaching footsteps. The tall sentinels of the forest gradually shaped themselves into form as the moon arose, gilding their dark tops and peopling the ground beneath with a thousand spectral shadows.

Beneath the light mantle which Evelyn wore she thrust the bundle given her by the mulatto. Whichever way she glanced, she seemed to encounter that repellent, yellow face, with its wild eyes and straggling hair. It glared at her from behind each tree, and rose, goblinlike, from the shadows in the white road. This shadow terrified her almost to the verge of insanity. At her right the deep ravine, previously referred to, divided the even ground, and yawned in channel-like chaos; while from its mysterious pits there issued the lonesome chirrup of myriads of insects. It was on

(167)

this very spot the evil spirit had seemed to mock Evelyn an hour previous. Suddenly remembering this she essayed to glide forward, but found herself held footfast, like one possessed with nightmare. Again she seemed to hear that fiendish spirit: "Misery, *misery!*" The atmosphere was astir with that one word, and she pressed her clammy palms hard against her throbbing temples, as if to assure herself that she was awake.

"I am surely going mad!" she cried aloud ; and the sound of her voice was certainly like some demented creature's. What awful information was this, written upon her brain in letters of flame? "Hazel Verne and Myrine Seymour!" Unconsciously she repeated the two names aloud; but the next moment she checked herself, and glanced shuddering about, as if to be sure that she had not been overheard.

At this moment two dark figures came into view, past an abrupt turn in the road, and with a glad cry she pressed forward to meet them. "Aunt!" she cried tremulously. "I heard your voice, and have been waiting for you here. I have had a fright, and could n't go another step alone."

"Hazel and I were alarmed at your long absence, and we started out to meet you," returned her aunt, as she placed an arm about Evelyn reassuringly. "We were on the road this side of the large gate," she continued, "when we were startled by a whistle, which Hazel recognized as

one which you use to call your deer in the park.
We were afraid you were in peril, and hurried on
as fast as possible. Oh, my dear! You gave us a
great fright. My breath is nearly gone! But
there! I am selfish; for I see you are pale and
excited. What has happened to alarm you?"

"Am I pale, really?" asked Evelyn with a
forced laugh. "Why, it was nothing, after all, —
nothing but an old negress, whom I saw as I looked
back over the road behind me. I fancied she was
following me with ill-will. More for amusement
than otherwise I sounded this little whistle, which
for years I have used to summon my pets, when
they stray too far away. Oh aunt, you should
have seen the creature run! You would have
laughed. At my sudden alarm she darted into the
forest like an antelope." Evelyn concluded her
distorted narrative with nervous laughter.

Marvelling much at her niece's want of dignity,
Mrs. Seymour said reprovingly: "You did wrong,
Evelyn, to frighten the poor woman. She may
have belonged to the Grange."

"No," replied Evelyn positively, "I saw her
face plainly, and it was strange to me."

"What then could have been her business in
this lonely place? Why did you not question
her?" continued her aunt seriously.

"I thought such a step uncalled for, as it was
clear to me that she was malicious, stealing catlike
about our premises after dark; but come, aunt,

why are we standing here? After all, no harm has been done. I am chilled, and anxious to get home." So the three, Mrs. Seymour with one arm about each niece, turned backward toward the house.

Evelyn still trembled, despite her effort at calmness, and her aunt, misinterpreting her tremor, presently said: "You were very imprudent to remain out so late, with so thin a cloak. These September evenings are sometimes sharp and frosty. You have not been quite well, and should have more regard for your health."

"I sat beside the graves deep in thought, unconscious of the cold and the lapse of time, till I was suddenly aware that the sun had set. Then I came away hurriedly, thinking I could still reach home before nightfall; but our twilights are so brief! I had walked but a short distance before dusk closed in. I was not in darkness long, however, for presently the moon rose; and then the darkened amphitheatre, as by some trick of enchantment, was abruptly transformed into a grandly illumined dome, — still as death, but populated by such fantastic shapes that I paused, glad to be there. I love these deep woods, especially when bathed in silver. — By the way, Aunt Lydia, did you ever see the moon so splendid as tonight? Look!"

As Evelyn concluded, Hazel lifted her eyes toward the Queen of Night, sailing in majestic

splendor; but Mrs. Seymour, instead of following
her gaze, looked with new solicitude into Evelyn's
countenance, which, like Hazel's, was lifted sky-
ward. Evelyn had spoken precipitately, and her
words had been partially incoherent. As her aunt
secretly watched the pale face, she believed she
saw in the dark eyes a look of wildness peculiar to
the victims of fever. "Poor, dear girl!" she
thought. "I fear her mind is overburdened by
sorrow!"

Mrs. Seymour sighed audibly; and Evelyn
mistaking this for a sigh of ecstacy over the beauty
of the scene, cried again: ●'Isn't she superb,
Aunt Lydia?"

"Who? — Oh, the moon! Certainly, my dear!"
stammered Mrs. Seymour, confused at her own
distraction. "I think I have never seen a more
perfect night," she added.

When they reached the Grange, dinner was
waiting; but Evelyn hurried to her chamber, to
leave her gloves and hat, — and the bundle wrapped
in oilskin.

During the dinner Mrs. Seymour watched her
niece covertly, feeling certain that she saw beneath
the calm exterior unmistakable signs of abnormal
excitement. Now and then she would see Evelyn's
cadaverous cheeks flush suddenly, and the same
wild look, noticeable in the moonlit forest, would
again leap into the brown eyes, making them glare
with a light not pleasant to behold. Twice Evelyn

had her glass refilled with the ruby elixir that warms the blood, and often inveigles men into deeds from which they would turn with abhorrence, if not under its influence. By the time the dessert was served, a hectic glow tinted both cheeks, and the girl became so jovial that her companions could do nothing but exchange questioning glances. Both Mrs. Seymour and Hazel were filled with amazement at the conduct of this changed woman, who usually looked upon claret with disgust, and scorned a jest, unless peculiarly brilliant.

"You are not well, dear niece!" her aunt could not resist saying, as they arose from table.

"I?" retorted Evelyn laughingly. "Why, dear aunt, you mistake! I was never in more perfect health and spirits."

"But," remonstrated her aunt, despite the ringing laugh, "your cheeks and eyes denote feverishness. Come with me to the cool veranda, and confide in me, if there is anything troubling you! Come, darling!" and she placed her caressing arms about the young girl's waist; while Hazel passed down the hall towards her own room, as Evelyn pressed a hot kiss upon her aunt's cheek.

"Why, best of aunts, you are needlessly concerned. I assure you I am perfectly well. I must beg you to excuse me tonight from remaining downstairs, however. I have several important letters to write, and have told Phebe to build a fire in my room. So now goodnight, dear; and remember, do not worry about me."

Another impulsive caress, and then the young lady ran upstairs quickly. "At last I shall be alone with my secret!" she whispered exultantly, as she glided along the dim upper corridor.

Having locked and bolted the door, she approached the chandelier, turning up the blaze to such a glare that not a recess in the apartment was left in shadow. Standing underneath the shimmering crystal pendants, she looked as Lady Macbeth might have looked, contemplating the sleeping Duncan. With an expression of ill intent her eyes sought the silk-draped bed in the alcove, and her bosom rose and fell tumultuously as she breathed the inaudible words: "It is there! It is there!!"

Next she took a full survey of the room, as if to make sure she was alone. The result was evidently unsatisfactory, for going to the window she pulled aside the heavy hangings, that she might have a clear view of the deep recess behind. Then she went to the closet, and peered searchingly within. Finally she crossed over to the alcove, and made a circuit around the bed, to convince herself that no-one was lurking behind those crimson draperies, to spy upon her deeds. This investigation ended, she gave a sigh of relief.

"I have no witnesses!" she said in a portentous whisper. "Walls are said to have ears; but fortunately they are blind and mute." The flush had heightened on Evelyn's cheeks, and her eyes glowed like coals of fire behind their raven fringes. Indeed she looked like a beautiful fiend, as she lifted one of the lace-trimmed pillows, and took from beneath the sheets the oilskin bundle which lay there concealed.

Seating herself on a hassock she untied the cord, though her fingers shook almost beyond control. At length the clumsy wrapper revealed something which once was white as the driven snow, but now bore the sallow tinge which time and exclusion from the light bring to linen.

For a moment Evelyn hesitated, ere she could touch it. "This once caressed the flesh of sweet infancy. It is too pure even to be fanned by my breath," she said to herself; but this thought haunted her but momentarily. She laughed at her own weakness. Lifting the topmost garment she shook out its long and soft folds. The delicate odor of some rare perfume still pervaded the linen, whose texture was elaborately inwrought with needlework; while on each shoulder was a tiny knot of faded blue ribbon.

Evelyn examined the baby-robe narrowly, in quest of some initial or mark which might corroborate the mulatto's story. Presently a low cry burst involuntarily from her lips. Written on the lining of the belt, with indelible ink, was the name, *Myrine.* "*Her* dress!" she said under her breath; and the color vanished from cheek and lip, making them the ghastly companions of the linen.

After awhile she went on, as in a dream, examining, one by one, the tiny garments, finding in
each the same carefully wrought needlework and
the same delicate scroll, wherein she read that
name, in bold letters, *Myrine.*

Evelyn inspected and refolded the last piece.
Then, inspired by that name, which seemed repeated by a hundred invisible spirits, and haunted
by the memory of the cry she had heard from her
aunt that day, " Can I forget the sorrow that has
haunted me for sixteen years ! "— she went to the
window, and flung open the broad sash to the cool
night air, thinking it might overcome the faintness
which seized her; as it did in a degree. Long
she remained behind the curtains, before she could
bring herself again to look at that little pile of
baby-garments.

At length she left the window. An awful look
gleamed in her eyes. Her lips were rigidly set, as
with a mighty resolve. As she once more drew
near the hassock she paused abruptly, arrested by
the sight of a folded paper, which had lain unnoticed on the carpet.

" What can this be?" she wondered. She was
not long in suspense. On the paper she read the
address, in crooked chirography :

*Mistis Weldon or to hoo somedever opens this
bundel.*

Divining, of course, that this note belonged with

the linen, but had slipped from the folds unseen, Evelyn opened it, and by dint of long perseverance, deciphered the crude negro expressions, which were meant to read thus:

MEMPHIS, July 3.

HEAR the confession of a dying woman, and grant her prayer!

On the nineteenth of January, 18—, I was dismissed for theft from the employ of my mistress, Mrs. Lydia Seymour, of New Orleans. I was angry, and resolved to be revenged on the woman who had turned me out of the shelter that had been mine from infancy. So when night came on, I crept to the nursery, where her twin-babies, Myrtle and Myrine, were sleeping in their cradle, and I took Myrine, aged two months, and wrapped her in a woollen shawl, and stole with her out into the night.

I walked to the ferry, and took a steamer the same night for Memphis; and one stormy night, about a week follow-ing, I placed the babe on the doorstep of Mr. Henry Verne, of 146 June Street, into whose service I entered as nurse three days afterward. I wished to be near the child, little Myrine, whom, despite my wickedness, I loved with all my soul. Mrs. Verne, her foster-mother, was an invalid, and died a few weeks after adopting the little babe; but Mr. Verne loved Myrine, and no one believed that she was not his own flesh and blood. None suspected me of bringing her to his door, and for nearly twelve years I remained with him as nurse to his adopted daughter.

They called her Hazel; but sometimes, when I was alone with my beautiful darling, I could not help calling her *Myrine*,—the name was so pretty, and seemed to suit her so well, with her large blue eyes and golden hair.

One day Mr. Verne was taken sick. He was paralyzed; and when he could no longer pay his bills, they came and sold the roof over his head,—my poor, kind master! He was good to me, and I loved him! He knew that he would soon die, and one day he asked me to take a despatch to the office. It was for his sister, Mrs. Gerald Weldon, who lived near the town of Jasper, in Florida. He told me afterward that he was going to ask her to take his little Hazel, and raise her to womanhood. I said nothing; but I ran away, for I did not want to see the lady who was coming to take away my darling.

That was four years ago. Consumption has been feeding upon me these years, and has about finished its work. Soon nothing will be left of me but a mass of dust. So I, Philias Ward, Myrine Seymour's wicked nurse, have made this statement, to take with me to Florida, where I am going to seek Mrs. Weldon, and give this, together with Myrine's baby-clothes, into her hands, or into those of some of her household. I shall then run away and hide myself, to die somewhere.

Do not try to find me. My guilty, black soul has punished me enough for my sin. It has eaten my life away, and there is nothing left for the law to feed upon. So pity me and grant my prayer. It is this: Do not tell Myrine that the mulatto nurse — Dosia, she called her — who watched over her faithfully for twelve years, was the wicked wretch who stole her from her mother's bosom. She loved me well. Do not let her love turn into a hate that would find me in my grave.

Ask my kind old mistress to forgive me. She will, I know, when her beautiful daughter is given back to her, and she knows I am sorry for my sin. Oh, if I could see the two sisters together once, I should die happy! but I can not bear to look my mistress in the face again. That is why I am going to Florida, and not to New Orleans. Mrs. Seymour lives in New Orleans.

This is the dying confession of

PHILIAS WARD.

Evelyn spelled out this letter twice. Then she deposited it in a private drawer in her desk, under lock and key, and sat down to think.

A mockingbird sang in the tree outside her

window; but she remained unconscious of its notes.
The bird sang on, as if to divert her thoughts from
the dangerous path into which they had strayed,
but she remained like a statue, her head thrown
back against the cushions of her chair, her eyes
closed; yet no slumber came to Evelyn that night.
She courted it not, but went on building mental
barriers between Hazel and the truth, — a truth
securely hidden from all save herself, — and —
God, who could not smile upon the wicked, or
sanction their dark deeds.

When Evelyn at last unclosed her eyes, the
silver clock was striking four. She went to the
window. The moon still held its vigil, but was
behind a dark cloud, and near its setting.

Noting the gloom a sudden determination seized
her. She hurried to the closet, and took therefrom
a long waterproof, in which she wrapped herself
closely. Carefully replacing the little garments in
the oilskin, she was ready to venture forth; but,
as if a new thought had occurred to her, she said
aloud: "I can not trust the weight of a chance
stone, but must have something heavy enough to
keep my secret down."

Going again to her desk she counted out twenty
dollars in silver coin, placed them in a strong
leathern purse, which she concealed inside the
bundle. Lifting this, and apparently satisfied with
the weight, she darkened her room and then went
noiselessly down the narrow back staircase, and

was soon speeding along the magnolia avenue, toward the orange orchard.

The sinking moon struggled behind a fretwork of clouds, so that Evelyn was in almost total darkness; but this was favorable. Knowing well her path she continued her way through the garden gate, and then over the path running through the orchard toward the lake. As she gained the willow skirting a faint light began to gleam over the quiet surface.

"All is favorable to me," she told herself. "I need a little light to select a good spot."

She stood on the brink of the shadowed waters, watching them grow brighter and brighter. Toward a tuft of lilypads she directed her eyes, as if calculating the intervening distance.

Presently there was a *whir-r-r*, a thud, a splash, followed by a sudden sparkling in the water, as though some magician had wrought a sudden transformation. There were widening circles near the lily-tuft, as if some object had broken into its placid surface.

The next instant Evelyn became conscious of a breathing presence near. She suppressed the cry which rose to her lips, and looked anxiously around. A moving object met her gaze. Bijou! First he fixed his eloquent eyes upon her face. Then he looked out upon the water, and howled.

CHAPTER XX.

A SISTER'S LEGACY.

No compunctious visitings of nature shall
Shake my fell purpose. MACBETH.

AT the close of another fortnight came Mrs.
Ormsby, a middle-aged Creole of genteel
address, to act as chaperon to Evelyn. When
she was duly installed, Mrs. Seymour announced
her own early departure, as Myrtle had written
that the Heights were no longer bearable without
her mother's presence. Vainly did Evelyn entreat
her aunt to protract her stay for at least another
fortnight.

"I can not bear to look forward to the lonely
days that must follow your leave-taking, Aunt
Lydia," she said, with genuine tears in her eyes,
as they stood, one chilly evening, before the
library grate, wherein the cannel coal crackled
cheerfully.

If there was any real affection left in this
revengeful woman, it was centred upon her
mother's sister. Though guilty of the crime of
concealment towards her aunt, this was not because
she loved Mrs. Seymour less, but that she loved
self more; for jealousy outstripped the purer
sentiment.

Evelyn felt the hypocrisy of her words, even while she uttered them, and the soft caress which fell upon her cheek became hateful to her. She averted her face from her aunt's glance, to conceal the flush of shame which she felt glowing within. The flesh seemed to burn, as though caustic had touched the spot where Mrs. Seymour's kiss had rested.

Noting Evelyn's trouble, and mistaking it for grief, Mrs. Seymour discreetly went to the window, partly to dry her own eyes.

"I have been thinking, Evelyn," said she, presently returning to the hearth-rug, "what I might ask of you in the way of a keepsake from Julia's jewel-case. The stone-cameo set she used to wear so much, — do you think you could part with that?"

"Certainly, Aunt Lydia! The cameos shall be yours without the asking, for they descended from your grandmother," returned Evelyn calmly. "I have thought several times of bringing out mamma's casket of treasures, that you might select some other relic besides the cameos. I will fetch it."

The side corridor which led to Mrs. Weldon's special apartments had been seldom trodden since her death, for the door which opened into them was usually locked. No one wished to enter rooms rendered sacred by death's presence. As Evelyn turned the key, and noiselessly crossed the threshold, she was struck with nameless awe, and felt herself in an accusing presence.

She alone could realize what had occurred since that gentle presence was called to Heaven. She had sinned; and the awful insight of condemnation was hers. She shrunk from the gloomy silence of the room. With clasped hands she uttered this wish in remorseful tones: "Oh God, had mother lived!"

Then she pondered silently, yet without altering her position: "Had my mother lived, what then? How many hearts might have been throbbing tonight with joy unutterable? Then Aubrey Deveréll would have exulted over a different union, leaving me to drink my cup of bitterness alone. Mine would have been the misery, — but not — not this guilty conscience! Oh, this darkness is unbearable! Mother, *mother!* Do not look at me so! I can not bear your accusing eyes."

She almost groped her way across the room to the window, and hastily pushed aside the shutters. A flood of light from the setting sun poured itself across the bright carpet, and brought each piece of furniture into plain relief. It put to flight some of Evelyn's dread; and she breathed more freely, as she suffered her eyes to wander about the familiar apartment. The tears gathered, as she saw the wicker basket, with its bit of needlework, folded neatly, lying on the top.

"Poor, poor mamma!" she murmured, touching

the delicate fabric reverently, as though it was an altar-cloth. "I would kiss your work, but my lips are unworthy! They would stain the flowers your pure fingers were so patiently tracing."

Faster and faster fell the tears, and Evelyn cried out half-coherently: "If you had lived, this terrible temptation would not have come to me; but you were snatched away, and when it came, I fell. Oh — mother, *mother!* If you are looking down upon me now, pity, oh pity, and do not censure me wholly! I yielded to sin, because of my love for *him.* I loved him so! *I loved him so! She* robbed me, and I have sought revenge!"

For some moments her melting mood lasted, but no contrition hallowed it. No ministering angel came to warn Evelyn that there was yet time to repent of her wickedness, — that by one brief word she could weld the broken links of a home-circle, win to herself heartfelt gratitude, make herself a very goddess of salvation in the eyes of him whose name she worshipped. No! Heaven's appealing spirit came not to Evelyn's heart.

Gradually the tears dried upon her cheek, as vengeful thoughts outweighed her sorrow, and she moved toward the India cabinet, where her mother's jewels had always been kept. The cabinet was locked; but Evelyn found — in the bunch it was her mother's wont to carry — a small key, of peculiar workmanship, which she recognized as belonging to the box.

She had no difficulty in finding the casket of gems; but, instead of taking it from the cabinet, she set, about examining certain papers in the drawer near it. They seemed to contain nothing of special importance to her. There was however a packet of letters, yellow with age and tied with a blue ribbon. Evelyn recognized the handwriting as her father's; and there were a few old bank checks, which she listlessly tossed aside.

Presently, in a compartment all by itself, she espied something which attracted her keenest interest, — an envelop bearing a red seal, and this inscription:

Sacred to my dear Sister,
Mrs. Lydia Verne Seymour.

The tempter, once more sovereign in Evelyn's nature, needed but a moment to convince her that it would be wise to unravel the mystery of this sealed document. Held by a power she could not resist, she tore open the letter with steady fingers, and read the lines, never designed for other eyes than those of Mrs. Weldon's twin-sister.

WELL aware, my dear Lydia, that the dread malady, heart-disease, which through generations has been our family doom, will claim me as one of its heirs, and well knowing how unexpectedly it calls upon its subjects to relinquish earthly claims, I herein make an avowal to you which must ever remain a secret between you and your God.

Three years ago, when our brother Henry died, leaving little Hazel as a sacred charge to me, he also told me a secret attending her birth, which had never before passed beyond the knowledge of himself, his wife, and of one other person unknown.

It was this : Hazel was not his child by birthright but only by adoption. They reared her in ignorance of the truth ; and brother's dying prayer was, that this ignorance should remain with Hazel until her life's end. I have been true to his trust. Through three long years I have guarded my vow religiously. But you are part of me, Lydia, and I feel that in case of my sudden demise, ere Hazel attains majority, you will accept her as our departed brother bequeathed her to me — as a child whose origin is sacredly consecrated unto mystery, and must ever so remain.

Accept my legacy, dear sister, in memory of the dead ; and look upon my sunny-haired darling, whose nature corresponds in every way with the beauty of her face, as one God-given, to fill the vacancy of her whom you have long mourned. This is the will of

your affectionate sister,

JULIA VERNE WELDON.

Written, May 12, 18—.

The appealing voice had come at last to Evelyn. The duskiness had deepened, so that every object in the room now assumed a ghastly shape, and the close air seemed filled with the presence of the archangel.

Evelyn had stood by the window in order to decipher the small chirography of the hand now stilled forever. As she finished, and turned her face again toward the grayish gloom, her face shone like marble. She shrank from the solitude back into the window's recess, pulling the curtains together, to shut out the scene.

" Regard your dead mother's most holy wish ! "

a voice seemed to counsel. She groaned aloud in her anguish : "I can not! It is too late! I can not!" "*I can not!* I CAN NOT!" seemed to echo back to her from the silent chamber.

Faintness was overcoming Evelyn. She forced herself to come from behind the draperies and go to the cabinet. Thrusting the letter inside the little drawer, where she had found it, she securely locked the desk and turned to fly from the room. She had almost reached the door when, involuntarily glancing above the fireplace, she met her mother's solemn eyes, looking down upon her from a massive gold frame. In the gloaming they had a beseeching expression.

One low shriek Evelyn uttered. Then she tore herself from the apartment, and ran downstairs to the library, there to fall swooning to the floor, while flashing about her lay the scattered contents of the jewel-casket.

CHAPTER XXI.

So lonely 't was, that God himself
Scarce seemèd there to be.
COLERIDGE.

THE day of Mrs. Seymour's departure had arrived. It was early in the afternoon, and she sat alone in the library, her eyes directed wistfully towards the door, through which she momentarily expected Hazel to enter.

The elder lady had sent word to the dear girl that she wished to take a private farewell of her. All day long her heart had throbbed with an unutterable longing for this niece, whom she had begun to love with an affection almost as profound as that which she bore for her own Myrtle.

The thought of parting with Hazel for an indefinite time filled Mrs. Seymour with pain, but she strove bravely to repress the tears which veiled her eyes, for she wished to render the leave-taking less painful to Hazel.

At length she heard soft footsteps along the hallway. The door opened, and Hazel crossed the room, her hands clasped before her, in a manner peculiar to the girl when under strong

(187)

emotion. Her eyelids were red with weeping; her look was bent upon the floor.

"You sent for me, Aunt Lydia! I am come!"

"Have you been all day in your room, my love? I have not seen you since breakfast," said Mrs. Seymour, drawing Hazel gently toward her, and pressing a lingering kiss upon the tear-stained cheek.

"No, aunt, I have been down to the lake. I always go there when I am lonely." She lifted her beautiful eyes to Mrs. Seymour, and they were filled with a longing which reached to the heart.

"Myrtle shall come to Florida during her next summer vacation, and make you a long visit," pursued the lady, trying to throw cheerfulness into her tone. "When I am gone you must let the thought of her future coming serve as a barrier against loneliness."

At these words part of the sorrow in Hazel's face disappeared, like a cloud before a ray of sunshine.

"Oh dear Aunt Lydia, if you would indeed let Myrtle come! I think I could bear almost any degree of misery, if I were sure of seeing *her* again."

"Misery, child? *Misery?* Why should you utter that word? What do *you* know of misery?" cried Mrs Seymour, drawing the girl impulsively to her breast. "What is there of misery in your young life, my pet?" she entreated.

"It often makes me wretched to know that Cousin Evelyn dislikes me. Sometimes it seems as if my heart must break under her contempt. I so long for her love, Aunt Lydia! I pray, every night, for God to change her heart toward me."

Mrs. Seymour caressed the gold-touched hair, upon which her tears were now falling.

"You must not be discouraged, dear one. Persevere in your endeavors, and some day the light of your character will find its way into Evelyn's regard," she faltered, when she could trust herself to speak.

"No, no!" sobbed the girl bitterly. "Something tells me that she will never soften toward me. The days will be forlorn when you are gone. Oh Aunt Lydia, do n't go out of my life. I can't bear the thought. Take me with you!"

Mrs. Seymour could find no answer to this appeal. She only pressed the clinging form closer, and yielded secretly to her own grief as the other continued: "There is something in my heart that makes me yearn to be with you and Myrtle always! That is what I can not express in words, but it seems a part of me."

A moment of poignant silence followed. Mrs. Seymour was recalling her own child's words, spoken over the dead form of Mrs. Weldon, on the day of the funeral: "There is something in my heart that makes me yearn for Hazel, but I can not describe it in words."

These utterances of the two girls were almost alike, and Mrs. Seymour felt the same strange feeling again overcoming her which she had experienced that day.

"Show us the light, oh God," she whispered. Hazel heard this supplication, and felt scalding drops on her brow.

"Why are you crying, Aunt Lydia?" she whispered; but she only felt herself held tighter to that heaving bosom.

The two were still locked in close embrace when Evelyn entered the library abruptly. "Aunt Lydia," said she, striving to hide the annoyance this scene roused in her guilty soul, "the carriage is waiting. We have but little over an hour for our drive to the station."

Mrs. Seymour thereupon unclasped the clinging arms from her neck, whispering as she did so: "May Heaven forever bless you, darling!" Then she hurriedly crossed the room; but at the door she paused, and said interrogatively: "You will of course drive to the station with us, Hazel?"

"I have ordered the pony phaeton," Evelyn interposed quickly. "There is scarcely room in it for three!" Then she hastily closed the door behind them, leaving Hazel alone in the library, with a hopeless expression in her countenance.

In truth the girl felt that the last ray of happiness was flickering in its socket, and she crouched upon the floor, inwardly crying out to God to let her die. She had a faint remembrance of her aunt's afterward returning to the room to take a final farewell; but she must have been dazed, for she did not follow her out to the carriage, but remained where Mrs. Seymour left her, her face pressed against a cushion, and her bright hair falling about her like a halo, — that hair upon which her aunt's tears had glistened like diamonds.

Suddenly the rattle of carriage wheels awoke her to the conviction that her aunt was really gone. With a cry like that of some wounded creature she sprang to her feet, and rushed out of the house.

"Dey's done gone out o' sight, Missy Hazel," said the hostler, as she breathlessly reached the big gate, and questioned ·him in choking tones. "Dey's done been gone fibe minutes. Dey's done gone out o' sight, honey," he repeated with genuine feeling, as he regarded the grief-stained face, in its frame of tangled hair.

Hazel scarce waited to catch his words, but sped fleet-footed through the orchard, towards an opening in the hedge, which commanded a glimpse of the road over which the vehicle must pass. As she reached the spot, the fast-flying horses came for an instant into sight, and then were hidden by a cloud of dust.

"Aunty, aunty, come back to me!" wailed her isolated heart. "It is cruel of you to go out of my life, when I love you so! It is cruel of you to leave me so utterly alone. Oh Aunt Lydia, come back to me! *Come back*, come back!" She fell down on the soft grass, crying wretchedly.

Arline was away on her vacation; and so Hazel could not go to the kindly Frenchwoman, and be comforted by her sympathetic words. She could only go back to the desolate house, and bury herself in her own little room, weeping her heart sorer than it was already. Even Bijou had deserted her.

Suddenly it flashed upon Hazel that she had not seen her dog for two days. With this thought she hurriedly pressed back the tears with her wet handkerchief: "What has become of my dear old friend?" she cried aloud. The next moment she was bounding away to the kitchen, where she asked breathlessly, of Aunt Sarah the cook: "Black Mammy, what has become of Bijou? I have n't seen him for two whole days."

"Fore de Lawd, honey chile, now's ye ax Brack Mammy 'bout dat ar dog, I reckons I has ter tell ye as how he eenamos' kill hisse'f Sabbaday ebenin'," replied the negress, pausing to roll some flaky dough from her hands.

"Bijou hurt! How? Oh Black Mammy, how did it happen?" cried the girl, as she clutched old Sarah's dress excitedly.

The woman rolled the whites of her eyes about in a startling manner, and said evasively: "Run out to de stable, honey, 'n ax Nole 'bout de facks. He done 'tendin' de dog out dar, 'long wid de

hosses. Nole am a right down good-soul brack
un, 'n aint a gwine to let anythin' suffah wat
'longed to Marsa Wel'on. Sho 's ye bawn, honey
chile, ole marsa set heaps o' conf'rence on my
Nole; 'n now marsa 's gone, seems he 'specks dat
conf'rence heaps. Yes he do, chile, sho!"

Filled with solicitude for her noble Saint
Bernard, Hazel hastened to the barnyard. In her
precipitation she almost stumbled over Noel, who
was mending a halter near the gate.

" I came to see Bijou, Noel. Black Mammy says
my poor dog is hurt. Where is he? How did he
come to be hurt?"

" I done 'structed mammy ter keep mum 'bout
dat yah dog," returned the hostler, as he looked
angrily up from his work; but when his eyes fell
upon Hazel's sad face, he added more gently,
doffing his cap deferentially: " Ye sees, Missy
Hazel, I done tole mammy, 'n all de culled folks at
de house, not ter say as how Bijou 's hurt, case I
knowed you 'd take it bad like."

" Is he wounded? Is he suffering much? Oh
Noel, will he die?" cried the girl, and she covered
her face with both hands, and wept anew at the
very thought of losing her boon companion, her
one remaining friend.

Just then a prolonged whine came to her from
the loft; and before Noel could prevent, she was
bounding up the crazy stairs. The hostler followed, but paused on the topmost step, delighted

at the picture that met his gaze. Hazel had thrown herself on her knees beside her dog, and was talking to him in terms of endearment, such as a mother might use to her child, while she received his frantic kisses upon her hands, her face, her hair.

"Bress my soul, Missy Hazel, dat dog am de biggest possum out!" Noel shouted. After a convulsion of laughter he added: "He done lay like stone-dead all dis bressed day, 'n I could n't 'suade him ter budge or t' eat a mou'ful. — Wait!"

Noel was off like a shot, but returned speedily, with a piece of cooked meat. "Hol' out dis t' him, Missy Hazel. Ye see will he take it out you han'."

Hazel took the meat; and her whole face beamed when the dog seized and swallowed it hungrily, and then begged for more. Louder and louder became the negro's merriment, but he ceased laughing as his companion said: "You see what a successful nurse I am, Noel. I shall come every day to attend my poor dog. Now tell me how he came to be sick. I see no wound about him."

"Well, yer sees, little missy, 't was like dis," replied the hostler, as he perched himself on a bale of hay near by, and swung his feet awkwardly. "Fo' de las' two weeks, Bijou, he come in de barnyard ebery day shiverin', — cole and wet as

sop. Well, one day I says to myse'f, 'Now,' says
I, 'it's bad business, dat dog gwine in de watah so
much, 'n de wedah comin' on so termendeous cole.
It's bad business,' says I. 'De rumatiz'll settle
in his bones, sho.' Well, t' other ebenin', 's I's
comin' home from de ma'sh, whah I'd ben shootin'
teal, as I's comin' along side de lake, I heah a loud
yulp. Now, wen I heah dat yulp, I says t' myse'f,
'Now,' says I, 'dat fool dog am in de watah agin,
an' can't git out.' Well, den I runs like desperit
fro' dem willows, an' 'long side de lake, till I come
in sight ob dat dog; 'un jis as I specked, dah he
wuz in de watah, tangled up in a lot o' lily roots.
Well, I offn wid my close, 'n I jumps in dat lake.
Phoo-o-o-o! It makes my brood freeze now ter
t'ink how like ice dat watah wuz! Wall, I cuts de
tough roots from bout his feet 'n neck, un brung
him out plum friz stiff, poo' fellah! I toted him
home on my back, un he's done been sick ebber
sence. The rheumatiz settled in his bones, jis
'zactly as I profthesied."

As Noel concluded his story Hazel sprang to
her feet; and the next instant she was beside
him, with one of his rough hands pressed to her
lips. "Oh Noel," cried she, "how can I ever
compensate you? You saved my dear Bijou from
drowning!"

"I mought a' sabed de dog, missy; but I do n't
want no pay, I do n't want no *copesate* for doin' a
good turn for *you*. I'd risk my brack neck to

serbe you, Missy Hazel, — jes shuah's yer bawn, I would;" and the negro's black orbs beamed with pleasure at this demonstration of gratitude from Hazel, who presently said: "I can not imagine why Bijou should persist in his mad plunges. He has always hated the water in cold weather; but he will recover, of course he will recover?" she added, looking at Noel with troubled questioning in her aspect.

Noel's hopes in this direction having revived since she showed her wonderful influence over the dog, he replied, as he flung himself nimbly from his elevated seat on the hay: "Dat he will, missy, or dis coon's done missed his reck'non."

"And I shall come every day to attend you, my darling," said Hazel, her face all aglow, as she stooped to arrange Bijou's pallet, and bestow upon him a parting pat; but she was compelled to muffle her ears against his piteous whine, as she descended from the loft.

As she closed the gate, an uncontrollable desire came over her to see the place where her pet had nearly lost his life; so she went back to question Noel as to the exact spot, and then ran down to the lake.

She had no difficulty in recognizing the tuft of lilypads wherewith Bijou had been entangled, for they still floated on the bosom of the waters, a wreck of former beauty. The pink and white leaves had floated away, but she could see the

disturbed roots and broken stems; though little
she dreamed that under the dark water, and removed from human sight, lay a bundle of clothes
marked *Myrine,* which Evelyn Weldon had thrown
into the pool two weeks before.

CHAPTER XXII.

PARTING WAYS.

HOPE tells a flattering tale,
  Delusive, vain, and hollow;
Ah, let not hope prevail,
  Lest disappointment follow. WROTHER.

NEVER did time drag so wearily as during the next few weeks at Weldon Grange. Day after day found Evelyn at the library window, some open book lying idly in her lap. The pages she seldom turned, but suffered her glance to dwell listlessly on the clear autumnal landscape, or rest now and then upon the variegated foliage of magnolias and poplars.

In some remote corner of the same apartment Hazel was usually sitting, employed with light needlework or French lessons, in which she wished to be prepared against Arline's near return.

It was a dull October afternoon. A bright fire blazed on the hearth, and the room was filled with the odor of the wood. Yellow chrysanthemums, mingled with fine sprays of princess-pine, were tastefully arranged in the Dresden vases on the shelf, and gave cheerfulness to the room.

The pendulum swung lazily to and fro in the solid cathedral clock, and its monotonous *tick-tack*

was the only sound intruding• upon the silence
which for hours had reigned there, and almost
made the Parian busts of Shakespeare, Byron, and
Dickens frown morosely from their gilded pedestals.
In the fitful firelight they fairly blinked, and
imagination could fancy that they even lifted up
their heads and did address themselves to motion,
like as they would speak, after the manner of the
Ghost in Hamlet.

Evelyn sat in her accustomed place, in the deep
embrasure of the window, and today a piece of
embroidery lay neglected in her lap. She and
Hazel, who poured intently over her French,
might have been total strangers to each other,
so far as was indicated by conversation. One
may see people from opposite ends of the world
sit together for hours in a public parlor without
exchanging a word, yet there are glances of
human interest now and then between them; but
here was not a word or glance in unison.

Hazel occasionally glanced wistfully at the frigid
woman sitting by the window, whose impassive face
was always turned away, as Hazel supposed, but
was often turned full upon the girl when Hazel
was not looking; and those eyes were• cruelly
cold, expressing the thoughts of Evelyn's soul, —
thoughts which would have affrighted Hazel's
gentle spirit, could she have interpreted them
aright.

Seeing the younger girl in deep mourning, with

all her golden hair drawn into a loose coil in her neck, and her eyes so pensive, one would scarcely have recognized her as the gay butterfly-chaser of a half-year ago. She was not the same Hazel. Her mouth, then like a bud, bursting into dimples, had now settled into grave thoughtfulness. Though the smile lingered, it was restrained, while the dimples merely dinted the cheeks, being too shy to venture deeper.

The vivacious child, with little thought beyond Bijou and the birds, had been transformed into the premature woman, as a strong blast, sweeping through the garden, will suddenly hasten a half-open bud into untimely maturity; but the change had added to Hazel's charms. With sunny smiles and dimples, rosy cheeks and changeful eyes, she had been winsome; but now, with her shell-like complexion, thoughtful lips, and lustrous eyes, revealing a soul's subtle sorrow, Hazel was doubly attractive.

At length her lessons were learned. She closed her book, and arose to get her needlework, when Evelyn called imperatively: "Hazel, come here! Bring your book with you!"

The younger girl crossed the floor obediently. The thought of a few words with Evelyn, a thing of rare occurrence between them, made her heart leap with gladness. Was this the harbinger of reconciliation between them? The very thought caused a joyous flush, and she trembled visibly, with hopeful anticipation, as she stood before her foster-sister.

Poor, craving heart! How cruel to rouse such futile hopes! Mute and wondering she suffered Evelyn to take the volume from her hand, and then watched the dark face eagerly, as Evelyn rustled the leaves with her jewelled fingers. So intent was Hazel on her happy reflections, that she started like a frightened doe when Evelyn suddenly closed the book with an emphatic snap.

Raising her head, in her old arrogant fashion, the elder cousin said: "Why have you confined yourself exclusively to French this vacation? Are you so proficient in your other studies?"

The rebuke in her tone turned Hazel's short-lived hope into despair, and bore down her heart like lead.

"No, I am not, Evelyn; but Arline says my French accent is defective, and she told me to apply myself particularly to this study during her absence; but I have not obeyed her till recently. I thought —"

"No doubt you *have* thought much of perfecting yourself in this particular language! It is most fascinating. To appear really attractive to French people one should be able to converse fluently in their own tongue," interrupted Evelyn ironically; and she supplemented her words with a laugh which corresponded well with their metallic ring.

Hazel met her cousin's searching glance steadily.

She had not detected the hidden meaning of the words, though the unfeeling laugh seemed out of place, and wounded her to the quick. Those penetrating eyes seemed to burn into her childlike soul. Tears gathered in her gentle eyes, and her lips twitched painfully as she faltered: "You are mocking me, Evelyn!"

Another peal of hollow laughter broke from the darkling face. "Mocking you, indeed!" Evelyn returned, when her mirth had spent itself. "Am I far out of the way, when I say that, to appear doubly fascinating in the eyes of a French admirer, one must be qualified to speak his native tongue?"

"But why do you look at me so, Evelyn? Your eyes frighten me!"

"Actress! With what bewitching art you sustain your part! Now hear me, Hazel Verne! You can't mislead *me* by your crocodile tears and affected innocence. I understand you. I see through your mask!"

From the speaker's eyes gleamed a look so terrible as to cause the listener to draw back a step; for it was the lurid fire of jealousy, excited nearly to madness, which Hazel saw and felt, but was unable to understand.

Involuntarily she retreated further from the panting creature. "I—I don't understand you! I an actress? I wear a mask?" gasped the child.

"Yes, an *actress*,—of the most cowardly type!" hissed her cousin.

All at once an idea flashed across Hazel's dizzy brain. Surely Evelyn was delirious! She had worried herself too much, and this was the result. With this thought Hazel impulsively stepped forward, and laid an entreating hand upon the arm of her foster-sister.

"Evelyn, dear, I fear you are n't quite well today," she said, trying to assume a tone of quiet reasoning. "Let me help you to your room, where you can lie down and be made comfortable. I will be such a patient nurse, if you will only let me. Come!"

Evelyn's lips curled in scorn, but the light died out of her eyes; and her old hauteur returned, as she leaned back in her chair, agitated still, but otherwise outwardly calm. Perhaps it was more than hatred which made her shrink from Hazel's caress.

"Reassure yourself, please! I am quite well!" she vouchsafed to say. "As for nursing me, I do not want you. I could n't bring myself to tolerate a show of affection from one who has doomed me to despair. Our ways must lie apart; but bear in mind that you are entirely subject to my will until you come of age. After that you will be at liberty to choose your own way. Your future is well provided for by my father, and you can make it what you choose."

Keen surprise dried the tears from Hazel's eyes. She breathed intermittently, and she fluttered like a wounded dove, as she faltered : " I did not quite understand what you were saying, Evelyn. Do you mean that *I* have spoiled your life, — that *I* have caused you misery? Oh Evelyn, you could n't mean anything so untrue?"

"I mean *just* that! But for you I should be the happiest woman living! Perhaps — oh God! who knows? — I might be one of the best! As it is, — I am steeped in wretchedness."

" Won't you tell me what I have done? Once before you accused me of wrecking your life. Your words have tormented me ever since. I could not understand them. Sometimes I think you despise me for living here. If so, Evelyn, I will go away. Aunt Lydia loves me, — Aunt Lydia and Myrtle. I could go to *them.* Oh Evelyn, let me go to them, and then we shall both be happier! "

" You shall never go to New Orleans ! " was the answer to this beseeching cry; and the speaker's face was like stone, while she clinched her hands in her lap, to repress the demon which threatened her with another mad paroxysm. "I will bury you in a convent first ! "

A stifled sob fell from Hazel at this threat, — a sob from a broken heart, — and she quitted the room.

As the gray twilight stole into her pretty bed-room it found Hazel seated at the window, her aching head bowed on the ledge, weeping as only the wronged can weep.

"What have I ever done to warrant such unkind feelings? Oh that cruel accusation! What did she mean?"

Hazel carefully reviewed the past four years of her life, wherein she had tried so untiringly to win some generous feeling from her proud foster-sister, in return for which Hazel would so freely have lavished her own heart's warmest love; but how completely had she failed! To what a hopeless height the barriers now towered between herself and Evelyn!

When Hazel lifted her head from the window-ledge the evening had become so beautiful as to make her wonder if she had not been asleep, with a horrible dream. Away off in the east a broad halo of light heralded the moonlight, and the azure vault was ablaze with "the forget-me-nots of the angels." Through the wall of cypress and willow, at the southern extremity of the orchard, she could see the lake, glimmeringly reflecting the glory of God's firmament in its mirrored depths.

Suddenly fair Cynthia showed her red-barred face over the distant hilltops; and simultaneously, as if that glorious satellite had brought a message direct from the land of mystery, Monsieur Aubrey's last words came swiftly back: "If the time should come when you may need a friend, then will you turn to me as to one who would serve you at the peril of his own life?"

Oh if she could but see him now, this moment,

and ask him to explain Evelyn's cruel words. She wondered if he knew what they had suffered at the Grange since his visit. She wondered if he would come to her, if he knew how much she stood in need of a true friend!

The night promised to be as bright as day. As our child-heroine continued at the window she thought of the dear ones departed, and an unutterable longing came over her to go to their graves and pray. Perhaps there she could find some comfort in her unhappiness. "Yes," she thought, "I will go to Cypress Dell! No harm will come of it! It will be bright as day, and I shall fear nothing."

She was aroused from her revery by the entrance of Mrs. Ormsby, who was bringing her a tray of tea and toast. "I bring you a light supper, dear Miss Hazel," said the kind Creole. "You did not appear at table, and I feared you were not well. All in the dark? Well, well! This won't do, my child. I will strike a light."

Hazel protested gently against this proposal. "Please let me remain here at the window, Mrs. Ormsby. I shall enjoy my tea better with only the moonlight. Thanks! You are very kind!" She received the tray with averted face, lest her condition should reveal itself to this new friend.

"Is there anything else I can do for you? I would gladly help you, dear Miss Hazel," said the companion, as she was about to withdraw.

Motherly instinct had from the first drawn her to this sad-faced orphan. She knew, from the tremor in Hazel's voice, that she had been weeping, and longed to draw the girl to her sympathizing heart; but she went out, and closed the door softly behind her, as Hazel said : "There is nothing, thank you, but you are very kind!"

CHAPTER XXIII.

AVE MARIA.

How shall I bring the sunshine to thy face,
And dry thy tears, in bitter woe s despite? —
Love, my love, teaches me a certain way.
ALL THE YEAR ROUND.

IT was past ten when Hazel, warmly clad for her solitary walk to the Dell, left the house. As she passed through the large gate, opening from the town road into the one leading to the cemetery, she did not notice a saddled horse, hitched within the shadow of a wide-spreading poplar, a few yards away. She walked along beneath the arching pines, the soft moonbeams glinting through, rendering her pathway bright before her, and constituting a silver background for the embossed patterns of fern and late wild-flowers, which bestrewed the place.

Once, as she entered the shadow of a gigantic pine, the screech of a bird made her pause; but as she perceived the gray-feathered creature, perched on a low-protruding branch, a few yards off, and staring at her with eyes which looked as large as saucers in the moonlight, she waved her hand toward him, softly saying : "Pretty owl, I would not harm you !"

(208)

Then she resumed her walk, as fearless as before, some of her recent unhappiness absorbed in the peerless beauty of the night.

A few field daisies still grew by the wayside. These she gathered, to mingle with some fresh chrysanthemums she had plucked from the garden, — a tribute to the dead. She had stooped to cull a knot of maidenhair, to complete her bouquet, when a sudden burst of melody wakened the still night, like a chord from floating seraphim.

Hazel stood transfixed. Her face was upturned to the moonlight, her lips were parted, her hands were clasped in rapture, as she turned her ear to catch the dying cadence of that heavenly strain.

> *Ave Maria,* now we implore thee!
> Show us thy favor, grant us thy blessing!
> Amen, Amen!

Like a zephyr the last note died away; yet to Hazel the air still vibrated with the penetration of that voice. *Ave Maria! Ave Maria!* Everywhere the holy name seemed floating. It filled the night. It moved her as nothing before had done. Whose throat had sent forth such music, — and at such an hour, in such a place?

Surely it sounded like Deverell's singing. She had heard the same voice often in her dreams since he went away, but it always sounded far-off. Now it was near and real.

"Yes! It sounded as though he were very near me, — *very* near," she repeated to herself.

"I think I *am* half afraid, — not with the fear of something awful, but with fear which tells my heart to be glad. I think I will not go on to the graves. I will return to the house."

With an effort she retraced a few steps; but presently she paused again.

"Perhaps I am foolishly nervous," she told herself. "It might, after all, be only imagination. I have been thinking much of him tonight, and fancy may have brought back his voice, singing *Ave Maria.* It would be foolish to go home, now I am more than halfway to the Dell. Of course it was fancy, for he is far away, — perhaps on the other side of the Rocky Mountains."

Thus reassured she again turned her face toward the burying-ground; yet she involuntarily quickened her steps, until her little feet almost flew over the white road. Not until she had passed through the wicket did she pause to breathe.

As she neared the stone which marked the resting-place of a certain Weldon ancestor, who had lain in Cypress Dell for over a century, another owl — perched on the head of a marble cherub, and beguiling the night with his weird *too-whoo* — scurried away to another refuge, in the branches of the cypress which shaded the double grave Hazel was seeking. She watched him alight there, and then inadvertently glanced beneath the shadow of the tree; but she recoiled instantly, with a low cry, for on a rustic bench, near the grave, she saw a man reclining, his eyes intent upon the monumental inscription.

Hearing the girl's cry he leaped to his feet, and the moonbeams revealed the features of Monsieur Aubrey.

This sudden apparition caused her to reel like a wind-tossed flower. She would have fallen, had not strong arms encircled her. " Hazel, my little love ! " She heard this passionate cry faintly, as in a dream.

A moment's silence ensued. Hazel did not speak, because she lacked strength; but she lay trembling, with her head on Aubrey's bosom. He did not speak, because joy and amazement contended within him for the mastery. His lips sought hers, but were instantly withdrawn, at the dictation of a sense of honor. However, he pressed her to his heart, and stroked her hair.

As Hazel's strength returned she realized vaguely what had happened, and struggled gently in the arms which held her so firmly. Then Aubrey released her, and led her to the seat he had vacated.

Seating himself beside her he took her fluttering hands, pressed them reassuringly, and said: " If you feel strong enough now, little one, tell me what actuated you to come hither at this strange hour."

His voice, low-toned and earnest, — as she had heard it in the past, — thrilled her. " I was lonely,

monsieur," she faltered, "and the night was so
like the day that I had no fear." ·

"You are safer than ever now, child. — There,
there, do not weep!" entreated he, as she sobbed
violently. "You do not fear me, *petite?*" he
added with tender reproach.

"No, no, monsieur, it is not that. — I have no
fear of you," she said, closing her fingers over his
confidingly and almost involuntarily. "You must
forgive me if I cry. I — I — oh, you know it was
so sudden, — my seeing you here, — and — *everything!* I heard you singing *Ave Maria*, but I
tried to believe it was only my imagination. I am
so nervous. It seemed more like an angel singing.
Oh monsieur, I am so glad it was *you*, — your very
self! Were you singing over our dear graves?"

"Yes! The place seemed sacredly quiet, and
filled me with reverence. I did not know I sang
so loud!"

"You didn't sing too loud. It was the wind
which bore your voice to me. It was sweet, —
and, — oh monsieur, I can not express it, but it
sounded like a strain from an angel's harp!" cried
Hazel. Then she added: "I prayed tonight for
God to send me some true friend, and He has
answered my prayer. You are —" She hesitated, and Aubrey saw that she was blushing.

"What is it my little Hazel would say?" he
asked, lowering his handsome face until it almost
touched hers. "Tell me, my sweet one!" he

added; and in his ardor he crushed her little hand, — he did not know how painfully.

Hazel answered not. Lower and lower fell her veiling lashes; though, unknown to herself, her eyes were full of undefined love. She was conscious of a new sensation, but this she could not rightly interpret. She did not know the meaning of the flush in her cheek and the fluttering of her heart. She did not know why the pressure of his hand should move her so much. She did not know why an unutterable longing possessed her to be near this man always, — to feel his strength every day, to hear his voice saying, " My sweet one ! " What a refuge such a friend would be.

At length Aubrey spoke again. Mistaking her silence for childish timidity he said gravely : " I too have been praying, Hazel. I prayed that you might be delivered from all unhappiness. I believe this meeting was preordained of Heaven ! You speak as if suffering, — as though you needed friends. If this be true, then surely I have been guided to you by the Supreme Power. Can you doubt it ? "

" But monsieur, I expected to see you least of anybody," returned the girl, without looking up. " I believed you to be in California, or in some place far West. It seems like dreaming to see you here, and to hear your voice. Cousin Evelyn will be much surprised when she learns — "

" Mademoiselle Weldon must not know of our

meeting," interrupted the lover hastily. — "That is, she must not know of our meeting tonight."

He modulated his voice to almost a whisper as he continued: "I have been West. The news of your sad loss did not reach me until I had been in San Francisco a fortnight, as I did not read the papers regularly, and had a pleasant travelling-companion; but one day, as Hylton and I were dining at a French restaurant, I happened to scan the columns of a New Orleans paper, when my eyes fell upon a notice of your, — of Monsieur and Madame Weldon's sudden death. Ah, Mademoiselle Hazel, I shall not undertake to describe my great sorrow and surprise. My first thought was of you, little one. I remembered that your very best friends were now lying here, — no longer able to guard you."

"Do not sob so, little one! Your grief hurts me!" This he added, as her sighs lent a sad accompaniment to his voice.

"I wondered who would supply their place," he resumed when she had grown calmer. "This thought haunted me. I longed to return at once; but my friend was in poor health, and seemed to grow worse, and I felt in duty bound to stay longer on the Pacific Slope, — at least a few weeks longer. I went from place to place with him, like one in a maze. My thoughts were always with you. I wondered, hourly, how your life was getting on, whether you had one friend to shield

you from — from that *woman*, whom I knew to be
— not your friend, yet whom you would be with
daily. I lay awake, night after night, with this
one thought. I could picture for you a happy
future only from one standpoint. In one light
only would your life present itself as blessed with
love and tender care. In all other lights you
seemed to frown upon me from a fretwork of
sombreness, — oh such gloom. This framework
was so unfit for a . gentle nature like my little
friend's! "

He paused, overcome by emotion. Then with
one hand pressed over his eyes, the other still
clasping Hazel's closely, he sat awhile without
speaking.

She longed to speak some comforting word, but
she could not bring herself to break the hushed
stillness. So she sat quietly, wondering what
might be the one bright view he had taken of her
future. To her it seemed as if she had left joy
and sunshine forever in the beautiful past of her
childhood, and that she must go forth with an
aching heart into the vista of years to come, with
a hunger which threatened to endure till life's end,
— hunger for love, which, to a warm and respon-
sive nature like hers, is as essential as air to the
birds or sunlight to the flowers.

She lost herself in thoughts of those happy and
careless days, when she had roamed with Bijou
through the dells, or skimmed the lake in her little
boat, in quest of a certain pink lily.

Then the sound of Aubrey's voice interrupted the retrospect: "I have no right to describe to my little friend the roseate vision in which I saw her life as it should be, — in which I saw it gleaming in felicity. I have no right, Hazel; yet have I travelled thousands of miles impelled by this one purpose. — I arrived in Jasper this evening. Believing it would be useless to seek communication with you before tomorrow, I resolved, as the night was so perfect, to ride over to Cypress Dell, where I could at least be near those who had been so dear to you. Little did I think this very spot was our Heaven-appointed place of meeting; but so it has proved. — I wrote a note, which I hoped to convey to you through some safe medium. I asked you to appoint a place where I could see you alone. I wished our meeting unknown. You are fortunately spared this clandestine step, which I did not like to propose; and now I must beg you to listen to what my heart aches to say, here in this holy field of the dead. Will you hear and try to understand me, Hazel darling?"

Hazel felt his quick breathing, and was half-frightened at his passionate pressure of her hand; yet she answered quietly: "I am listening, monsieur. I am sure I can understand what you wish to say, for you speak so earnestly, as though your heart was talking."

She lifted her trustful eyes, but they quickly fell, as again she saw the ardor in his expression.

"You are left absolutely alone in the world," said Aubrey presently. "Your — Mademoiselle Evelyn will never make your life what her parents desired. Ah, little one, you shiver, — because you know the truth! Your lives would be better apart. Yours should be transplanted beyond the reach of her blighting presence. A delicate flower can not survive in the dank shadows of a cellar. A lily droops and dies, when bruised by ruthless hands."

"I have made some good friends since aunt and uncle died," began Hazel as the Frenchman paused, — "oh, such dear friends! They are Aunt Lydia, Cousin Myrtle, and Uncle Seymour. They were here at the funeral, and Aunt Lydia stayed with us nearly two months afterward. I love her so! She seems like an own dear mother to me! It was like tearing a piece of my heart out when she went away. Then there is Myrtle! I could n't begin to tell you how we love each other. If I could be with her always, I should want no greater happiness; but of course that can never be. I must always go on living here, and she is away over the Gulf."

The girl's words came upon Aubrey's secret thoughts like a bombshell. For a moment he was hardly master of himself, and his next sentence cost him an inward struggle. "Why must it be thus? Why can you not go to New Orleans, and live with those you love?"

"It was only this afternoon that I begged Evelyn to grant me this happiness; but she would not! She said — she said — such cruel things to me! — I wanted to die."

"What cruel things? Tell me what mademoiselle said to make you so miserable!" rejoined Aubrey, unconscious of the strong resentment in his tones.

"She said she would bury me in a convent, sooner than let me live in New Orleans. She looked so white and terrible when she said it! My heart stopped beating with fear. Then she accused me of something so dreadful! She said I had doomed her to a life of despair! Those words will always stand out before me, they were so cruel; but I can not understand them. I would die sooner than bring misery to anybody! That is why I begged Evelyn to let me go to Aunt Lydia. I thought I had made her hate me by living at the Grange; for ever since I came she has repulsed me. I am sure she despises me for something besides my coming into her fam — "

Here Hazel found herself suddenly caught and held in Aubrey's arms, as by a vice.

"My darling, my pure one," he ejaculated, "give me the right to protect you from the woman who makes you suffer! Take my name, and let it be a safeguard against such misery. The inhuman wickedness of this world makes me shudder for your innocence! I am unworthy to receive a flower so guileless; yet, oh Hazel, I love you, darling! I have loved you since that evening I found you crying at the window, wounded by Evelyn's sneers. Even before that I believe I loved you, — yes, from the very first! Only trust me, little one, — that is enough! I am satisfied with taking your simple confidence in exchange for the great love I bear you. I will trust to the future for a sweeter reward. Will you believe me, Hazel? Will you be my wife?"

"Your *wife*, — your *wife?*" faltered the white lips so near his own. "Why — I — I — Do you wish to marry me? Do you wish to take me away from the Grange?"

"I would take you to my own beautiful home on the Mississippi," said Aubrey, — smiling, despite himself, at the young girl's guileless surprise.

"Once installed at Deveréll Hall you could see your aunt every day, and have Myrtle with you constantly, if you liked. Then I should always be near to protect you."

"But a wife! It seems so strange to think of myself as a wife, when I am scarcely sixteen!" and Hazel concluded with a little deprecatory laugh.

She seemed to be lifted from the ground, and scarcely breathed. She could see the white monuments and the dark cypresses. She could see his love-lighted face. She could hear his soft voice; but it was as if she saw and heard in a vision.

" I have read of girls in the Orient being wedded at ten and twelve," he was saying; " but I will not urge your answer tonight, sweetheart. Come to me tomorrow night at eleven o'clock, down by the lake where I first saw you, and give me your answer there. Oh my little love, let your answer be this, *I will be your wife.* The next day I will come and claim you, in the presence of Mademoiselle Weldon, as my promised bride, of whom no earthly power can rob me. Will you promise? "

" I do not yet understand what such a promise would involve, monsieur. To come to you at that hour of the night would seem treacherous, — unjust to Evelyn. It would be deceit! "

" I promise you that no word of censure shall fall on your dear head. Come to me, and I will face the results. Not for worlds must you allow a syllable to escape your lips as to what has passed between us tonight."

A few happy moments followed, after which they placed Hazel's forgotten flowers by the graves. Then, at her request, Aubrey repeated the low sweet measures, as they both knelt there :

> *Ave Maria,* now we implore thee,
> Show us thy favor, grant us thy blessing!
> Let us more love thee, thy love possessing!
> Guide us, protect us, we are thy children.
> Amen, Amen!

CHAPTER XXIV.

FATE GOETH FIRST.

How canst thou tell how far from thee
Fate or caprice may lead his steps,
   ere that tomorrow comes?
Men have been known lightly to turn
   the corner of a street;
And days have grown to months,
And months to lagging years, ere they
Have looked in loving eyes again.
              COVENTRY PATMORE.

HAZEL slept little that night. How could she close her eyes in stolid slumber, with that beautiful picture filling the darkness of her bedroom? His words possessed her: "Take my name, and let it be a safeguard against the misery that may await you. Be my wife!"

She could not define the rapture roused by this memory. She only knew that she was unspeakably happy; and she regretted when morning came, lest it should bring the knowledge that she had only been straying in delicious dreamland.

When the first streak of sunlight kissed her pillow, and found her with eyes wide open, she was convinced that all was dear reality. She could yet hear that fervent voice. Indeed, the thought of his heart-throbs almost frightened her, as she remembered how he had embraced her within his manly arms.

"It was not a dream!" she whispered with delirious joy, and tucked her head beneath the coverlet, as if to hide her maidenly blushes from the light. "I have seen him — my king! He knelt by the graves, there in the beautiful moonlight, and sang *Ave Maria*. I have promised to meet him again tonight, — *this very night.*"

Hazel arose; but, before dressing herself, she knelt beside her little bed, and prayed long and earnestly, looking like some suppliant angel, in her snow-white robe; for her glorious hair was unbound, and rippled almost to the floor in waves of golden glory, the slanting sunbeams touching it here and there, causing it to fairly blaze. She prayed that God would direct her mind aright through the day, and prepare her heart with an answer to him who professed to love her, and wished her for his wife.

Often during that day she stole away to her room, to reflect for a moment, — to ask her soul if she had sinned in confiding so implicitly in Aubrey Deverèll, the man who seemed a very king amongst men. The answer was always: "No, you have not sinned in trusting completely in him." Yet something seemed to tell her that she could have him only as a friend. She must not promise what he had asked. She could not be his wife. He could only be her friend, — her very dearest, noblest friend.

Then would come to her a vague realization that there was not enough in friendship to satisfy her heart, upon which the impression of a sweeter word had now been stamped; yet she would go on trying to accustom herself to the thought that she must go to him that night, and say: "I will continue living at Weldon Grange. I must stay here for years, perhaps, — trying, as I have done, to win my cousin's favor. By-and-by, perhaps in four or five years, when I am of age, I shall go out into the world."

The words were dictated by her conscience; but they seemed bitter as she repeated them, even though she felt them to be the outcome of truth and honor. She would not shrink. *Integrity* had always been a golden word. She felt that to steal away in the dead of night, to pledge herself in betrothal to this man, would be hateful and low, and would confirm Evelyn's words, that Hazel was a stealthy actress.

Sometimes Hazel's weaker spirit would rise uppermost, remembering Aubrey, as he stood in the moonlight, tall, noble, princely. Then she found herself wishing to be always near him. It seemed last night, with him beside her, that nothing could do her harm. She felt so safe, so happy. But now — oh now — everything looked dark and foreboding, — darker than before his coming!

Her sense of duty and the joy of her love conflicting, her cheek was pale and her eyes downcast.

Daylight waned at last, and evening came on apace. Hazel saw little of Evelyn except at table, when scarce a word or glance was exchanged between them. The only time when their eyes met Hazel believed she saw beneath the severity of Evelyn's a look full of despair, — a look which troubled Hazel all the afternoon, and increased her pity for her cousin; for it smote her with remorse at having cherished a deceptive thought.

Could our innocent have rightly interpreted that look, she would have recoiled from the very memory of her recent meeting with Aubrey; but no knowledge came to her of the envy which was petrifying Evelyn's life, and Hazel went on looking forward to the time when she would see him again, unconscious that she was treading on the coils of a serpent, and that soon the viper would raise its fearful crest against her. By degrees an unnatural brilliancy crept into Hazel's look. The very thought of once again beholding her *king*, as she secretly called Aubrey, filled her with bliss.

After dinner, when she had sought her room as usual, Hazel put on her plainest mourning dress, adjusted a creamy fichu about her neck, arranged her bright hair into a diadem, and leaned toward the mirror, until her soft warm lips met those of the reflection therein. It was a childish action; but one that must appeal to any heart realizing the girl's loneliness, her desire for something to love, something to caress.

A smile curled her coral lips as she did so. Then she exclaimed with amazement: "Why, how like Myrtle I look!" Once more she kissed the reflection. "I will make believe it is you, Myrtle darling! Oh, I love you!"

The face smiled back, and she seemed to hear Myrtle's voice saying: "I love you too! I love you, I love you!" From the distance that voice seemed borne to her; and long she stood there, gazing devotedly into her own face, but seeing, instead of blue eyes and gold-brown hair, orbs of soft brown and a crown of topaz.

The time now passed tediously. Almost for the first time in her life, Hazel began to experience the gnawing of suspense. She watched unceasingly the dial of the clock on the dressing-table. With every breath she wondered if ever minutes so loitered before.

As to all things else, there came an end to Hazel's probation. The hands pointed to a quarter of eleven. It would certainly require fifteen minutes to reach the trysting-place; so, putting on a warm circular, and tossing a scarf over her head, she noiselessly glided from her room.

She had only to pass down the back hallway, open a window looking into the garden, and she was outside. Her feet once safely on the ground, and the sweet breath of flowers about her, she hastily plucked a cluster of chrysanthemums, and bestowed them amid the lace covering her bosom. Then she sped across the lawn, down the magnolia avenue, keeping well within the shadows. ·

At length she reached the wide driveway and gate. She felt free from discovery, and was in the act of drawing the heavy bolt, when, *Hark!* Was that the sound of footsteps, falling suddenly upon the tranquil air? Yes! Faster and faster, nearer and nearer they came.

Hazel's first impulse was to lift the hook, rush out into the forest, and conceal herself behind the trunk of some great tree; for she felt a presentiment that Evelyn was in pursuit; but her feet were as heavy as though "to the soil they had taken root," and she stood helpless, as fixed as one of the statues in the shrubbery.

One hand was on the gate. Her eyes were directed towards an abrupt bend in the driveway, around which she knew her follower must soon appear. How soon indeed! The next instant a woman's figure dashed into sight, and the moonbeams fell upon a beautiful face disfigured with anger.

CHAPTER XXV.

Love can hope, where reason would despair.
BULWER.

ON returning from her usual horseback ride that evening, the only recreation in which Evelyn now indulged, she lingered in the stable-yard to give Noel some instructions about the removal of a span of horses to Fairacre the next day. She had finished her orders, when the hostler said abruptly: "Missy Eb'lyn, I see de gem'lin t'day wot stop at de Grange afo marsa and missus die."

His young mistress turned upon him, a mad hope kindling in her eyes and deluging her cheek. "Whom do you mean?" she managed to say.

Vainly she strove to crowd back the image of Aubrey. The bare idea of his being the visitor rendered her, for a moment, scarcely mistress of herself.

The boy's next words brought with them a bewildering sensation. "I means de gem'lin wot was call Marsa Deberall."

"You're mistaken! Do you hear me? I say you are mistaken! It is incredible. He is hundreds of miles away."

(227)

" Fo' de Lawd, Missy Ebelyn, I seed him," persisted Noel.

Then he added, with a peculiar jerk of the head : " I seed Mounsour Deberall, shuah 's my name 's Noel Johnsing. I seed him a sittin' on de hotel poach in Jaspah, smokin' a segah; un' I says to myself, 'Now,' says I, 'dat am de berry gem'lin, as was at de Grange las' summah.' I says ter myself, says I, 'Him 'll be gwine ober to de Grange dis ebenin', fo' ter see Missy Eb'ly;' un' if he do n't now, chile, I 's miss my reck'non, dat 's — Gimminy! Missy Eb'lyn, wot ails ye ? "

He stepped forward to support her, for she seemed about to faint; but, suddenly collecting herself, she motioned him back with a nervous gesture. "A — nothing is the matter with me!" Flashing an angry look upon him she added, " You 're an idiot!" and then hurried from the barnyard.

" Gimminy! Dat am a she-tiger!" soliloquized Noel, when she was well beyond earshot. " Guess her 's in lub wid dat gem'lin, dat Mounsour Deberall. Bet my las' coppah he 'd nebber marry dat gal if he knowed what dis yah niggah do. I knows her! Yes, I does! Reckon I 's got two eyes for to see de teahs in Missy Hazel mos' eb'ry day since old marsa and missus die. How de bressed chile am change since den! Her use ter be playful-like, as a kitten. Up in de mo'nin', afo de sun riz, chasin' de butterflies, along wid de dog,

— rompin', singin'. Um golly! How dat pooty froat did make de air ring! Happy as de birds! Now her goes about wid dem eyes full o' teahs, 'n wid de roses all gone f'om her pooty face. Oh, it a'mos' breaks my heart, fo' ter see how pale and sad-like she looks! Un' who 'm 'sponsible fo' all dis yah? Dat she-tiger! Bah! Her aint fit t' tie my honey's shoes!" In no amiable mood the darkey tossed the saddle roughly aside, and led Alcides to his stall.

Aubrey Deverell in Jasper! Impossible! Yet how positive that boy was. Dear Heaven, if she could be convinced his words were true! If she could feel assured *he* were near. "My darling, would that you were coming to me!" was the cry of Evelyn's heart.

Sinking into an armchair, she did not leave her room until darkness closed about her. At one moment she strove to put Noel's words from her as idle chatter. The next she yielded herself to feverish imaginations, born of faith in the boy's report.

If Aubrey were in Jasper he was surely on his way to the Grange! Yet why had he loitered a whole afternoon in that drowsy village, when he might easily procure a horse and ride over in an hour? How could he be in Florida and in California at the same time? Had he not told her that his trip West would be extended far into the winter, possibly into spring? Had he heard of her affliction, and therefore altered his plans? Perhaps he had written to apprise her of his coming, and the letter might have miscarried. Perhaps he had been awaiting some word from her in Jasper. She would send a messenger immediately to town to make inquiries at the hotel, —and deliver a note, should he indeed be there.

Finally she roused herself from her revery, resolved to act at once upon this impulse; but when she realized that it was already evening, she also perceived the foolishness of her plan, prompted by naught save a servant's gossip. She was foolish to give Noel's speeches a moment's consideration, — yes, very foolish.

With this conclusion she went across the room to strike a light; but her feet became entangled in her riding-habit, which, in her distraction, she had forgotten to remove. She laughed at her stupidity; but her laugh was unnatural, as she tore her habit off in the uncertain light, and flung it from her.

After she had lighted the chandelier she moved towards the mirror, to smooth her hair; but she recoiled upon beholding the reflection of her image, and exclaimed: "Great Heavens! Can that demented-looking thing be Evelyn Weldon?"

The transformation was truly marked. Her cheeks, which had grown so cadaverous since the death of her parents, were now glowing. Her dark eyes shone like diamonds in their deep setting. In the mirror she could see the bits of rich bricabrac on the mantle, and the . clock whose hands pointed exactly to seven.

"Seven o'clock!" she exclaimed; and as hope revived the inward conflict she added: "He may be on his way at this very moment."

A sudden rap at the door made her heart stand still with expectation; but it was only her maid, who came to inquire if she would not come down to dinner. "Bofe bells done rung, an Mist'is Ormsby an' Missy Hazel am a'waitin'."

Evelyn had not heard either bell. "I won't come down tonight, Phebe," she responded, sinking languidly upon the sofa; "but you may bring me a strong cup of tea. Stay!" she exclaimed, as the maid was about to withdraw, "bring me a glass of sherry, instead. My ride has quite upset me. I may want some tea later."

After drinking the wine thirstily, she dismissed Phebe for the night, locked her door, and began a superb toilet, selecting from her wardrobe a rich lavender satin, over which were filmy folds of black lace. "If he *should* come," she said to herself, "I must be looking my best."

Oh that invincible *if*. How often suspense would give place to joy if we could bridge this little gulf! How often do we battle against grim despair with this one word burning in our bosoms, inciting us to hope for what reason forbids. If, *if*, IF, goes on the alluring spirit-voice within us; and we hearken to the muffled cry, half-doubting, half-believing. With strained pulse we anticipate, and yet dread, the instant which must bring us face to face with the inevitable.

Thus was it with Evelyn. Her heart had long been a stranger to the hope that she could ever again be to Aubrey Deveréll what once she was. She had moreover schooled herself to the belief that they would never cross each other's paths again. Yet here she was, a struggling victim to that unattainable *if*, trying now to thrust the negro's statement aside, and anon catching his words on the rebound, and hugging them to her breast, in breathless readiness to believe; for the wish is ever "father to the thought."

At length, completely mastered by this delusive influence, she seated herself at the open window, her eyes directed toward the magnolia avenue, along which she hoped — against hope — to see her idol pass.

Little she dreamed that not far away sat Hazel in her chamber, her heart also astir with anxiety, born of the hours which depicted the same image.

Yes, before them each was the same face; but while one looked with strained eyes from the window, feeling her heart gradually settle back into the darkness from which it had been rudely summoned, — as the hours dragged on, and Aubrey came not, — the other's blue eyes were fixed upon the face of the clock, noting each moment with a heart-throb, and sure that each brought her king a step nearer.

Queen Constance, who looked down upon Evelyn with solemn eyes from her silvered frame, seemed no more lifeless than Evelyn.

The indescribable beauty of the night was unmarked. Softly the moonbeams fell on each flower and shrub in the garden below. Brightly they glanced athwart the fountain, and turned the jets into pearly spray. The green sward and the blue ether were alike resplendent with scintillating gems; while the white-winged cherubim and the Naiad Queen, smiling and flinging kisses to the stars, made the garden a fairyland.

A flood of silver came streaming through the window where Evelyn sat, and turned the curtains into folds of frostwork, putting to shame the glaring light of the chandelier; but the moonlight softened not the human visage, framed in its coronal of cruel hair. Like a statue she sat, her queenly head defined against the glistening gauze, — her shapely hands, folded listlessly in her lap, gleaming like carved ivory, against meshes of dead-black' lace.

Surely painter never chose a better model for Despair. Ever since half-past nine had she remained thus statuesquely posed, her eyes gazing out into the night, — whose stars she saw not, whose beauty was ugliness to her; and now it was nearly eleven.

Suddenly a dark-clad figure glided along the avenue, beneath her casement. The incident would ordinarily have passed unnoticed; but there was something about the movement which recalled Evelyn to herself, and caused her to rub her eyes, like one awakening from unpleasant slumber. Then she looked after that retreating form, — but only for a moment. The next she bounded to her feet. With an exclamation of frenzy she rushed from the room, and ran down the stairway like one bewitched. Out of the front door and across the lawn she dashed, a goblin driven by a blast of fury.

CHAPTER XXVI.

FACE TO FACE.

THAT it should come to this.
HAMLET.

FULL a moment elapsed ere the painful silence which followed Evelyn's apparition in the pathway was broken. She was the first to speak.

"Well, what is the motive of this midnight adventure, Hazel? I demand an explanation!" In her voice were blended triumph and menace.

For one moment Hazel looked appealingly into the cruel face before her; but seeing no mercy there she began brokenly: "I—Evelyn—I—"

The pale lips refused to speak further. She could not bring them to form a falsehood. She had never acquired the tricks of diplomacy. Had her life depended upon it, she could not have given utterance to deceit.

She tried to meet Evelyn's eyes unflinchingly, but her own fell before them, and she shuddered as she beheld their unholy glitter.

"Why do you stand there trembling like some impostor? Speak! Where are you going at this unseemly hour?"

"Going?" echoed the other in a dazed way. "I was going—"

Suddenly she seemed to realize her helplessness, and tried to arouse herself to the necessity of making an effort in her own defence. "Oh Evelyn, trust me! Only believe in me!"

Her very attitude seemed to develop Evelyn's suspicion into certainty. She moved spasmodically. Her eyes were almost green in the moonlight. Her white lips twitched, as she grasped one of Hazel's wrists and hissed: "You wretch! Tell me what has taken you from my house this night, or I swear I will measure your punishment by my aversion."

Her grip was so tight on Hazel's wrist that the younger girl suffered acutely from the cutting nails; but she did not flinch nor cry out; she only said, with forced calmness: "Evelyn, I entreat you, have pity! You do not know the injustice you do me. I have done nothing wrong, I swear it!"

"You swear!" repeated Evelyn with a Satanic laugh. A mockingbird, who had been filling the night with melody, now hushed his rich notes, as if in fear of that strange voice.

"Oaths coming from lips false as yours, Hazel Verne, pollute the very air," she continued. "You have stolen from your room tonight to hold a clandestine meeting with Aubrey Deveréll. Though you should summon an angel from Heaven to deny this, I would not hold you innocent."

She pushed the fainting girl violently from her.

After a moment's burning surveillance she was about to speak again, when, as if aided by some unseen influence, Hazel lifted her head proudly, and said, in a voice strangely subdued: "Evelyn, if in the past you had shown the slightest friendship for me, the least tender sentiment of any kind, there would be no cause for your lack of confidence now. When I entered your father's home four years ago, a lonely and inexperienced child, I cherished a conviction that you would receive me with something of a cousin's affection; but my disappointment was greater than words can express."

She went on hurriedly, anxious to pour out her heart's pent-up misery: "You were cold toward me, — cruelly cold, — from the very first moment we met. Though your treatment wounded me deeply, it did not discourage my ambition to make you my friend. In this I persisted from day to day, to the time when aunt and uncle died; but I never succeeded in winning a really kind word or glance. Often have I wept my heart sore, because of your utter contempt. My life seemed sometimes unbearable; but at other times I forgot all else, and was happy in the love of my dear aunt and uncle. They died! If you were cruel and cold before, you were utterly heartless afterward. You seem to forget that I am of your own flesh and blood. You seem in nowise to appreciate my lonely position in the .

world; though your own is much the same, and
should prompt you to some sense of sympathy.
From day to day you show your hatred for me.
If you deign to notice me at all, it is to brand
me with unjust accusations."

Here Hazel paused, and the glistening tears
declared that her short-lived spirit of independence
had spent itself.

A few moments of silence followed, when only
Evelyn's labored breathing and Hazel's quavering
sobs could be heard. Did "compunctious visitings" silence the former? Whatever the cause,
Hazel was suffered to proceed awhile longer, as
she spoke with visible effort.

"I have found generous friends, with whom I
am offered a home, — friends before whom I could
kneel, so deeply do I reverence them; but I have
pleaded with you in vain to let me go to them.
You say you will send me to a convent, rather
than see me attain the happiness I feel to be
rightfully mine, — offered me, as it is, by my dead
father's sister, who has seemed, since the first time
I saw her, like my own mother — "

Evelyn started spasmodically at that word
mother, and a low cry escaped her lips. She
recovered herself immediately, however, and said
sneeringly, as she bent her dark face nearer, that
she might look straight into those true eyes before
her: "You grow sensational! Pray let me impress you with the fact that this is no time for

dramatics. You have wandered far from our subject, so I will recall it. You owe me some explanation of your midnight wanderings. I say you have an assignation with Aubrey Deveréll, and are on your way to the trysting-place. I happen to know he is in the neighborhood, so any attempt to mislead me will be useless. Confess!"

"Evelyn, my lips are sealed," began Hazel; but the next instant she reeled under a stinging blow.

"Shameless coward! Not alone have you enticed my lover from me, but you have stooped to infamy. Oh, I thank God my parents have been spared the knowledge of their foster-child's character! Better they should die, than live to be disgraced by one they delivered from beggary and the slums. Go back to the house, you ingrate!"

Hazel did not move, but lifted her eyes to the distorted face. The poor child was choking, and nervously unclasped the mantle from about her throat. Then all was darkness. That messenger of mercy, unconsciousness, came to alleviate her sufferings for a time; but her awakening was terrible, for she felt herself dragged towards the house, with the words ringing in her ear: "Your home shall henceforth be the Magdalen Asylum!"

CHAPTER XXVII.

THE FALLEN PORTRAIT.

Look here upon this picture.

HAMLET.

AFTER thrusting Hazel within the governess's room, — which Evelyn concluded would be the safest place, because situated in the less-frequented part of the house, and at present vacant, — she locked the door on the outside. Then she tottered, sick and half-fainting, to her own apartments.

She went toward the grate, in which a few bright coals still glowed, feeling a tremor in every limb, — a tremor not caused by the temperature of the night, but by the shattered condition of her nerves, and then gave vent to a cry which vibrated with agony.

Then she sank into a chair, with both hands pressed to her face. In appearance she had aged years within an hour. Let us not attempt to describe the thoughts which thronged her aching brain as she thus sat, hugged in the arms of misery worse than death. Words are inadequate to the portrayal of such sufferings as hers.

She was in a stupor. Before her eyes a mist gathered, as she let them wander aimlessly about the room. A smile, in which there was something indescribably pitiable, wreathed the lips, which moved continuously, though nothing audible escaped them. Once or twice she attempted to rouse herself; but she was like an inebriate, who bestirs his paralyzed faculties for one instant, only to let them sink deeper into oblivion.

Slowly the night dragged on. At length dawn gleamed into the open window, bringing with it a current of chilly air. Every spark of fire had been long exhausted on the hearth, but Evelyn no longer felt the cold. The sun rose. The early birds flew by the window, some of them alighting on the ledge, and peeping in upon that silent figure, sitting where the light fell upon her stony face.

The bell in the barn-tower struck the hour of six, the signal for all the servants about the premises to be up and doing. Dreamlike sounded each clamorous peal. As the last echo died away, Evelyn slowly turned her eyes toward the window, as if vaguely realizing that a new day had begun. At the same time she became conscious of a living figure in the room. She walked toward it, and saw only her own image reflected in an opposite mirror. This insane-looking creature, with dark hair falling in tangled masses about her shoulders, had a weird fascination, though she scarcely recognized it as herself.

Walking gradually toward the mirror, with arms

outstretched, a piteous smile still lurking about her lips, she spoke as one might to a beggar: "Poor thing! Poor suffering woman! What do you wish? Food, drink? I will give you anything. See!"

Mechanically her fingers wandered to her ears, disengaging the priceless diamonds therefrom. "Take these," she cried, "and these," — stripping two rings from her fingers, and holding the glittering cluster toward the image, whose hands were also outstretched, seemingly to grasp the offering.

Just as Evelyn's hand came into contact with the cold surface of the glass, there was a fearful crash behind her. She turned with a terrified shriek. Her mother's portrait, which for years had hung above the mantel, lay on the floor, together with rare curios carried along by the heavy frame in its fall, broken into a hundred pieces.

The portrait had fallen face upward. From beneath the thin glass, shivered into innumerable fragments, a pair of gray eyes looked straight into Evelyn's, — looked up reproachfully, yet with holy tenderness, as if her mother's heart were speaking from their depths: "Thou hast wounded a spirit that loved thee! Thy wicked words have come to me in Heaven! Thou hast sinned against the dead! Thou hast outraged the living!"

For a moment Evelyn met this painted gaze

with returning reason. Then, with extended arms and a low cry of *mother, mother!* she fell forward upon her face, and lay there motionless beside the fallen portrait.

Monsieur Deveréll, having waited until past midnight for Hazel at the appointed place, turned his horse back toward Jasper with a keen sense of disappointment. Convinced that something unforeseen had detained Hazel at the Grange, he resolved to convey to her a secret message in the morning.

Fortune favored him in this. After breakfast he sauntered out to the esplanade, to indulge in a cigar. Glancing casually up the narrow street he saw a negro on horseback, whom he recognized as the hostler from the Grange, galloping hurriedly in the direction of the hotel. Recognizing Monsieur Aubrey as he came nearer, Noel doffed his hat politely. At Aubrey's signal he drew rein.

" You are from Weldon Grange ? "

" I is ! Yes-sah ! "

" And you go back this morning ? "

" Yes-sah ! I 's gwine back d'rectly, sah. "

" Can I trust you with a note to Miss Verne, to be delivered to her privately ? "

" Missy Berne ? Oh, yes-sah ! but has yer got de note ready writ, marsa ? Yer sees, I 's in a termendious hurry dis mo'nin'."

Hereupon he would have made known his errand

to town, which was to summon the family physician to Evelyn's bedside, but he was interrupted by Aubrey: " Well, I won't detain you; but if you are passing back this way, say in twenty minutes, I will have the note ready, and trust to you for its safety."

" Yes-sah ! " said Noel ; and, touching his hat again, he added that he would return within half an hour. Then he was off like the wind, for he was astride of Don Carlos.

The young Frenchman hastened at once to his room in the hotel, and wrote to Hazel hastily :

I AWAITED you at the appointed place until after midnight. That some impediment prevented your coming as you promised is clear enough; for I know you trust me wholly, little one, and would not wilfully disappoint me. Would I could make you realize the strength of my love for you! It would lead me to defy the world to place any barrier between us that I could not surmount. Will you let me prove this? Will you let me come to Weldon Grange today, and claim you before the household as my bride? Should you bid me come, your pure heart may be wounded by revenge, sharp as a serpent's tooth; but should its sting be yours to endure, remember, little one, that I will be there to shield you with my love, and the pain will only endure for a time, — only for a little time, — when I will carry you far from the enemy, where you will forget that unhappiness ever existed.

Doubtless some of my words will puzzle you. In your ignorance of the world's inhumanity you will be little able to interpret that bitter word *revenge;* nor would I seek to instill into your heart such impure knowledge; but in my experience I have learned that a vengeful thirst is much like intemperance. It waits not the guidance of reason. It is impulsive, unjust, and can smite to bleeding a guileless heart, even as a wind-blast can smite a lily to the earth.

I pray you, my pure one, bear this in mind, and be brave when I come to you. I can not doubt that you will bid me come. Remember, Hazel, this is the most earnest appeal of a lifetime. Refusing to grant it, you may be submitting yourself to an experience more bitter than death. Once more I charge you, *be brave*, darling, and surrender your future, without fear or hesitation, to one who loves you unselfishly, and would sacrifice all else to gain you for his own.

I will await your reply at noon, today, down at the lake. Either come, or send some word to me.

AUBREY DEVERÉLL.

Having sealed and addressed the letter Aubrey descended to the veranda to await Noel's return; but he was surprised to find the boy already there. Urging him to great precaution in the delivery of the letter, Aubrey thrust a five-dollar bill into the yellow palm, at the same time declining any thanks, with an expressive sweep of his hand. Then he watched the rider out of sight before ordering a horse to be saddled for his own immediate use.

CHAPTER XXVIII.

GATHERING MISTS.

THE child of misery, baptized in tears.
LANGHORN.

AND our heroine? Daylight found her lying on Arline's bed, as she lay when the door was closed and locked behind her a few hours earlier. She might be dead, so still did she lie, her face buried in the pillows, and her unbound hair streaming over their whiteness; but Hazel was not lifeless, though she wondered, with almost every breath, why the death-angel did not reach her before life was reduced to such chaos. The knell of her happiness had been tolled in those words: "You have enticed my lover from me. You have stooped to infamy. Your home shall henceforth be the Magdalen Asylum!"

Oh, if she could find herself once more in her own little bedroom, with the conviction that she heard such dreadful words in a trance! Poor bruised heart!

The bell in the tower tolled six,—the same sound which had roused Evelyn to half-consciousness. Like her persecutor, Hazel stirred as the discordant clang jarred upon her. She lifted her fevered

(246)

face from the pillow. As through a mist she
dimly observed the various objects in the room, —
the good old-fashioned furniture, a bureau with
mediæval carvings, the mahogany bookcase with
well-filled shelves, and the spotted muslin curtains,
unlike any others in the house.

"Arline, dear Arline! If *you* were only here
to comfort me!" came from Hazel's dry lips, as
she realized that she was indeed in the governess's
room. Then her tearless eyes wandered to the
fireplace. Above it still hung the picture of Ellen
Douglas, — beautiful Ellen, poised in her little
shallop, where the water touched the strand. The
eyes, with solemn sadness, seemed fixed upon
Hazel in mute sympathy. Hazel gazed at the
picture a moment, and then resumed her old
position on the bed, once more sobbing in the
gray solitude.

Presently two golden arrows came swiftly
through the window, as if shot by angel-hands.
They touched the rippling waves of the child's
hair, and began a game of hide-and-seek amid its
meshes, glad to find so fair a playground; but
they were selfish sunbeams, for no thought gave
they to the lacerated heart. All regardless of
Hazel's misery the sunshine danced merrily away.

"Oh Evelyn, Evelyn!" she sobbed. "How have
I wronged you! How have I blindly robbed you
of what you held dearer than life! I *have* doomed
you to misery! I see it all now, — Heaven help

mie, I see it all; but it is too late. I see the
bitter meaning of your words. Like you, I wish
the dark pool had engulfed me before I first saw
Monsieur Deveréll!"

How far away that happy morning seemed!
How completely the intervening time had been
given over to infelicity! How Evelyn must have
suffered!

Hazel recalled many incidents connected with
Aubrey's visit. She remembered how Evelyn had
looked at her that morning, down by the lake,
when she had been rowing with their guest. She
recollected Evelyn's glance in the evening, when
Hazel stole into the parlor to hear the stranger
sing. She thought of the suddenness of Evelyn's
exit from the room. Now she could interpret the
meaning of it all! Evelyn loved Aubrey, and
was jealous of every syllable and glance bestowed
upon the little cousin, whom she hated for being
at the Grange while he was there, and whom she
suspected of secret wiles. These thoughts probed
Hazel to the quick.

"How could I have been so blind as not to see
that she worshipped him! Yet what was I, a
child, to know of love's ways? I wonder if they
were engaged. Monsieur must have thought much
of Evelyn; else, why had he travelled all the way
from New Orleans to see her? Yes, they must
have been betrothed! He would have married
her, had he not seen me, — *had he not seen me!*
What is it, beneath all my sorrow for Evelyn, that

makes me glad of knowing him? I try to make myself believe I would rather die, than be a blight to anyone; yet I find myself back in Cypress Dell, listening to his voice. I feel again that strange sensation, when I recall his words, his pressure of my hand. This is all wrong. I must put such thoughts from me forever! To cherish a *look* of his would be wicked! I will try — oh how hard will I try — to forget him, my king. I will remember only Evelyn's misery, and that her love has been wrecked through me. I will pray God to restore him to her. After all that has passed, what if I should be the medium of reuniting these two hearts? Surely, if Aubrey loves me as he says, he will be willing to make any sacrifice for my happiness. Surely — "

Her meditations were suddenly interrupted by a clinking sound, as of a key turning in the door. Filled with terror Hazel pressed her face deeper among the pillows, for she believed Evelyn was returning to chide her victim afresh.

Her heart stood still with this dread anticipation, and the seconds were as hours, before she heard the rustle of clothing and the approach of footsteps. Then, oh merciful tenderness, whose hand was laid upon her hair, with gentleness that might have been a mother's? Surely not Evelyn's! And that voice, so low and sweet: "*Chère* Hazel! *Chère petite amie!*"

"Arline, Arline, is it you?" went up Hazel's glad cry, as she sprang into the governess's arms.

CHAPTER XXIX.

DOUBTS.

So when a raging fever burns.

A HALF–HOUR later, when Phebe came to perform her usual morning duties, she found Evelyn prostrate beside her mother's portrait. The alarm was given that something had befallen their young mistress, and the servants speedily lifted the powerless form to the bed. It took but a moment to remove the silk dress, bedraggled with dust and soiled with dew. Then they applied restoratives and chafed the lifeless hands.

Soon nature began to reassert itself, and at length Evelyn opened her bloodshot eyes. There was no intelligence in their stare, — only an awful vacancy, which caused the attendants to exchange gruesome looks. Life had returned, but all was confusion with poor Evelyn. Her face seemed fanned by stifling air, as from a furnace. Her cheeks flamed brighter and brighter, till their hue matched the tapestries about her bed. Then her lips moved in incoherent phrases. At times she would clinch her hands savagely, brandishing them at her attendants, and forbidding them to touch her.

(250)

"You have dressed that infamous girl in wedding-robes, and put orange-blossoms in her hair! You have made her a marvel of loveliness, for *his* eyes to rest upon. You pierce me all over with thorns, you minxes, you worms! I will poison you. I will tie silver round your necks, and sink you into the lake! Ha, ha! Nobody can find you there! The money will hold you down. The lilies will swim above you! You will lie there and rot till the Judgment Day! Not even the dog will miss you."

Again she would break wildly forth: "Look! That hideous face with the red scar! It is hiding there behind the tree, leering at me! See! — Ugh, how horrible! The forest is full of goblins and witches. They will not let me pass. They are coming toward me, all of them! They will take it from me — the bundle. Help, help! One of them has wrenched it from my bosom, — that one there, with a face like Aunt Lydia's! She will see the name and read the letter, and then they will tie me to a stake and burn me for — for throwing Myrine in the lake! — "

The startling intelligence soon ran over the estate that the young mistress was dangerously ill, — mad; and as soon as Noel could saddle Don Carlos, he was off to Jasper after Doctor Weaver.

As Aubrey rode at an even pace along the lane toward the Grange, the doctor passed him. The young Frenchman noted, with vague apprehensions, the old-time saddlebags. Knowing the lane led direct towards the Grange, he inferred that this must be the doctor's destination, and wondered why Noel had not told him of any sickness there. His remembrance of the colored man's haste corroborated his forebodings.

Upon further reflection, however, he decided that the doctor's mission could concern neither of the young ladies of the house. Doubtless one of the servants had been taken ill.

With a mind more at ease, Aubrey continued leisurely on his way, soon losing sight of the other horse and rider, as they trotted around a sudden bend.

A few minutes later, as Aubrey was about to double the same bend, his horse suddenly made a violent plunge into the air, almost unseating the rider. Looking around for the cause of this alarm he saw an aged mulatto woman, crouching among the rank weeds near the fence.

Mistaking her for a beggar, with his ever-ready desire to alleviate suffering Aubrey took a half-dollar from his pocket, and tossed it toward the creature, saying as he did so : " You look needy. Take this money ! "

He did not wait for a word of thanks, but rode forward, not even looking to see if the woman picked up the money. A sudden thought made him check his horse, and look searchingly back at the tawny face, still half-concealed among the weeds. The woman also looked up, meeting his penetrating eyes; but the next instant she averted her face, and he saw her sink backward, while a sickening aspect settled on her features.

" By what thread does that repulsive face connect itself with my past life?" he repeated to himself over and over again. " I can not be mistaken! Somewhere I have seen it before."

Presently, as guided by some magic wand, he was again in his boyhood, accompanying his mother on a round of friendly visits. Why should that yellow and red-scarred countenance link itself with those visits? More and more enigmatical became the question.

Aubrey had not removed his glance from the woman's face; but so unconscious was his look, he did not observe she had straightened herself, and was retreating gradually.

A sudden attack of coughing led him to watch her movements. There was something in that rattling cough to evoke pity, for it betokened a fatal disease.

Her rags were the mouthpieces of stringent poverty. Her coarse black hair lay in wisps over a threadbare shawl. A frock, of some rusty-black cotton stuff, was rudely patched, while bare toes betrayed themselves through mismated shoes, and she was without head-covering. As she ceased coughing, and staggered on at a quicker pace, Aubrey called after her: " Here, woman! "

She hesitated, and then reluctantly looked at him once more, with timid eyes.

" Come nearer! "

She slowly approached, until she stood within a few yards of her questioner.

" Have you ever lived in New Orleans?" he asked, almost gruffly.

She did not reply, but turned her bare head first this way and then that, like a haunted creature eluding her pursuer.

" Have you ever lived in New Orleans?" he repeated more gently; for a conviction dawned upon him that the woman was demented.

Still she was silent. The fearsome look deepened, while she quaked with cold.

" I am a brute! I have frightened her! " thought he, as sympathy overruled his curiosity. " There is your money, lying in the dust! Pick it up, and put this with it." Thereupon he tossed her a second half-dollar.

" Go to the village, and get yourself food and clothing. Here are five dollars for it! " This he added, as he observed how ragged she was.

She accepted the note, picked up the silver from the dust, and then sank upon her knees, crying: " Oh bress yer, *bress* yer, marsa! You's got a angel's heart, 'n dis po' soul 'll bress yer till her dyin' day! "

She might as well have blessed the sentinel pines by the roadside, or the dust upon which her tears were falling; for when she looked up, her benefactor was no longer in sight. He had spurred away as she stooped for the money, trying to assure himself that only his overwrought brain led him to behold anything familiar in the woman's face; but his attempts to waive his remembrance of her proved useless.

He rode on beneath the interlaced foliage, feeling a pang of remorse for having loitered so long, when Hazel's answer was probably awaiting him at that very moment.

He felt not a little annoyed at the indelible impression that red-scarred visage had left on his mind.

Would that he could have seen the mulatto when, finding herself alone, she cried aloud, in such tones as only guilt can awaken: "Oh my brack soul, my brack soul! Dey's on my track! I'll hide! I'll hide away yondah, in de great city!" — meaning Tallahassee; yet she gripped the money in her yellow palm, as she repeated triumphantly: "I'll hide in de great city!"

Then she plodded along the road toward Jasper, which she reached by noon, and there purchased a ticket for Tallahassee.

CHAPTER XXX.

I KNEW, I knew it could not last;
'T was bright, 't was heavenly, but 't is past.

MOORE.

"HAZEL, what has happened? Why do I find you like this, — locked in my room, and so troubled? You have been crying, little friend. What has happened in my absence, to make you so changed?" Thus asked Arline, when Hazel became more subdued.

As yet the girl could not bring herself to disclose the facts. She only clasped her arms around the governess's neck, and said: "I can't tell you now. Wait till I'm stronger. It is enough for me to know that you are beside me, with your kind heart. Let me rest my aching head upon it. Heaven has been merciful in sending back my friend!"

The girl looked into the Frenchwoman's face, which showed supreme anxiety. "Arline," she cried, "promise me that you will never give up your faith in me, even though you should hear terrible things about me. Believe me, — never in my life have I knowingly done wrong!"

(256)

"Dear love, I know your guileless heart too well to let censure enter mine," said the governess, wiping the tears from the sweet face. Then with a kiss she continued: "I had my doubts that all was not going well with you, and I decided to come at once, without advising Mademoiselle Evelyn of my intention. It was some divine influence, warning me of trouble and sickness."

"Sickness, Arline?"

"I make reference to Mademoiselle Evelyn's illness. Surely you know of it!"

"Evelyn sick? No, no, Arline, I know nothing! I have been here all night, without seeing even a servant. This is terrible! You do not mean that she is really ill — confined to her bed!"

Arline had secretly believed that a scene had taken place between her charge and the proud daughter of the Grange; but now Hazel's ignorance of Evelyn's condition was mysterious, and the governess's eyes dilated with astonishment. She stated how very ill they considered Evelyn, and noted how that look of anguish deepened in Hazel's eyes.

"Arline, Arline!" she wailed, as the governess paused, "I have been the cause of it all. I have perhaps killed her! Merciful Heaven, what shall I do? Why, oh why was I ever born? My birth was ill-starred!"

Speechless alarm arose in the Frenchwoman's heart, as Hazel fell writhing to the floor. "*Mon*

Dieu," thought she, " the child's mind is amiss ! "
Kneeling she took the sufferer's head in her lap,
and caressed the curls as she whispered : " You
are not well, my wee lamb.   Come, lie down again
on my bed, and let me bathe your head and bind
your hair.   That will soothe you."

Hazel lifted her hand deprecatingly.   " No,
no ! " she moaned, " you mistake my sufferings.   I
am not ill in body.   It is my conscience.   You
would despise me if you knew all ; but believe
me, it has all come from blindness.   You shall
judge my heart some day.   If your faith remains
unshaken I will go away with you somewhere, and
devote my life to your happiness.   If you condemn
me,— then,— oh then, I shudder for myself ! "

Marvelling more and more at Hazel's words, yet
steadfast in believing that the brain was over-
strained, Arline continued to reason quietly : " *Ma
chère* need not be distressed as to her cousin's
illness.   She will recover.   If a fracas has been
between you, there will be reconciliation.   Your
sensitive nature may make you blame yourself as
most in the wrong ; the good and generous always
do.; but you are not in the least guilty,— certainly
not !   You fancy that mademoiselle's illness had
its cause in this dissension ; but you mistake !   It
is the result of an *affaire d'amour*."

" You know this ! " cried Hazel.

" *Oui, ma petite !* I have known it many months.
Mademoiselle Evelyn was enamored of my country-

man, Monsieur Deveréll, who was here last summer.
I watched them often from my window, as they
strolled in the garden below. I guessed her secret,
and had a conviction that her feelings were not
reciprocated. I could not help pitying her, when
her face grew thinner every day."

"Arline, you knew all this, yet said not one word
to warn me,— to save me from bringing her such
misery?"

"Ah, but listen! Mademoiselle Evelyn will be
duly compensated for what she suffers through her
love, for he is very near. Nay, he may be with her
at this moment. While I was waiting in the *salon*
at Jasper,— waiting for the carriage,— a gentleman,
whom I at once recognized as Monsieur Deveréll,
ordered a horse to be saddled. Without a doubt
it was to ride here! He has heard of mademoiselle's
misfortune, and sympathy impelled his return."

Hazel was walking toward the window.

Arline understood this action as arising from
eagerness to see if there was any sign of an
arrival. She placed herself immediately behind
Hazel, and could see Noel in the garden. He was
looking up, and gesticulating unintelligibly, but
evidently trying to catch Hazel's eye.

"He wishes to make me understand something.
I will go down and see what it is." With this
Hazel ran down the short corridor which led to
the back stairs.

Another moment and she stood in the garden

below. Here she was met by Noel, who noted her disappearance from the window above, anticipated her coming down by the back way, and so reached the side gate just in time to meet her. Finding the coast clear for the delivery of Deveréll's letter, the boy slipped the white missive through the wicket into her hand.

"Don't let nobody see ye read it, Missy Hazel!" Having given this advice in a stealthy undertone, the negro went away awkwardly on tiptoe, with a gait that would have been in itself sufficient to convict him of misdemeanor, had there been an inquisitive onlooker.

Hurrying to her own room with the letter, her heart all of a flutter, Hazel locked herself safely against intrusion, and read the loving lines. She longed to see him; but this longing she restrained, whispering to herself : "It can not, it *must* not be! Evelyn's love must be restored to her. I have no right to think of him, except as a friend, — my *king* of friends. How true are his words! How deeply the shaft of jealousy has been thrust into my heart he shall never know. I will go to him, and say that I can never, *never* be his wife; but that, if he loves me, he must save Cousin Evelyn by going at once to her. He is noble, generous. Surely he will do this, when I tell him it will make *me* happy. I have read how women test their lovers' hearts. I will weigh my king's heart of gold."

Awhile she prayed. Then she questioned her heart. Would the self-abnegation be mostly hers or his? for at last she knew that she loved him with all her soul.

CHAPTER XXXI.

SWEET whispered the breeze, but it whispered of woe;
And bitterness flowed in the soft-gliding stream.

AUBREY paced up and down the margin of the lake, close by the spot where Hazel's little boat was moored. His face was pale and anxious, his step quick and impatient. Momentarily he expected Hazel, or some message from her. More and more unsupportable became his suspense. At length he leaped into the boat, and tried to cool his temples by laving them with the cool water. Somewhat pacified he found himself able to reflect more calmly.

"More than likely Hazel was detained by her cousin, who perhaps forced the dear child to confess everything. In such a case, what rash act might not that woman commit!"

He glanced at the placid water, and suddenly recalled the words he had overheard Evelyn use on one memorable occasion: "I wish the lake had covered you forever, before that fatal morning when first he saw you."

He could not believe Evelyn as criminal in deed as she was vengeful in thought; but the longer he

(262)

dwelt upon her utterances, the more apprehensive he became.

The sun sailed higher and higher over a sea of celestial blue, and golden fire rained through the foliage over Aubrey's head. Did those bright beams come as good omens?

A loud splash attracted his attention. He saw Bijou swimming rapidly toward a mass of lily-roots. A horrible thought took possession of Aubrey. He pictured the cold form of his love beneath the water, her white face upturned, her hair entangled in the undergrowth,— dead, drowned! It was an awful moment. He sat powerless, in presence of the image thus conjured up in his mind's eye.

How the dog panted in his heroic efforts to fight his way through the cold pathway to the aquatic plants. His respiration grew hoarser till, in apparent exhaustion, he disappeared beneath the surface. This roused Aubrey's power of speech, and he cried out in consternation: "Bijou, Bijou, old fellow!"

A moment after, and the creature reappeared. He turned his large eyes toward the man in the boat; and then, as if encouraged by a human presence, he resumed his struggle, plunging and whining. At length the dog reached the lilies, and with one loud bark disappeared the second time. Aubrey cut the boat adrift, and rowed rapidly toward the spot. When within a few yards of it he saw a black object rise to view, floating lifeless

on the water. Another instant, and the canine
hero would have sunk forever, but with a sweep of
the oars Aubrey was beside the poor fellow. He
held him afloat with one strong hand, while with
the other he steadied the boat, in order to pull the
dog aboard.

Five minutes later Bijou was lying on the sunny
embankment, rapidly coming to himself.

"Had a cold bath, and not much the worse for
it, eh, my good fellow?" said his rescuer, as he
rubbed the dog vigorously with a piece of burlap,
which he luckily found in the boat. The dog could
only make dumb signs of gratitude, looking
yearningly into Aubrey's face, and occasionally
lapping his hand, as it came within reach.

The young Frenchman never paused in his gentle
ministrations, until he was rewarded by seeing
Bijou on all fours, shaking himself vigorously.
Presently the dog walked slowly away, — not,
however, without casting a wistful look toward the
spot which had twice been his bane.

Despite this unexpected rescue Deveréll had by
no means forgotten Hazel. Her name was his
underlying thought, and he could hardly endure
her delay. Again he paced feverishly up and
down the lakeside, with hands clasped behind him,
his lips compressed.

Occasionally he consulted his watch. When it
indicated a quarter after one he grew desperate,
and walked toward the aperture in the willows,

goaded by an impulse to rush into the house, and demand a sight of her whom he loved so sacredly.

A shout of joy burst from him as he gained the opening, for in a moment Hazel was clasped in his arms.

CHAPTER XXXII.

THE TEST.

Give sorrow words! The grief that can not speak
Whispers the o'erfraught heart, and bids it break.
SHAKESPEARE.

"CAN it be you, my love, my love?" cried
Aubrey rapturously. Holding the girl at
arm's length he scanned her face with worshipful
eyes; but when he saw how changed she was, he
snatched her to his heart again.

"Great God! What has happened to you,
darling? Tell me everything!"

It was many minutes before Hazel could bring
herself to speak. Then she gently extricated herself from his arms, and said tremulously: "I have
been troubled. I did not come to you last night
as I promised, — because — because — trouble kept
me away. Cousin Evelyn has suddenly been taken
ill. Oh Monsieur Deveréll, already her fever has
reached such a height that serious fears are
entertained, lest she has not strength to battle
with it."

In her emotion Hazel slowly raised her troubled
eyes till they rested upon her companion's countenance. He was silent; but she could read deep
consternation in his face, as he waited for her to
proceed.

(266)

"The doctor has been here all the morning. He is over her constantly. It requires all his strength to quiet Evelyn's ravings. If you could but see her! I looked into the sick-room just before coming to you. I saw her glaring eyes and heard her shrieks. One name was constantly repeated."

Again Hazel paused. Still Aubrey spoke not, but his heart rose and fell again with her words. She watched his face, filled with mingled love and pity, and abruptly placed one hand upon his arm, as she asked pleadingly: "Monsieur, can you not guess whose name?"

"Yes! I can not pretend to misunderstand you, *petite. Mon Dieu*, that it should come to this, just when I was on the eve of attaining my sweetest ambition!" He put her from him almost roughly, and turned away. One hand was on his aching brow, and the other lifted in a hopeless gesture.

Presently his manhood returned and he said huskily: "Forgive me, my pure one, if I have scared you! I was mad to so far forget myself. Go on! I will listen!"

"You know then that — that she loved you, — that she has loved you all the while!" cried the girl, and poignant disappointment was in her voice.

He saw her eyes fill with tears, and her lips tremble uncontrollably, and again his manhood was forgotten. He took an impulsive step forward, and snatched her to himself, whispering: "Oh darling, even if I did know, what does it signify! I might in a small degree have appreciated her affection, had not your face dawned upon me. *You* are my fate. Why should aught but death come between us and happiness, — aught but death? You love me, darling! Your true eyes tell me so! Do not send me from you, when I have won your heart!"

By main force Hazel detached herself from his clasp. She looked at him, her slender form drawn up to its full height, her face flushing, her eyes flashing with indignation.

"Monsieur Deverell, I have misjudged you. I believed in you, as one whose integrity was beyond reproach, as the stars are beyond sin. I am grieved to learn my mistake, — that your estimate of me is so much at fault. In one breath you proclaim me angelic; the next you seek to ensnare me by words such as no true woman should listen to without shame. I will take an oath, that no suspicion of Evelyn's feelings ever entered my heart until last night. As my conscience is now alive to what she suffers, I am filled with speechless guilt, for being the innocent cause of her misery. If in your bosom there lives a compassionate feeling for womankind, reflect upon the untold pain my cousin has endured since you went away last summer, — endured through you! Her

love has slowly eaten her life away. She lies
at death's threshold, calling for you. I would
sacrifice my life to restore her happiness. Monsieur, do you remember the day when you made a
declaration of eternal friendship for me? Do you
remember how you begged me to look to you, if
ever I found myself in need of a true friend?"

"Let me prove my remembrance. Ask anything of me," came reverently from the Frenchman,
as he bowed before her with uncovered head;
though he believed her next words would sound
the death-knell of his joyful hopes.

"That day has come. I am standing alone in a
forest of despair, from which you alone can lead
me; but you can do it with a single brave effort.
Be my true benefactor! Rescue me from a life
threatened with endless darkness! One glimpse of
your face will stay the madness that consumes
Evelyn's life. Will you save *her*, and make *me*
happy?"

Aubrey suppressed a groan. Trembling in every
limb he rubbed his hands across his forehead,
as if to smooth out the wrinkles of his brain, and
answered: "Angel of purity, what you ask me I
will grant, though it tear out my heart."

Lifting her hand to his lips he kissed it once,
twice, thrice, and added: "Show me the way. I
will walk in it, though the pathway lead to
martyrdom. Come, I am your slave! Lead me in
the right direction."

She smiled and blessed him, as she said: "No, not my slave, my savior!"

With bent head and dilatory step he followed her to the house.

CHAPTER XXXIII.

AUBREY'S TRIAL.

> THE past is past. I see the future stretch
> All dark and barren, as a rainy sea.
> > ALEXANDER.

NO light was permitted in the chamber; but the red-tongued flames, holding revelry in the grate, sent a ghastly glimmer over the invalid's face. Evelyn's restless hands twisted the sheet. They clutched imaginary objects, which she wrung hatefully. When these demonstrations ceased, she sank back into the bed, crying out for Aubrey, as a wailing child cries for its mother.

Sometimes she called in frenzied accents: "Aubrey, Aubrey! Do not abandon me for that designing girl! Tear off her bridal dress. Deck me in her stead. See," — touching her black locks proudly, — "orange-blossoms will better grace my dark beauty. On her tawny hair they lose their loveliness; they droop under her breath. She will poison you, when your lips meet!"

Evelyn was in the midst of one of these outbreaks when the door opened softly, and a slight figure moved cautiously across the room toward the window, where the doctor was meditating.

(271)

Hazel walked carefully around the room, so as to avoid the sick woman's glance; but as by some intuition Evelyn shrieked out in painful accents: "It is *she!* I tell you, it is *Myrine Seymour!*"

Hazel paused a short distance from the doctor, and by the fitful firelight he could see a puzzled expression come over her face.

"I tell you it is *Myrine Seymour!* She has come to give me up to justice!" raved the demented woman.

The look of bewilderment deepened on Hazel's face. She went to Doctor Weaver and whispered: "Whom does she mean?"

"I can not tell you, my little girl. Perhaps she refers to one of her friends. Don't you know anyone of that name?"

"I know a *Myrtle* Seymour; but Myrine — Myrine," — dwelling upon the beautiful name as though she loved to repeat it, — "I never knew anyone by that name. I never heard it but once or twice in my life, and then — then my old nurse applied it to *me!*"

After a moment's silence Hazel spoke again: "Doctor!" Her expression changed, and it was plain to Doctor Weaver that she wished to say something important.

"Well?" he asked encouragingly.

"I was forgetting! I came in to say that a gentleman wants to speak with you in the entry, just there, outside the door, — Monsieur Aubrey Deveréll!"

" Aubrey ? " repeated the doctor in an astonished whisper. " Can it be the Aubrey for whom my patient calls so often ? "

" It is the same," returned the girl calmly.

" This is a godsend ! " she heard the physician exclaim, as he abruptly left her side.

Hazel herself did not tarry in the chamber, but went out through Evelyn's dressing-room, for her cousin's ravings were unbearable ; yet a smile transfigured Hazel's expression into one of saintliness, when she pictured to herself the scene that must ensue when Evelyn awoke to the consciousness of her lover's presence.

" What will her thoughts be of *me?* " she wondered. " Will her prejudice vanish, or will her happiness make her forget me altogether? If there is any womanly sentiment in her she will repent her misunderstanding. To see her smile, to hear her say, ' I have wronged you, Hazel, and I am sorry,' would be enough ! I might then look for some compensation for all I have suffered. In the light of her confidence, I may forget my heart's sacrifice, — its lost hope. A deeper joy may find its way into my life, which seems so barren without *him.*"

" Aubrey ! Aubrey ! "

" I am here, Mademoiselle Evelyn. Have courage ! "

He stood beside the bed, looking down upon the

delirious woman in pity blended with rigor; yet on his brow was the peace of resignation.

His voice had its old magic effect upon the invalid. She raised herself on one elbow, and gazed upon him. During a brief and unbroken silence her eyes never left his face, but rested now upon his dark mustache, now upon his white brow. She then looked at the hand which clasped hers gently, as it lay listlessly outside the coverlet.

"Have courage, mademoiselle. I shall stay with you till you are strong again. Be troubled not, but rest — sleep!"

"Bend down!" commanded the sick woman, in a voice strangely subdued. "Is it really Aubrey, in the flesh? I have stayed here at the window hours, waiting for you. Noel said he had seen you with Hazel, — that you were married? Is it true? *Is it true?*"

She stared at him, and drove her nails into his palm so that he felt the pain. He bent down, however, until he felt her breath upon his face. Then her fingers twined in his hair, and a hot touch was on his head. He scarcely dared trust himself to meet her glance again, lest his courage forsake him.

Presently she spoke: "Kiss me! I shall not be satisfied until you have kissed me, Aubrey! Ah, you hesitate! Now I am convinced! I am the victim of a sham!"

Her voice ended in a scream. She thrust him

from her with both hands, and tore the counter-
pane wildly. Seeing the folly of weakness he
again approached her. " Evelyn, for your own
sake, try to calm yourself."

" Calm myself! Calm myself! What, in this
prison, — doomed to death by *her* hand? They
have hunted me down; they have — "

Suddenly her mood changed. " Come nearer,
warden!" she whispered. " I have a secret to tell
you."

Yielding to this new caprice Aubrey drew a
chair to the bedside,. and bent his ear close to
her lips. He waited for Evelyn to speak again.
Wondering at her continued silence he at first
moved his head in mute interrogation, and then
sprang to his feet in consternation. She lay with
head thrown back and arms outstretched, in deathlike stillness. He hastily called Doctor Weaver,
who was waiting in the hall.

The swoon was long, but at the doctor's request
Aubrey remained within hearing. It was well he
did so, for no sooner did Evelyn open her eyes
than her lips again formed the one name : " Aubrey, I want Aubrey!"

The doctor again gave place to the Frenchman,
who came hurriedly to the bedside. She looked
rationally into his face; but the hand she tried to
reach out to him fell listlessly. Tears gathered in
her eyes, the first since her illness, — nay, since a
long time before. Aubrey tried to soothe her, and
finally succeeded.

"I thought you had gone out of my life forever," she said. "How comes it you are here?"

"Because of your illness. — Now I bid you rest. Rest is essential to your recovery; and recover you must, —*for my sake!*"

These three words cost him a mighty effort; but they were said, and their effect was magical. The sick girl's fingers closed over his; and presently, with one blissful sigh, she passed into slumberland.

CHAPTER XXXIV.

Wo have been friends together,
In sunshine and in shade.

C. E. S. N.

NOTWITHSTANDING the fever had been checked in its earliest stages, November was waning before Evelyn was pronounced sufficiently convalescent to leave her apartments; but she gave little heed to the lapse of time. Whether a day, a week, or a month had passed, since she basked once more in the light of Aubrey's smiles, was immaterial to her. Her knight was there to prove her visions real.

She had consented to drive with him one morning, in accordance with the doctor's advice, and advanced to greet her betrothed when he crossed the threshold. As he pressed one of her hands lightly to his lips, her worn face was transfigured with a lovelight which made it indeed beautiful. No trace of the old hardness was visible in the countenance uplifted in gratitude for the bunch of exquisite flowers he had brought from a Jasper conservatory.

Aubrey could not help wondering how treason

(277)

could ever dwell where now righteousness only seemed to abide. He found himself wishing to erase his knowledge of her evil-mindedness, and undividedly consecrate himself to her happiness; but this could never be. What had been was written indelibly on the pages of memory. As he helped her on with her wraps he compressed his lips into a hard smile, saying to himself: "The past is moulded. That invincible priest called Providence has decreed this faulty piece of humanity to be mine, and I must bow in self-abnegation."

"I hope you are dressed warm enough," he said aloud, as he lifted her into the carriage. "Even here, in this tropical clime, one must be prepared for frosty snaps."

The beautiful grays pranced gaily away, and were soon dashing along the open country road, toward Fairacre. The last time Evelyn had driven with him, over this same quiet highway, her hopes were levelled with the dust. Now they were exalted to the skies, for she was the promised wife of the man who sat beside her. What a world of meaning in those three words, *his promised wife.* They gave the world a new garb, such as she had never believed could exist outside of Paradise.

"I have been born again," Evelyn told herself, as they traversed the white road through the forest. "My heart beats with devout love for all nature. Why have I never before been so impressed with the stateliness of these pines, and their varied wood-coloring? Why are the notes of the birds so sweet? It is the magic of love! Love has transformed these monotonous fields into a veritable Eden!"

What of him who sat beside her? Where were the hopes which had made his life so golden? His youth, his vivacity, his reverence for the inexhaustible beauties of nature, — how had they vanished so abruptly? Where was his aspiration, his ambition? Alas, he now lived in listless unconcern for the future. Providence had torn from his heart the image graven there. Aubrey had waked from a dream of bliss, to find himself ensnared in trammels he had regarded with abhorrence.

Honor bound him to Evelyn, bound him to her indissolubly; and his heart cried out in rebellion. Thus he pondered: "Oh the unpardonable cruelty of Fate! How could it smite one who loves with such devotion as mine!"

Did Evelyn surmise aught of this despair? Nay! It was enough that he came into her presence daily, that he read to her, that he brought her flowers, that he kissed her hand, that he inquired solicitously after her welfare. She saw him through worshipful eyes. She believed he had come back into her life of his own accord; and this was enough.

She seldom thought of the unknown medium of this reunion. If in a moment of contrition her

mind turned to Hazel, she decided to seek an
early interview, when they might be reconciled.
Thereupon would follow a mental conflict between
pride and remorse; and Evelyn would swerve from
her good purpose, which must involve a forfeiture
of her dignity. Then she resolved to compromise
the matter, and make amends by kinder treatment
of her foster-sister.

The tragic scene between herself and Hazel was
completely obliterated from her recollection by the
fever. She recalled nothing of her frantic pursuit
of her cousin, nor of the painful interview which
followed.

One day, while looking over her wardrobe,
Evelyn suddenly came across her lavender silk.
The lace was torn and the train was soiled. For
a moment she was puzzled. Then she peremptorily
summoned Phebe.

"Can you account for this?" questioned the
mistress, as she held the injured dress before the
surprised girl.

" No, Missy Eb'lyn," rejoined Phebe, retreating
before her mistress's accusing demeanor.

"Don't prevaricate! You *must* know how my
dress come to be ruined. Look!" Evelyn held
the folds of her ill-fated finery nearer, so that the
girl could get a better view. "Tell me the truth,
Phebe. How did this mud come on my train?
How was this lace torn?"

"'Deed, Missy Eb'lyn, I can't say, honey! —

I can't say's I know how all dat dirt come on de bottom, 'n how de lace got tored. 'T war in dat ar condistion de mo'nin' I found ye in a heap, heah on de flo'. I's done puzzle my topknot more'n a little 'bout de way you come all dress up, un' lyin' like stone dead, wid you' hah all down, un' you close in such a way —"

"Don't try to shield your cunning with my illness. I understand I was found in my own room, in an · unconscious condition; but in this dress? — Preposterous! Don't seek to mislead *me*, Phebe! You have evidently taken advantage of my sickness, to wear this dress at some of your darkey frolics. You may as well confess!"

The girl drew back in scorn, the indignant blood surging beneath her tawny skin. Seeing the defiant look Evelyn became more deliberate. She had certainly never known the young mulatto guilty of such impertinence. It dawned upon Evelyn that she might give her servant the benefit of the doubt, inasmuch as her own memory of that night was a blank.

Suddenly that scene came rushing back to her brain, like a lightning flash. In a dazed way she put her hand to her eyes, as if to think. Again she saw that vision of herself in the mirror, arrayed in lavender, with the diamonds in her ears and on her fingers.

Presently she said to the maid: "I have been hasty, Phebe. I remember putting on this dress

now. It was the night before I was taken ill.
The occurrence is faint, almost indistinct to me,
and I do not remember what followed. I may
have wandered into the garden, under the spell of
coming delirium. You can never know *how*
troubled and miserable I was."

To conceal her embarrassment she burst out
laughing, and then added, by way of atonement:
"I only meant to tease you a little! You have
always been an obedient girl, never giving cause
for fault-finding. I will make you a present of
this dress. Take it, and let your best beau see
how you can grace the next ball. Now go, and
return to me at two o'clock. I shall want you to
arrange my hair."

Phebe would have lingered to speak her
gratitude, but her mistress turned away, so the
girl straightway left the room; but once in the
hall, beyond observation, she made all sorts of
grimaces over her new frock, which she declared,
in a stage whisper, would "fairly stan' alone, and
make Dixy Sloane turn green with jealous."

It was late in the forenoon when the young
couple returned from their drive. As they walked
through the gate, it was plain that something
unusual had occurred during their absence. On
the lawn the servants were assembled, with
troubled countenances; while beyond stood Mrs.
Ormsby, close beside Hazel, who was in a kneeling

posture, her head bowed over something dark stretched on the grass.

"Aubrey, what can be the meaning of this excitement among the servants? There are Hazel and Mrs. Ormsby! Pardon me, dearest, if I run and see."

Evelyn hastened on, leaving her companion to follow. As he drew nearer he could hear Hazel weeping bitterly. A spasm of pain passed over his face when he noted the cause of her sorrow. There, on the green sward, he saw her beautiful Bijou, — dead. His black coat was wet. In the silvered clasp of his collar was entangled a limp water-leaf.

Evelyn turned toward her lover as he approached, and said, in an undertone: "Only think, Aubrey, — how dreadful! Bijou, Hazel's great Saint Bernard, is dead,— drowned in the lake, it seems."

He noticed that her face was ghastly, while a hunted look came into her eyes. She could not bear his questioning gaze, but turned quickly away, ostensibly to console the mourner.

"Come Hazel," she said entreatingly, "come with me into the house. We all sympathize with you, but grief can't recall the poor fellow."

A smothered sob was at first the only response. At last Hazel said: "I can't give him up, — my one faithful friend! We have loved each other so! We were always together. In happiness and in trouble he was my companion!"

With unsteady fingers Evelyn disengaged the leaf from the dog's collar. It seemed to mock her! Crushing it in her hand she threw it away. Then she whispered to her foster-sister, so that no one else distinguished the words: "I will love you now! Let me love you now, Hazel! Let all the past be forgotten from this moment! Let us try to be happy in each other's friendship."

The next second Hazel was on her feet, with arms outstretched. "Evelyn, oh Evelyn! Surely you can not be in earnest!" cried she incredulously, yet with a countenance beaming like the sun through a veil of mist. "It is what I have been hoping, praying for; yet it can not be true! You can't wish to give me your love!"

For an answer Evelyn pressed her lips lightly upon the girl's wet cheek, and placed a comforting arm about her waist. Aubrey looked on spellbound, while the servants went slowly away, wondering.

CHAPTER XXXV.

RETROSPECTIVE AND PROSPECTIVE.

AND my soul from out the shadow
Shall be lifted nevermore.
POE.

OH heart, count not too high thy summer days.

"HAZEL, I will go with you to your room. I want to tell you about my plans," said Evelyn the following morning.

"Before we enter upon other topics," she continued, when they were comfortably seated together, "tell me all about poor Bijou. I have heard no particulars. How did he meet his death, —and by water, too?"

Evelyn toyed restlessly with the silken tassel of her gown as she spoke, yet she looked anxiously at Hazel. It was a moment before the little cousin could bring herself to speak of her loss; but at last she turned her head towards the garden, to hide her emotion, and told the story.

"I had to go down to the lake yesterday. I had accidently left a book there, and wanted to get it. It was Owen Meredith's Lucile. Bijou followed me as usual. Just before we reached the willows he bounded ahead. The next moment, to my

(285)

astonishment, I saw him plunge into the cold water, and swim toward a lily-patch. I watched him closely, for Noel had told me that the dear fellow had a recent mania for these plunges, and would invariably make his way to this particular spot. It is only a month ago since Noel one day rescued him from drowning, when he became entangled in the roots. Well, suddenly I saw him disappear. It must have been full sixty seconds before he came up. Then he looked at me, barked three or four times, and dived once more. The minutes passed, and I saw nothing more of my darling Bijou, — only a violent commotion of the water, which indicated a struggle below. I tried to call for assistance, but I don't think a sound escaped me. I don't know how long I stood there, but all at once I saw a dark mass floating toward me. Nearer and nearer it came, till I had only to stretch out my arm and touch it. Then I must have screamed aloud. Bijou was drowned! His once beautiful eyes were devoid of expression, and stared at me in an awful way. It was a sight to remain in memory always."

She paused, quite overcome, and laid her head upon the window-sill. Had she seen her cousin's face at that moment Hazel would have been thoroughly perplexed. Evelyn was grateful for the child's grief, as it afforded a refuge for her own feelings. While Hazel sobbed, Evelyn's hands lay interlaced tightly in her lap, for the suspense was almost intolerable.

" Well, Hazel, I am listening," she muttered.

" There is nothing more to relate, except that I dragged the poor fellow from the water, placed him on the grass, and ran to the house for help."

" And those mysterious plunges, — their motive? Have you any idea about that?"

" Not the slightest. I heard Noel say he meant to drag that part of the lake. He thinks there must be something buried there. Dogs have such an instinct about such things, you know."

Hearing a low gasp from her foster-sister Hazel looked up quickly. " Evelyn, what is it? You are ill again! You have exerted yourself too much."

" It is nothing," said Evelyn faintly, " nothing but a sharp pain here," — indicating her heart. " I have had such a pain frequently since — since — since *they* died."

To herself she added: " I shall keep a sharp lookout that the lake is not meddled with."

Hazel said that Noel would dig a grave beneath the willows, where the dog and she had passed so many hours together; and then the conversation drifted from the past to the future.

" In my new prospects," said Evelyn, " I have seen my past life in what a poet calls the hollow mirror of remorse. My conscience has not been an affable companion during the past few weeks. My pride might have stood its ground, but for yesterday's catastrophe. I know I have wronged you in my thoughts, Hazel. I can never make due

reparation for the taunts with which I have
humiliated you. Pride has been the household
foe of our Weldon race; and I should perhaps
have followed in the footsteps of my ancestors,
and let it change me into gall, but for this chance.
Yes, chance has led me blindfold to the altar of
contrition. Full well I know the generous nature
to which I appeal. I was not surprised at the joy
in your face, dear Hazel, when I asked you to
forget the past; yet do not think I can take
advantage of your forgiving spirit, and consider
the breach entirely healed, for this can never be.
I have wronged you irrevocably, and shall always
be pricked by accusing conscience in your presence.
I must look up to you, as a sinful woman *must* look
up to one beyond reproach."

She broke off with a dry sob, which roused new
compassion in Hazel, who flung herself upon her
knees before Evelyn.

"Why do you accuse yourself of having sinned
beyond redemption? Is it not enough that I have
forgiven you, — forgiven you tenfold? That we
might be bound together in friendship has been
my constant prayer. Now that this prayer is
granted, why should we not both be above regret?
You have Monsieur Aubrey, — a king amongst
noble men. I have *you*, — you and your love!
Is not this enough?"

"That I have Aubrey is bliss indeed; but," she
added, with a sensibility new to Hazel, "there is a

shadow on my soul which will not be lifted!—
Child, child, rise! Don't kneel! I can't bear
it!"

Hazel arose. She was filled with fear lest
Evelyn was threatened with a relapse of the fever;
but she was reassured when her foster-sister bade
her be seated, and listen while she spoke of the
future.

"My marriage has been arranged for the twenty-
fifth of next month,—Christmas," she resumed,
growing animated, as thoughts of coming happiness revived. "I have made Aunt Lydia and Uncle
Seymour acquainted with my plans, and expect
them, with Myrtle, by the fifteenth, if not earlier.
You are pleased? Yes, I knew you would be. You
and Myrtle will be nice companions. I intend
to have you both for bridemaids. My wedding will
be without display, on account of our mourning; I
shall send no invitations, except to immediate relatives; yet, as the date will mark three events in
one, I shall expect it to be a memorable and happy
time. I say *three events in one*, because on Christmas night Uncle Elmer Weldon will be installed
as future master of the Grange. This was a request of my father to his lawyer. He did not
wish the home of his ancestors to pass into strange
hands, should I ever leave it. I shall feel no regret
in resigning our beautiful place to a master so
worthy as Uncle Elmer, for he and his two sons
will maintain it creditably. Fairacre, by papa's

will, will come to you at your majority. Till then
Uncle Elmer will be your guardian; so it is for
your interest, as well as for mine, to have him
established here, as he will see your estate well
cared for, at least till you marry, or come of age.
Meanwhile, you can make it your home with Aunt
Lydia, as you wish."

"Oh Evelyn!" interrupted Hazel, unable to
listen composedly a moment longer. "Heaven
itself seems suddenly to open before me. You
have set the bright gates ajar with your own hands,
and that is more than I can realize!"

"Myrtle's governess has returned recently to
England," added Evelyn, disturbed by Hazel's
words, though outwardly calm. "Ah," thought
she, "if Hazel dreamed how much nearer Heaven
I could place her!"

Then she continued: "Myrtle's governess has
returned to England, and I have been thinking
how pleasant it would be for both you girls to
have Arline in New Orleans. Your personal at-
tachment to her would of course make you regret
a separation. I have referred the matter to Aunt
Lydia. I am sure she will highly commend
the arrangement. — Almost ten o'clock? I am
expecting Aubrey at ten, so I must get ready for
our drive, — the last for some time, as he goes
to New Orleans tomorrow. Come to me on our
return, and you and I will discuss your dress
for the wedding."

Touching Hazel's pure brow with her lips Evelyn sailed from the room, leaving the girl silent with new-found pleasure. Long she remained by the window after Evelyn and her betrothed had driven away. How intently did this womanly child listen to the song in her heart: "Myrtle is coming! Myrtle is coming! We two as Evelyn's bridemaids! Myrtle and I to be inseparable!"

The day set in triumphal flashes, dispelling all fears of the brooding storm. Like a benediction, soft-tinted shadows fell athwart the graves at Cypress Dell, and over the golden hair of a maiden who had gone thither to whisper to her departed loved ones her new joy.

CHAPTER XXXV.

DEVERÉLL HALL.

THERE is occasion and cause, why and wherefore,
in all things.

SHAKESPEARE.

THROUGH the day the cold rain had been falling in New Orleans; but toward night-fall the down-pour ceased, giving place to a cutting wind, which froze the sodden roadway and interfered with the flickering duty of the street lamps.

About the steamer-landing the prospect was forbidding enough. Shrill steam-whistles and the lusty cry of five-and-twenty hotel-drummers mingled in deafening chorus. In conjunction with the impenetrable gloom and the angry roar of the waters, this noise might well dishearten the tired and shivering passengers who thronged the dock.

Among these was Aubrey, who found himself drifting with a stream of miscellaneous humanity, now jostled against a burly negro, now treading on some demoiselle's toes, and almost grating his teeth over her exclamations. He fairly wished himself in Jericho when a young creole begged him to have regard for her babe, which he was heartlessly squeezing.

Monsieur might as well look for the King of

(292)

Mardigras in that crowd, as for his coachman, whom he had telegraphed to meet him; and the young master felt out of temper, as he wondered what transit he could find for Deveréll Hall, in case Joice was not on hand.

Once clear of the crowd Aubrey stood looking about him, when a hand fell heavily upon his shoulder and he felt his portmanteau snatched rudely from his grasp. "The Lacléde Hotel? Right this way! Follow me! The only first-class — Holy Saints!"

The tooter had mistaken his man for once. At least he so concluded, when his parrot speech was abruptly snapped by a smart blow from the Frenchman's fist, causing the man to drop his prey in a twinkling, and stagger backward to recover his breath.

"Ruffian! Mind you make no such attacks in future, lest you be dealt with as you deserve," exclaimed Deveréll, as he repossessed himself of his valise.

"Pardon, monsieur!" returned the fellow doggedly, as he managed to lose himself in the crowd, — none the wiser for his recent defeat, however.

Having regained his self-possession Aubrey moved on, bent upon finding a cab, if one was to be had at any price; but he had gone only a few steps when again he was arrested, this time by a familiar voice, with a strong cockney accent: "Mounseer Deverhall, I thought ye 'ad n't harrived has wuz expected. I wuz jest hon the point hof drivin' back to the 'All, when hall on a suddint I seed ye from the kerridge-box. This way, mounseer!"

"Good! I thought you had missed my telegram, Joice. It is so thundering dark one can't see a foot ahead. — Yes, I'm all right. Take the shortest cuts and drive fast! I'm hungry and chilled!" Aubrey closed the door with a bang, drew the silk shades, to shut out the dismal air and prospect, and settled himself for a tedious drive, over miles of rough roads.

Notwithstanding Joice took the shortest way, it seemed hours before the carriage finally halted. Bright lights shone from many a window, and cheered Aubrey with their welcoming rays; but before ascending to the front door he glanced toward a certain suite of rooms in the east wing, as if to ascertain whether they were occupied. A light answered his look in the affirmative, and he mounted the steps with a pleased exclamation.

Having duly greeted his housekeeper, an aged creole of aristocratic bearing, who had served the Deverélls through three generations, he mounted to the second floor, where were situated the rooms just alluded to.

He entered without warning, and saw, at a table strewn with miscellaneous reading-matter, a young man, whose fair hair and frank eyes may be recognized as belonging to Wilford Hylton.

"Well Hylton, old boy," exclaimed Aubrey cheerily, "I am glad to find you still domiciled at the Hall — shut up, as Shakespeare says, in measureless content; yet I confess it is a pleasure I hardly dared anticipate, after my cavalier treatment of you."

It may be well here to explain that, on returning from the West, Deveréll had insisted that his companion should take up his quarters at the Hall for a time; and then Aubrey had immediately departed for Florida, simply saying that private matters necessitated his absence.

"Another twenty-four hours *would* have shaken my faith," rejoined Hilton, as he grasped his host's hand. "Candidly," he went on more gravely, "the servants have all come to regard me in the light of an impostor. Madame Housekeeper scarcely tolerates me. I verily believe your protracted absence led her to suspect foul play, I posing as the villain! Faith, I'm not jesting!"

Deveréll laughed. "If you are not jesting, you have grown morbid and fanciful, my friend! Madame Corrilla assures me she has not worried in the least. You see your injustice. Absence has long been regarded by the servants here as one of my idiosyncrasies. — But come, we will dine, and then discuss affairs in general."

"Firstly," resumed the young host, when they again sought Wilford's cheerful quarters, "I presume you wish to know my recent movements, —

where I have been, what doing? Well, to condense a long chapter, I have been over to Florida, to Weldon Grange, and, — well, I have become engaged to the daughter of that house."

"To Ev — to — to Miss Weldon!" gasped Wilford, stirred by the shock; but suddenly collecting himself, and feigning unconcern, he added, "I wonder!"

"You wonder?" laughed Aubrey with a shrug. "Now soberly, what is your candid opinion of my venture? Remember, as somebody says, that a generous friend no cool medium knows."

"Your engagement, was it one you had long premeditated?"

"On the contrary! When I took leave of you, three weeks ago, I had no thought, however vague, of asking Mademoiselle Weldon's hand; but I am a victim of circumstances."

"I am to conclude that, seeing the lady's misfortunes, you have been more in pity than in love with her," said Wilford, looking searchingly at his friend, whose uneasiness he could not choose but note.

"There is a why and wherefore in all things, as the immortal bard has said," returned Aubrey presently. "It is an affair of honor. All I ask of you is this: Do you not think my fiancée will bear her prospective title with dignity?"

"With such grace, such undeniable beauty and accomplishments as Miss Weldon possesses, she would do honor to a queen's drawing-room," declared Hylton earnestly; and his face grew a shade paler as he thus referred to the woman whose image he had been striving to efface.

"Good! Now will you grace the nuptials by acting as best man?" continued Aubrey, little knowing that he was adding fuel to a smothered flame.

"For what date is your marriage appointed?"

"For Christmas."

"Business will keep me away, I regret to say."

"Of a pressing nature?"

"The most pressing. The past three weeks have not been altogether a season of idleness. I have stumbled upon an old friend of my uncle, one who will soon be a kinsman of yours, the Honorable Franklin Seymour, who desires me to enter his office."

"And you have accepted the proposal?"

"Yes, the compact is sealed. I shall enter my official duties the first of the month."

Deveréll puffed away at his cigar in silence for a moment, and then said, in a tone of keen disappointment: "I had hoped for a different turn of affairs. I had planned to appoint you my private adviser."

"You are always generous and considerate, Deveréll."

"And you, to balance the compliment, are devilishly hot-headed; else you would have waited for my return, before closing this business."

" I am grieved at your displeasure, but I gain a footing that points to future prosperity."

Aubrey softened visibly, and mentally branded himself an unmitigated and selfish ass, for wishing to consign his friend to the narrow sphere of a private secretaryship.

" At anyrate, we won't quarrel. Let us compromise the matter by having you keep your quarters here. It will be preferable to a bachelor den. With a Madame Deveréll at the head of the establishment we can promise you endless social pastimes, which will of themselves aid your profession."

What excuse could Hylton make for declining this generous offer? Yet could he accede to an arrangement which would bring him into daily contact with the woman who had so ruthlessly discarded him? Never! For Evelyn's sake, if not for his own, they could not live under the same roof.

" You hesitate," said Aubrey, annoyed at Wilford's reluctance. " Perhaps you desire to shake me off altogether."

" No, no! It is not that, believe me, my dear friend! How *could* you judge me so ungrateful, after your unselfish interest? You do not understand, you can never understand, my motive in declining your hospitality. I can not explain myself! This I beg of you, Deveréll: in the name of God, believe anything of me, think me wanting in anything but gratitude, if I say I can not live at Deveréll Hall."

Their eyes met. Instantaneously divining the truth Aubrey covered his face with both hands, groaned aloud, and bowed his head upon the table.

Thus Wilford left him, and stepped out upon the piazza, where he bared his hot temples to the damp air. Halcyon promises the future held for him, fame, and perhaps a wife with a jewel-heart, to whom he would consecrate a holier love than the mad infatuation he had bestowed upon Evelyn.

She was waiting for him, — Myrtle, with soft eyes and wavy hair. Already his spirit-voice was going out to her in the silence, " Coming, my love, coming."

Though the Deverélls were loyal Americans, intermarriage and preference had so perpetuated the stamp of a transatlantic origin, both upon their collective life and personal habits, as to make them seem like French people. Indeed Aubrey was so Gallic in temperament that he was constantly called the young Frenchman, — as he has been designated in this narrative; yet it was several generations since the family had paid allegiance to any power outside their adopted nation. Their estate was called by a good English name, the Hall; yet when the young master's expectations were known, the household felt as if the bridal was to be the bringing home of a *grande dame* to the chateau of a seigneur of the old regime.

Lively scenes ensued. Despite the inclement weather, every door and window was thrown open. Upholsterers, painters, and carpenters, were on duty.

Nearly a half-century had elapsed since the old place had been surrendered to decorators; and since the death of Aubrey's mother there had been little social life in these lofty apartments, where once the beauty, wealth, and chivalry of the Crescent City danced and sang. For twenty years these rooms had been the abode of silence. The servants, when they entered the old parlors, walked on tiptoe; for the older ones reverenced the memory of a gentle presence that had been the light of the place.

The crisp air fanned each apartment, as it assumed some new aspect. Faded tapestry gave place to India silk and Turkish damask. Heavy mahogany chairs and sofas disappeared, with their dark cushions and grotesque carvings, and hammered brass and polished ebony usurped stations so long guarded by their clumsier predecessors. There was one object left untouched, — the square piano, over whose keys Madame Claudine's fingers had so often wandered, her sweet contralto voice charming many a listener. This remained in the back parlor, unmolested.

"Monsieur," suggested a French artist, who had ·

been engaged to give the finishing touches, "I vould zay, you put vun upright in place of ze square piano, vitch do look exceedingly ungraceful in ze drawing-room, wiz all zis moderne furniture."

"That piano shall remain where it is," said monsieur with brief emphasis, as he looked at it with reverence. "It was my mother's!"

Finally the curtains were lowered, and the rooms left once more to dark silence, awaiting the advent of a new mistress.

Aubrey, however, had yet much to accomplish before Christmas. His business agent urged his attention to certain buildings that needed improvement. In overseeing the repairs of the old, and planning the construction of new tenements, he was inevitably detained in New Orleans far into December.

CHAPTER XXXVII.

THE WEDDING EVENING.

Thus grief still treads upon the heels of pleasure.

CHRISTMAS night at last! At Weldon Grange were assembled the favored guests, — all relatives of the happy pair.

Despite the well-filled parlors, the quietness which brooded over the house was singularly at variance with such festivities. Richly dressed ladies conversed together with hushed voices, or promenaded the spacious rooms, pausing to admire some exquisite floral decoration or bridal gift. There were fair maids and handsome lads, who would fain have engaged in holiday frolics, had not the disapproving glances from their elders prevented.

"Children, do you forget? Children, remember, sorrow has reigned in these very rooms!" So said the fathers and mothers.

But is not sorrow akin to pleasure? Where yesterday rested the burial-casket, and mourners bowed in grief, today kneel the bride and groom, to accept the marriage trust.

Upstairs in her bright boudoir stood Evelyn, — a marvel of loveliness, as her fair attendants declared.

We have seen Hazel and Myrtle as they stood over Mrs. Weldon's coffin in their mourning robes. Now they were decked in pure white. No distinction had been made in their simple attire, except that in the folds of Hazel's dress lay delicate sprays of lily-of-the valley; while Myrtle's gauzy drapery was caught here and there with clustering stephenotis. Evelyn had at first chosen lilies-of-the-valley for both; but some artistic prompting led her to make this floral variation.

Hazel's hair fell in a glory of ripples to her waist, and in its bronze meshes lay a circlet of pearls, — Evelyn's bridal gift, — and her arms and throat were also encircled with pearly strands.

Myrtle's topaz tresses were similarly arranged, and pearls were her ornaments also. What an elf she appeared, her dancing eyes and glowing cheeks full of happy expectancy!

"Now Evy," cried Myrtle, when every detail of the bride's toilet was complete, "take a parade on the floor, to satisfy us that nothing is lacking."

Evelyn did her sweet cousin's bidding, and could not suppress a smile of vanity at their admiration.

"Beautiful as a dream!" cried Hazel; while Myrtle, in her girlish romance, called the bride a veritable Cleopatra.

"Now," continued Myrtle, "Hazel and I have exhausted our compliments; so pray tell us how *we* look. I have been dying for your opinion about my hair. Mamma thought my pearl brooch would serve as a clasp to confine it, but I wanted my hair exactly like Hazel's, so she finally consented. What do you think now, — honestly?"

Evelyn let her eyes wander from Myrtle to Hazel, and back again. By degrees the flush of excitement died out, leaving her face almost as white as the orange-blossoms. At last she said nervously: "Candidly, Myrtle, I do not like your hair flowing. It does not suit your face. Take my advice! Let Phebe arrange it in a coronet, with the pearls clasping it at the top."

Myrtle pursed her pretty lips and said, "And Hazel's too?" — willing to submit to any change, could her hair only be like her companion's.

"No, Hazel's shall remain as it is. I — oh yes, there is yet another change! I want red roses in your drapery, in place of those faded flowers. Some exquisite roses were sent me today. Phebe, go and bring them. They are on the table in my sitting-room. Quick!"

Myrtle suppressed a tear of vexation, but at Evelyn's imperturbable look she surrendered herself to the maid's dexterous hands.

The sole child of indulgent parents, Myrtle had been much petted. She was wont to consult her own pleasure in all things. This change was no small disappointment, for she and Hazel had talked of little else but their twin toilets. No wonder she thought Evelyn harsh, and mentally called her a capricious tyrant, not at all artistic in this new choice of flowers for a bridemaid. "Red roses! How horrid and awkward! I wish mamma would come in directly and interfere, I do! Mamma thought me just perfect as I *was*. Why don't she —"

At that instant the door opened and Mrs. Seymour entered. She looked at her daughter in surprise: "Why these changes in your toilet, Myrtle?" she asked abruptly.

"Cousin Evelyn suggested them," returned the girl pettishly; whereupon the mother turned toward Evelyn, who feigned unconcern, and busied herself with retying the ribbons of her bouquet. "I thought the pale and starry stephenotis perfectly suited to Myrtle!—And her hair! Why Evelyn, are you quite certain it looks better in a coronet?"

Seeing that diplomacy was unavoidable, Evelyn whispered, so that neither of the bridemaids overheard her words: "It was for *your* sake, dear auntie. They looked so like each other, I feared —"

Mrs. Seymour was touched. "You were very considerate, my dear! I have dreaded seeing Myrtle and Hazel together tonight, dressed so much alike. I saw them in black at sister's funeral, and was completely unnerved by the resemblance."

"Mamma, I believe you are conspiring with Cousin Evelyn after all!" As Phebe adjusted the last rose in the drapery Myrtle flounced across the room, and stood before her mother rebelliously. "Look at me now! How horrid, in comparison with what I was before!"

"Oh Myrtle, you look a very Goddess of Love in those red roses!" chimed in Hazel, who had been a silent but sisterly sympathizer with Myrtle's disappointment.

"I agree with Hazel! Your hair is done beautifully, my pet," said Mrs. Seymour; then, seeing that her daughter's displeasure was modified by her words, she added, as she turned again to her niece: "We must go down at once! They are already playing the Wedding March."

They kissed the bride, and wished her godspeed; and then the four met the gentlemen, already waiting in the hall, — Mr. Elmer Weldon, who was to give away the bride; his two handsome sons, who were to be groomsmen; and the Honorable Franklin Seymour.

A few moments more, and Aubrey Deverell had accepted Evelyn Weldon as his wife, promising to love and honor her until death. Then they received congratulations, but it was mockery to Aubrey.

Mockery! Pity the bridegroom whose heart thus cries out ere the breath of wedding vows is cold! Pity the man and pity the woman!

Evelyn leaned heavily on her husband's arm,

for her joy was overpowering. He felt her hand tremble, and its cold touch might be felt through her glove. "You are not quite well, I fear," he whispered solicitously.

She answered his look with one of triumph. "It is the close rooms," her lips managed to say; but presently she cried earnestly: "Aubrey, Aubrey! Take me into the air!"

He led her along the hall to a low window, looking into the garden. Throwing open the sash he bade her lean out, so that she could drink in the breeze.

"There, I am already better, — much better, Aub — My God! What was that?" She broke from him suddenly, with a fear-stricken face.

She had heard a rustling among the dead leaves, thickly strewn below the window.

"Someone is hiding outside! Aubrey, oh Aubrey!"

"Come away! You are nervous! You need rest," returned her new-made husband, gently placing his arm about her.

As if she heard him not she again leaned forth into the darkness, scanning it narrowly; for she was impressed with the idea that a human being was lurking near. Yes, distinctly she heard labored breathing! What was that gleaming out of the darkness like two steel points? A pair of piercing eyes? Once before she had seen them, — once, before, as she came home from Cypress Dell!

Aubrey heard her timid cry, and saw her white hand hesitatingly seek the window-ledge. "You are fainting, — Evelyn, my wife!"

She did not answer, but fell back into his arms. The guests were surprised, though not seriously alarmed, when the word went about that Mrs. Deveréll was ill, and had retired unceremoniously to her own room; and they were reassured, half-an-hour later, when the bridegroom rejoined them, with the tidings that his wife was sleeping peacefully, after a slight swoon. They therefore repaired to the banquet-room, the groom and Mrs. Seymour leading the way, though regret at the bride's absence hung over them like a pall.

CHAPTER XXXVIII.

LIGHT THROUGH NIGHT.

THE thorns which I have reaped are of the tree
I planted; they have torn me, and I bleed;
I should have known what fruit would spring
from such a seed.
CHILDE HAROLD.

"SLEEPING peacefully!" Aubrey was the victim of deceit when he went from his wife's couch with those words on his lips. He did not see the long lashes lift themselves slightly. He did not see the cunning look as he bade Phebe sit near her mistress, and call him if she became restless.

Scarcely had the door closed when Evelyn opened her eyes with feigned surprise.

"Phebe, that light annoys me! I can not sleep, with it shining so bright. Why are you here? I sha' n't need you again till morning. Turn the light very low, and then leave me alone."

"I 's afeard to leabe y' alone, Missy Eb'lyn. I 'll jis' lay down on de flo', heah by de fiah, so 's ye can call me, honey, if ye wants me." .

"Will you obey me, and go?"

"Yes 'm! I is; but marsa done tol' me, —"

" How dare you parry words, when you know I am dying for sleep ? "

The girl went away crestfallen.

No sooner was she gone than her mistress locked the door, hurriedly dressed herself in plain attire, drew a waterproof close about her face, and then stole forth into the night.

The cold light of the stars guided her to the spot where she had encountered those eyes. In dread uncertainty she turned her gaze in every direction, meeting naught but darkness, which seemed sent on purpose to baffle her.

From the house came the suppressed hum of voices, but there was none of the merry-making which characterizes a wedding party. No music and laughter cheered the midnight air.

Only the youngest guests had done justice to the tempting viands. The disappointed servants, who had spent days of toil over the feast, carried the meats, salads, pastries, and ices, all back to the kitchen.

" Dah 'm de bridecake, what took me a bressed day ter stir and bake, — not teched ! Dah it am, wi' de reef ob flow's 'bout it, zackly like it went on de table. Fo' de Lawd, chillum, I 's bressed if I ebber see sich doin's, 'fo' or since the 'mancipation. It do seem more nor a funeral as a weddin'. Bridecake not cut foh de ring ! Dat am bad luck. Now ye heahs me, brack uns, it am bad luck, sho's you bo'n ! "

So spake old Aunt Sarah, as she deposited on the dresser the snowy pyramid in question, with its garland of smilax and hyacinths.

The bridecake uncut! It must indeed have been a sad wedding supper! The ruby wine was still in the crystal decanters, and no toasts had been proposed in honor of the bride!

At midnight the guests began to retire to their respective apartments. By one o'clock the parlors were empty, only Mrs. Seymour and the house-keeper remaining below.

"I have been to Evelyn's door, Aubrey," said the aunt, as he returned from bidding the last guest farewell. "I found her room perfectly quiet, so I did n't go in. Phebe says she does n't wish to be disturbed."

Aubrey said he would go out for a walk before retiring, as he had a wretched headache, and a few breaths of fresh air might do him good.

Really he wanted to be alone in his misery. The bondage galled him, in which he had been so suddenly ensnared. He felt the iron in his heart, and could have cried aloud in his agony. He had spoken to Hazel but once that evening, and then his brief words were: " Are you happy now, little one?"

She had tried to throw gladness into her words: " I am happy for *her* sake ; " but her voice faltered, and she turned away quickly, lest he discover what she now knew to be true.

Meanwhile Evelyn was grouping her way hither and thither in the darkness, a despairing cry going up from her heart: "Merciful Heaven, guide me to her, lest my new life be ruined ere it begin!"

At length a suppressed cough broke the fateful stillness.

"She is here; thank God!" Evelyn exclaimed aloud, as she parted the shrubberies whence the sound seemed to issue.

Suddenly her foot came in contact with someone crouching in the darkness.

"Philias Ward?" called Evelyn hoarsely.

Another spell of coughing came on, and then a response, half-defiant: "Yes, I's Philias Ward. I's come here to die, miss."

"You do not know your peril," panted Mrs. Deveréll, laying an imperious hand upon the mulatto.

"What matter if I *is* found out?" asked the woman in a dogged tone. I can't live but a day longer. For tree days I's been draggin' myself heah to see you, an' be tol' she — Hazel — had ben resto'ed to her own home. You' p'omise! Hab you gib Mis' Seymour — ?"

"Hush! There are those within hearing who would kill you if they knew you were here. Philias Ward, beware! A terrible punishment will follow, if you expose yourself to my kinsmen. A score of them are here tonight, in this house; for this is my wedding night."

"You' weddin'!" echoed the other, still un-
daunted, "you' weddin'! Is dey here, — Hazel,
Myrine, — wid her mudder 'n little Myrtle? I
looked in de hall windah, and saw many ladies
and some young gals, but not Myrine, not Myrtle.
Oh, I'd know 'em, even after dese many yeahs!
How lubly dey mus' look togeder, — de twin
sisters!"

"I saw you outside the window, and have come
to warn you of your danger."

"Danger? I ain't afeard. I'd face my deah
old mistus, if I knowed she was at de weddin',
along wid Myrine an' Myrtle. I'd rush in dar, 'n
fall on my knees, un' I'd let my old mistus know
how sorrow I is for my 'havior."

"My God!" groaned Evelyn.

"Hain't you' aunt come from New Orleans to
de weddin'?" the mulatto asked, grasping Evelyn's
cloak as she spoke.

"No," returned Evelyn, — and the lie choked
her, — "they are not here; and it is well for you!
— Come with me. I will make you comfortable
till morning. I will give you food and drink."
Mentally she added: "It would be no great sin
should I give her a draught that would put her to
sleep forever. She is already at death's door.
She must go!"

"I can sleep here, and I aint hung'y," said the
mulatto obdurately.

"Sleep here, to be trampled upon? No, you
must come with me."

"Wait! It's a comin' on agin, — de cough. It'll soon — tah me — to pieces. One or two more sick spells 'll finish — "

A struggle ensued. When the cough subsided both women were startled by the sound of some-one raising a sash, and Evelyn could see her aunt leaning from a back window, to close the outside shutters.

Philias also saw Mrs. Seymour, and staggered to her feet, gasping: "My mistus, my mistus!" Like a maniac she wrenched her hand from Eve-lyn's grasp, and rushed through the shrubbery, toward that wide stream of light, wherein her old mistress's face was distinctly outlined.

Evelyn stood transfixed, her heart crying piti-fully: "I am lost, — lost, *lost*, LOST!"

She saw the mulatto fall forward, her head striking against the casement, and heard Mrs. Seymour's cry of alarm! "It is Philias Ward! Merciful God!" No answer came in response to her cry.

Unconsciously Evelyn pressed forward a few steps, repeating the words audibly: "God grant she is dead! Grant that her lips are closed for-ever! Then I shall be saved, *saved for him!*"

"And your wickedness would endure until nothing remained of your humanity. No, by the Eternal! If Philias Ward dies, her secret un-revealed, *I* shall deliver to Mrs. Seymour her long-lost child!" These words, spoken, with the vengeance of Gallic blood, made Evelyn reel as though struck by a bullet.

"You here! You know all!"

"*Everything!* Would to Heaven I had died, rather than live to bestow my father's name upon such a woman. You have robbed an innocent child of her birthright, a mother of her child!"

There was a gasp and a fall. For humanity's sake Aubrey lifted his wife from the ground, but without a single heart-pang learned the truth. She had fallen at death's door, though not quite across the threshold.

All the next day his bride heard a voice calling to her from the valley of shadows; but just before answering to that call she opened her eyes, and whispered her husband's name.

He approached the bedside, his face almost as white as hers, and looked down upon her; but he could not speak. What words of kind farewell could his betrayed heart utter to this guilty and dying woman?

"I have been wicked, Aubrey, — but it was all, *all*, through my disappointed heart! I thought you loved *her*. I sought revenge! When you came again I would have acknowledged my sin; but it was too late! Rather than lose you I would have carried my treason to the grave! I might have known what fruit must spring from the seed of my bitter sowing!"

She closed her eyes, her face was distorted with

the pain which was so soon to close her account with the world.

The agony passed, and she spoke again: "Aubrey, I can't ask forgiveness; but darling, do n't judge me wholly wicked. I am not so false as I seem, — as I know you think me. As your wife, I would have outlived every taint of evil."

Another spasm, and then she said: "My aunt, Hazel, Myrtle! I want them. Quick, or it will be too late."

They came speedily, and then she said: "Come near, very near, all of you!"

Mrs. Seymour pressed one of her niece's hands forgivingly within her own, and bent to kiss her, but Evelyn pushed her back.

"No, no! Do n't touch me until you have heard. Perhaps you *have* heard! Perhaps she — the — Philias —"

"Does Evelyn know Philias is here?" asked Mrs. Seymour in bewilderment.

Aubrey bowed assent. "Hear what your niece has to say, Madame Seymour. She has revived from this last attack."

The aunt leaned over, that she might hear more distinctly.

"Philias Ward! You saw her last night?"

"Yes; she came to the window, just as I was closing the shutters. She called my name, and then fell to the ground. Before I could go to her assistance she was dead, — with hemorrhage."

" She died before confessing ? "

" Yes! I am deeper in the dark than ever about my lost babe, my little Myrine! " said Mrs. Seymour hopelessly.

Evelyn rose with an effort to a sitting posture, and beckoned to her two young cousins, who wept at the foot of the bed. At this signal they came to her side.

" Look, Aunt Lydia, look! You always thought them so like! Hear the truth — from my lips! Hazel is your long-lost daughter, — your Myrine! Look! In my desk — look there, and find a rose-wood box and two letters. One is from — from my dead mother, to *you*. The other is in Philias Ward's crabbed hand — her confession, — the abduction of — of — of Hazel. Read, — you will be convinced. The bundle of baby-clothes, — in the letter — I threw — The dog saw me, — Bijou, and strove to bring my crime to light. Don't censure me after I am gone. Let my contrite blessing abide with you all — now — and — for — ever! "

Another struggle and Evelyn Weldon Deveréll had passed the unseen gates.

In Cypress Dell, beside her parents, Aubrey laid his bride of a day. It was not in cruelty, it was not in triumph, that he turned from her tomb, and breathed more freely.

A year later, when he led the beautiful Myrine Seymour to the altar, his hair was prematurely

gray. In his furrowed face was the shadow of a
bitter sorrow; but this did not lessen his love for
Myrine, when he conducted her through the por-
tals of Deveréll Hall, bared his noble brow, lifted
her bridal veil, and placed upon her true lips the
first kiss of wedlock.

From their terrace windows they could look
down the avenue and see a picturesque little
villa, destined to be the home of Wilford Hylton
and his bride-elect, Myrtle Seymour.

One night, as they stood in the gloaming together,
Aubrey with his arm about his young wife, her
head resting trustingly on his shoulder, Hazel
whispered: "Tomorrow will be my sister's wedding day. Tomorrow Myrtle also will be very
happy. Aubrey, see how the moon smiles upon
their pretty home, — a benediction!"

He drew her closer to him, and silently prayed
that the coming union might be as blessed as their
own.

www.ingramcontent.com/pod-product-compliance
Lightning Source LLC
Chambersburg PA
CBHW060518030726
47498CB00004B/988